MONGREL

LEE COLGIN

ACKNOWLEDGMENTS

I owe so many people my thanks. Kat Silver, I couldn't write without you. Dextre, for alpha reading. My critique partners: Sierra Charleston, Stephanie Briarton, Barbara Leftih, Nicole Renee, Jenn Bass, Elizebeth Michaels, and Helen Bold. And my beta readers: W.M. Fawkes, Kim, and Hellie Heat. I love you all, and thank you for the help!

ABOUT THIS BOOK

Mongrel, a creature more wolf than man, leads a lonely life on the fringes of pack society—until the night a handsome vampire shows up with a mysterious request.

Bowie, a vampire cursed to a life of endless nights, maintains close ties with his human family. When young girls in their village go missing, he must act quickly. But to find them, he'll need to convince the local werewolf pack to loan him their best tracker—a wolf known as the Mongrel.

Though he hates the slur, Andras is used to being called *Mongrel*. When Bowie refuses to refer to him by anything but his given name, Andras can't help a flicker of unexpected trust toward the stranger. He volunteers to help Bowie, risking banishment.

Can two tenderhearted men overcome their traumatic pasts and work together to rescue the girls before it's too late? Or will the world's most prolific killer snuff the flames of their passion along with the lives of the captives?

This steamy love story spans the country of Hungary as Andras and Bowie journey through cities and wilderness on their quest to right a villain's wicked wrongs. Mongrel features a sweetly possessive werewolf, a cinnamon roll of a vampire, and the worst killer in history. A surprisingly fluffy MM Paranormal/Historical Romance considering the subject matter.

HEA guaranteed with loads of laughs along the way and no cliffhanger ending!

CHAPTER 1

*T*he Kingdom of Hungary, 1610

I WATCH the ground pass by beneath my paws rather than risk meeting the eyes of the other wolves. They probably aren't looking anyway, having better things to do than greet the *mongrel*, even on a full moon. I've spent so long pretending not to care it's almost worked. Who needs them? Not me.

I give a full-body shake to settle my fur how I like it and amble toward the heart of the village, a cool night breeze keeping me company. The chattering of insects pings from the forest beyond a row of humble cottages as I continue past.

Anticipating tonight's run has me eager. I imagine the frantic heartbeat of my prey as I target my dinner. Pent-up energy dances in my muscles, tickling every nerve and rumbling in my chest.

I love the hunt. Nothing else in my life brings the satisfaction I take from stalking, chasing, and tearing into my prize. It's one of the few activities where the others tolerate my presence.

Though they'll never admit I'm the better predator, they're always willing to devour the feast I provide.

Only Ava treats me as equal. She's too old and frail to hunt for herself these days, but I'll be sure to bring her a choice portion. Nothing beats a fresh meal, and she deserves the pleasure more than anyone.

It wasn't always like this. I had friends once when childhood still sang with innocence and the world had yet to slam its doors on me. But remembering better times only brings sorrow, so I move forward to whatever tonight might hold.

Voices sound from fifty paces ahead. Odd because most of the pack would normally have shifted by dusk. Among them, a voice I don't recognize floats to my ears.

"I must speak with your alpha," says a smooth tenor, calm, though his timbre vibrates with urgency. "The matter is vital."

Risking an upward glance, I scan the gathering. Jolan and Ozor, the pack's enforcers, stand in their human forms facing the speaker, both tense and braced for a fight. But the stranger's posture isn't threatening. He's neat, wearing charcoal stockings under a crisp blue tunic. Knee-high black boots gleam with a recent polish. Spine straight, shoulders back, weight settled in the heels, not the toes. Nut-brown hair hangs tied at his nape, most of it hidden beneath a fashionable black hat. If his features weren't puckered with annoyance, he might be handsome.

I creep closer on silent paws, ears flicked forward.

"We're busy," barks Ozor. "Or hadn't you noticed the moon? Come back another night."

The stranger's lips part, but before he can reply, Farkas storms through his front door.

Clad only in a pair of worn tan breeches, the pack alpha thunders down the porch stairs and into the commons. Even barefoot, Farkas is intimidating, towering head and shoulders over the others. His black eyes land on the stranger in a threatening glower, but the man isn't shaken.

"You're the alpha, I presume?" The stranger extends a hand, his movement graceful, as if he's been invited to a friendly tea instead of invading hostile werewolf territory on a full moon.

Farkas ignores the proffered hand. "Your kind isn't welcome here."

Your kind. Wondering what that means, I inch forward so I can scent him for myself.

The stranger returns his arm to his side, fingers curled but not fisted. "And you have my apologies, but this couldn't be avoided." His eyebrows arch as he inclines his head. "We must speak."

I sniff the air. His scent is masked by soaps. Lavender was used for his clothes, rose for his skin and hair, but beneath the added fragrance lies the spiced scent of blood—his own, yes, but also…someone else's? That's odd.

"Then speak," growls Farkas. "What do you want from me, vampire?"

A vampire! I've never seen one before. He looks so…human. Fragile. Not what I'd expect of a blood-drinking night terror at all.

The vampire casts a glance at the gathered group. Farkas looms before him with Jolan and Ozor on either side. Shifted wolves have enclosed him within a loose circle. I remain farther back, watching. His gaze drifts calmly over me. Blue eyes land on mine, startling in their intensity, like a summer's sky darkening before an afternoon storm. I blink, and his attention shifts back to Farkas. If the lone vampire is bothered at being surrounded, he doesn't show it.

"Panic rises in the village of Varad and beyond. Young girls are going missing, stolen in the night, no trace as to where." Though the vampire's words are shocking, his voice remains calm. "The people need help."

"You'd better not be accusing us." Farkas puffs out his naked chest, ready for a brawl. "We have nothing to do with it."

The vampire raises his eyes skyward as if he's suppressed the urge to roll them. I don't blame him. Farkas may be enormous, with the strength of ten wolves and the arrogance of twenty, but he's about as quick-witted as a moth headed toward a fire.

"I'm not accusing you," says the vampire, his crisp tone bordering on irritation. "As I said, they need our help. I'm here because werewolves are excellent trackers. Your expertise is required to find the girls."

"You want *us* to help find missing humans?"

The vampire presses his lips into a thin line. "Precisely. There's no time to waste."

"Why would we help you?" asks Jolan. "And for that matter, why is a vampire concerned with human villagers?"

Like the strike of a snake, the vampire's gaze darts to Jolan. "These are the same people your pack trades with," he explains. "Where will you acquire fabrics, grain, or anything else you don't produce yourselves if the villagers are so frantic with worry they can't work? A single tracker is all I need, your best one. Then I'll leave you to"—he waves his hand absently toward the forest—"whatever it is werewolves do on the full moon."

I'm the pack's best tracker, but Farkas won't send me. He's too paranoid to let me out of his territory. I'm banned from excursions to nearby villages, but I go anyway. I like humans. They're simple. Friendly. Not like wolves.

For years, I've known I must escape this pack if I ever want to find a day's peace, but I've been reluctant to take the risk. What if I leave one terrible situation, only to discover something worse? No other pack will have me, and lone wolves are known to go feral. Still, I've considered it. This vampire could be my chance.

With a huff, Farkas nods to his second. "Go with him, Ozor. Put him on the scent trail and lead him to the girls, then return. Surely a vampire can handle a petty human squabble from there."

"Fine," grunts Ozor. "Let's get this over with, blood bandit. I have a bitch to breed."

The vampire doesn't hide the distaste emblazoned across his features as his glower settles on Ozor. I understand. The wolf wouldn't know a bar of soap if it hit him square across his pinched face. And if you can make it past the stench, Ozor remains unpleasant company with his stubborn arrogance and aggressive personality. I wouldn't want to be alone with him either.

The vampire lifts his chin, directing his next inquiry to Farkas. "Ozor is your best tracker?" He doesn't sound convinced. And he shouldn't be. Ozor is a shit tracker.

I make my decision.

Before Farkas can answer, I force a rapid shift. It's painful when performed this fast, my bones snapping and reforming into place as I rise from all fours to two feet and step forward.

"I'm the best tracker." I harden my glare, daring Farkas to suggest otherwise. "I volunteer."

The vampire's full attention hits me like the crackling energy of a lightning bolt, alive with heat. I meet his eyes and watch as his expression morphs from interest to shocked curiosity. His lips part.

I don't have a fully human form like the others, only something close to it—a mix of wolf and man, not quite either. There's no denying the animal in me; it's written where skin becomes fur. Farkas will be angry I've let the vampire see this. He'd prefer my existence remain secret, but I don't care. I like the way the vampire is looking at me. I flick my tufted ears toward him, unbothered by my nudity.

Farkas shoulders me out of the way, inserting himself between me and the vampire. "No. You'll take Ozor, or you'll have no one. The mongrel isn't to leave pack land."

As usual, he's spoken about me as if I'm not here. An old wound festers, but I ignore it. "I'll stay in wolf form. No one will see beyond the animal. I'm faster than Ozor, and he doesn't want to go anyway."

Farkas snarls at me. "Ozor knows how to obey a command, which is more than I can say for you."

"I'm the better tracker," I argue before common sense convinces me not to. I can't let the opportunity pass without a fight. With a desperate look I beg the vampire to insist. He stands a better chance of convincing Farkas than I do.

"I want him," says the vampire, picking up my cue with flawless timing.

Farkas shakes his head. "The mongrel cannot leave."

"Why not?" The vampire lifts a shoulder in an elegant shrug. "Keeping him in wolf form suits me fine if you insist he must be hidden."

I don't love the sound of that, but I can disagree later, once we've gone.

"Consider this," the vampire continues, sounding almost bored. It's smart of him. "We don't know how far the girls have been taken. This mission might take longer than you expect."

Irritation curls Farkas's upper lip. "How long?"

"No way to tell, maybe weeks. Remember, I'm limited to searching only by night. Can you really spare Ozor? He is your second, is he not? Or shall I have…" He hesitates as if he doesn't want to say the word. In this moment, he earns the beginnings of my respect. "The mongrel instead?"

It's a clever strategy, appealing to Farkas's disdain for me, pointing out I am the lesser offering. One look at Farkas tells me it's worked.

"The villagers must never see him," Farkas warns. "They already suspect your kind of running amok. Wolves must remain secret."

"Of course." The vampire bows his head. "You have my word. And I shall escort him home safely when our business has concluded."

I have other plans, but the vampire doesn't need to know that.

Farkas grabs me by the biceps and spins me to face him. "Do what he says, and don't be a burden."

"Yes, Alpha." My voice comes out sincere, but inside, I'm already celebrating. I don't mind obeying a vampire if it will help the villagers, and weeks of travel will give me an idea of what life could hold outside werewolf territory.

"If you muck this up, you might not survive the punishment," Farkas threatens me, then glares at the vampire. "And you don't want me as an enemy."

"Certainly not," says the vampire, somehow maintaining his polite, if irritated, manner.

With a grunt, Farkas turns his back on us. He and the rest of the pack prepare to take to the woods for the rest of the night. I cast a victory glance at my tour guide and watch as he saunters toward me. Up close, his blue eyes sparkle like lapis lazuli. He's several inches taller but somehow manages not to look down on me.

"Thank you for offering your assistance." A sincere smile reveals a tantalizing glimpse of his fanged canines. "I cannot follow the trail on my own. Your expertise will be invaluable, and afterward, I will owe you a debt."

Snickers erupt from nearby pack members who overheard, but for once, I don't let them bother me. I'm itching to leave.

I meet the vampire's gaze. "I'll do my best. No payment required."

He gestures toward the valley, where the villagers live. "Shall we?"

My excitement turns heavy as I realize what must happen next. The change must show on my face because his expression reflects concern.

I make sure not to sound as choked up as I feel. "There's one thing I need to do first. It won't take long."

CHAPTER 2

"Of course, whatever you need," says the vampire. "Can I help?"

He really can't. The thought of saying goodbye to Ava hardens my soft heart to stone, but I've always known that to be free of this pack would mean losing her in the bargain. "No, but don't worry. I'll be quick."

"You don't need to rush." He glances at the other wolves still milling around, their wary gazes not exactly welcoming. "But could I tag along? I seem to have overstayed my welcome in your"—he scans our shabby, overgrown common area—"town square?"

The urge to laugh briefly overcomes my sadness about the task ahead. "Town square" is rather generous for what's little more than an untamed garden between rundown huts.

"This way." I lead him past the circling wolves. Has Ava ever met a vampire? In all our years together, it's never occurred to me to ask.

"What's your name?" He pitches his voice low, but I know the others will still be able to hear us.

"Mongrel," I say through clenched teeth because it's not

worth asking him to call me by my real name. If I do end up back here, I'll be teased for having made the request.

"I can't call you that." He looks genuinely appalled, his eyebrows nearly meeting in the middle.

I quicken our pace to get out of eavesdropping distance. "Why not?"

He keeps up easily enough, trotting along behind me. "It's…unkind."

I manage a shrug, though my stomach quivers. "It's what I am."

"But it's not *all* you are." He talks with his hands, gesturing to insist on his point. "For instance, I'm not called Muck-Spout because I swear a lot. Though I do swear a lot, mind you." He raises an elegant finger with its neatly manicured nail at nothing in particular. "I'm called Bowie because that's my name, and I'd like to know yours."

I don't answer. My head is crammed full of racing thoughts, a jumbled tangle that shuts down my ability to continue the conversation.

It occurs to me, as the vampire—Bowie—follows, that I'm naked, while he's fully dressed. My tail hides the crack of my bottom, but I'm still presenting him with a view of my ass while we climb the path to Ava's.

Though modesty isn't a common trait among shifters and certainly not me, a flicker of self-consciousness lifts the fur along my spine. Before I can overthink it, I shift back to the comfort of the animal form, slower this time so it doesn't hurt.

"All right. Don't ask for your name. Duly noted," says Bowie, unruffled as he hurries to catch up.

As my paws hit the dirt, the bashful feeling recedes, leaving a messy pile of emotions in its wake: the exciting possibility of freedom, fear of the unknown, a tingle of nervous energy that tightens my throat when Bowie watches me.

I don't pause to sort this out; it's safer to ignore the turmoil until I'm alone. Instead, I focus on Ava. What should I say to her when this could be goodbye?

"That was truly spectacular. I've never witnessed a werewolf shift before, and now I've seen you do it twice. I'll admit to a fair bit of jealousy on the matter. Contrary to superstition, I cannot transform myself into a bat. Or even mist. What must it feel like?"

Since he's handling the conversation for both of us, I'm free to wonder what being stuck in only one form might be like. Though a form like Bowie's—tall and slender with lean-muscled shoulders and thighs—might not be so bad. I, on the other hand, am the normal shape as a wolf. But on two legs, I'm too short. Too much wolf and not enough human to have attained average height. Smaller than the others when in human form, scrawny, with fur along my spine from nape to tail, pointy-tufted ears, and fanged incisors that must rival any vampire's. Since I can't pass for human, I'm left with only other wolves for company, and they decided I was a freak long ago.

Bowie's stare is different. His eyes shine with interest rather than disdain. He's playful rather than mocking, at least for now. I glance away. Best not set my expectations of him any higher than basic toleration. Even that is more than what I'm used to.

We pass through the far gate, me leaping over it and Bowie carefully unlatching the rickety wooden door, then swinging it shut behind him. Ava's flock of hens rushes to greet me. They spot Bowie and avoid getting too close to him. If his musical chuckle is anything to go by, he's not lost to the irony of a dozen chickens running straight toward the muzzle of a hungry wolf. But I'd never harm them. Ava derives great joy from their care, and they lay enough eggs for half the pack's supply.

Ava's little stone cottage stands alone among towering evergreens. It's dark now, but even in daylight, a pleasant shade hugs the home. Somehow, despite the hour, the house is cheery. Perhaps it's the glow of the fireplace through the oval windows or the flowers that cover the sills, but even without those signs of warmth, the cottage would be welcoming because Ava is welcoming.

As if anticipating our arrival, her age-bent form appears from the opening door. A friendly smile beckons, and curiosity gleams in her golden-brown eyes.

"Andras, is that you?" she calls.

Bowie shoots a triumphant glance my way. He points to me and mouths the name "Andras." then he smiles, teeth gleaming. I shake my head and snuffle at the ground before breaking into a trot, assuming he'll follow.

At the threshold, I gently rub my flank along Ava's thigh in greeting. Her hand finds my forehead and scratches behind my right ear, my favorite spot. My weakest spot. With no small amount of horror on my part, my leg begins to twitch against my will as if possessed by some demon of phantom itches. I growl in protest, but Ava only chuckles. Glancing backward, I see that to my utter embarrassment, Bowie has noticed this exchange. His rose petal-pink lips have curled into a delighted grin, and mirth sparkles in his gaze.

"Oh, lovely trick," says Bowie to Ava. "Will he do that for anyone, or am I right that you're someone special?"

Ava extends her hand. "More than one person can be special."

Bowie takes her fingers in his and ever so gracefully plants a kiss on her knuckles. "Enchanted, my dear. Since Andras here is in no shape to make the introductions, I shall stumble forth myself. Bowie of Varad, at your service."

"Handsome *and* charming? I see you're a double threat."

I can hear Ava's smile in her voice as she reclaims her hand. Of course she likes him—he's well dressed, polite, and not-so-subtly captivating. Ava and I stand no chance in this exchange.

"You may call me Ava."

"It will be my pleasure, Ava, as it is to make your acquaintance," Bowie croons. "And what a beautiful home you have. So lovely."

He isn't wrong, though he's laying it on thick. We've taken good care of the old cottage over the years, but it's modest at best. The stones are clean of moss and grime, the porch is swept tidy, and the surrounding plants are carefully tended and groomed.

"Thank you. Come along and see the inside." Ava steps back to make room for him to enter. "I'd offer you tea, but I have a feeling you'd decline."

How does she know? Granted, I smelled the blood on him, but even then, I wasn't sure, and her senses have dulled with age. Yet somehow she'd pegged him for the vampire he is. Ava never ceases to amaze me. And here I thought she'd taught me everything she knew, but our talk of vampires was limited to the human folktales in several of her many books.

"You're right. I cannot drink tea," says Bowie, his tone tinged with regret. "But I do enjoy the scent and the warmth of holding the mug."

"I'll put on my kettle." She leads Bowie inside and asks casually, "What are your intentions with my Andras?"

Far too mortified to stick around, I take her question as my cue to exit. I leave Ava to her interrogation and Bowie to conjure his defense as I slip past the bookshelves to my room. Bumping the door closed with a hip, I let out the breath I've been holding and ease into my two-legged form to dress. Farkas might have demanded I keep to the animal, but I'll need to communicate with Bowie from time to time, and I don't fancy being naked while I do.

I resist the temptation to listen in on their conversation as I choose a sturdy pair of gray woolen pants and a cream linen shirt to put on. I shove a second shirt, a lighter pair of pants, and the hat that best hides my ears into a leather satchel. Should I take anything else? Seeing as I'll have to ask Bowie to carry my pack whenever I'm in wolf form, I should keep it light, and I need to leave space for what I'm wearing. I'll be sad to leave my books behind, but even bringing only one would be weight I don't need.

My gaze land on a prized possession from my childhood: a rag doll made from the scraps of Ava's sewing projects. I named her Marta, after my mother, and kept her even after the other boys taunted me for having a doll. Her black button eyes stare back at me, and though I know I'm being stupid and sentimental, I can't leave her.

Into the bag she goes, crammed under the clothes. "Sorry, Marta."

I shut the satchel, throw it over my shoulder, and sit to fasten my soft leather shoes. I'd like to at least begin this trip on two feet. I have questions for Bowie before I shift back to wolf form, and he seems the talkative type. Whatever he knows about the missing girls, I need to know too, anything that might make them easier to track. I'm also curious why he's involved at all. I mean, I like humans, but most of my pack doesn't. Wouldn't a vampire think of them as…food? I shudder. Bowie doesn't look like a killer, but he must be. That's what vampires do, right?

I listen for the sound of their voices and hear laughter. Perhaps it shouldn't surprise me they've charmed one another. With a deep breath, I say goodbye to my room and head to the kitchen What have they been discussing? Hopefully nothing too embarrassing. Ava knows all my secrets.

Bowie sits casually at our little round dining table, leaning forward on his elbow, one leg crossed over the other. For all appearances, he's deeply engaged in Ava's story. She's in the chair across from him, her back as straight as it goes these days, proper as rain, though the story flowing from her lips is not.

"Well, you should have seen little Farkas that day." Ava shakes her head, looking every bit the disapproving pack grandmother. "Running through the middle of the village, naked as the day he was born, and hollering like a banshee in heat!"

Oh, that story. We aren't too fond of Farkas in this household.

Bowie's glittering eyes are wide, and so is his grin. "Well, what happened?"

Farkas snatched a bear cub that day. Still a cub himself, he was no match for the mother bear and should have known better.

"Our old alpha, Vuk, rest his soul—now that was a good man, I tell you. He came flying out of his house, shifted in midair, and kept the mother bear from killing Farkas. 'Let loose the cub!' he ordered, but Farkas has always had a stubborn streak." Ava's gaze shifts downward. "He killed that baby bear. I'll never forget the sound of the mother bear's wail. Vuk had to kill her too."

I chime in. "If Farkas had just given up the baby like the alpha said, he could have led the mother off. Such a waste." I mostly remember how arrogant he'd been after he'd gotten away with it. "Farkas made the other boys call him Bear Killer after that."

Bowie leans back in his chair and crosses his arms. "Disgusting," he huffs.

Ava picks up the story. "Well, Andras refused. Said he couldn't understand why Farkas would be so proud of killing a baby. He came home with a bloody lip and two black eyes, but my boy has something you can actually be proud of." She sets her mug on the table with a thunk to emphasize her point. "A conscience."

"Indeed." Bowie lifts the mug from which he's clearly not been drinking to affirm Ava's words.

Heat creeps into my cheeks. That story has always made me uncomfortable. Ava doesn't realize it, and I've never told her because I like the sound of pride in her voice too much. But I remember the mother's wail.

Bowie studies me, his features fond, though he doesn't actually know me. I wonder what else Ava has told him.

"I'm ready," I say.

"Must you leave so soon?" asks Ava.

She loves visitors, and we get so few. I hate to drag Bowie away from her, but the matter of the missing girls is quite serious. Looking at her face, so marked now with age but still cheerful as always, I know I can't say goodbye, not forever at least. As much as I'd like to build a life away from this hateful pack, Ava still needs me. The others will take care of her, of course, but not like I do. I must return, if only to convince her to leave with me next time.

I lean down to embrace her. "The villagers could use my help. I don't know how long it will take, but I'll come back straight after."

Her arms come around my waist. "Don't hurry on my account. Have some fun while you're away, and bring me back some of those mint candies from town."

I chuckle. Ava and her sweet tooth. "Of course." I kiss her cheek, then pull away. "Don't let the chickens in the house while I'm gone. I built them a good coop, and they can stay in it."

Ava grants me the courtesy of looking sheepish. She's far too softhearted when it comes to her hens.

And to me.

Bowie rises gracefully and bows to Ava. "Thank you for the delightful conversation and the loan of your dear Andras. I promise to return him to you no worse for wear."

"See that you do. Now get on." She shoos us away with the flick of her thin wrist. "It's past my bedtime."

I lead Bowie from the cottage and close the door behind us. It's perhaps a two-hour walk to the village, shorter if he can run as fast as me, but I don't know anything about vampires. I suppose I'm about to find out. "Shall we?"

His smirk spreads wide. "Come along, dear *Andras*." He overenunciates my name like it's a prize he's stolen from the rightful winner. Then his face turns serious as he reconsiders. "May I call you Andras? It's a lovely name and suits you better than…"

"Mongrel?" I finish for him, shrugging. "I'm used to it, but you can call me Andras now that we're leaving."

The grin returns. It lights his face like the full moon's reflection in a tranquil pond. "All right, Andras, I will."

Together, we leave my home behind and head downhill toward the valley. I don't look back.

CHAPTER 3

$\mathcal{M}$y stomach rumbles before we've gone far, loud enough that Bowie doesn't ignore it.

"I've kept you from the hunt, haven't I?" he asks with an amount of sincerity I don't often hear from others. "You're hungry. Should I wait while you…I don't know…stalk and kill something?"

The distaste in his tone at those last words, along with the vague waving motion of his hand toward the trees, makes me laugh. "Don't you also kill things?"

His eyes widen with shock, then narrow. "Not if I can help it."

I stare at his face. He's so expressive, nose scrunching and lips pursing.

"Sorry, but you're a vampire. I just figured."

"I can feed without killing," he says in that precise way of his.

Well, that's interesting and not what I imagined. Still, it doesn't change the fact that *I* need to kill something. "I'll need to hunt."

"Don't let me stop you. I cannot have my best tracker going hungry."

"I'm your only tracker." My ears flick forward, then back, listening for the telltale signs of prey hiding in the bush. I run my tongue along my sharp teeth. I caught wind of deer earlier, but I don't need something that big to feed only myself. "I'll cut away when the opportunity arises. Could you carry my pack when that happens?"

"Of course. I can carry it now if you like."

"I've got it." The weight of the pack is oddly comforting, a bit of home tagging along on the adventure.

The silvery glow of the full moon brightens the cloudless night sky. A thousand stars twinkle in the distance. The wolf in me itches to stretch his legs, to race through the forest, to lift his chin and howl. But the human in me has questions, and Bowie is chatty.

I start with the most pressing. "Why are you helping the villagers?"

"Why wouldn't I help the villagers?" he challenges, though his features remain relaxed, and there's no hostility in his response.

I think on my answer as we make our way down the path, which has turned into a narrow dirt road. Wide enough for horses or a small cart, though not quite big enough for wagons. Bowie's stride is naturally quick but not rushed. I match it easily.

"Aren't they scared of you?" I ask. Though it's not a valid reason not to help them, it would be a drawback. Rumors and legends of vampires abound in these parts, the foothills of the Carpathian Mountains. In human stories, the hunt and subsequent slaughter of vampires tend to involve fire, stakes, and beheadings. Reason enough to keep one's distance.

Bowie puffs a breath through his nose. "I only interact with a few. Most of them know my family by name. I rely on my sister to keep me informed. She, her husband, and their steward are the only ones who know of"—his hand joins in on the conversation, waving delicately in front of him—"my condition."

I nod and look him over more thoroughly. His clothes have the appearance of merchant class, but upon closer inspection, I notice the fine silken fabric of his fitted stockings, the sturdy and expertly dyed wool of his blue coat, a bright hue surely designed to bring out his eyes, the sort of luxury money buys. It's cut to such perfection it would fit no one but him. His elegant hands, which he uses so frequently to dance along with his words, have exquisitely manicured nails, perfectly clean, not a speck of dirt to be seen. Leather boots nearly as tall as his knees shine black with polish. Even his matching hat is of the best quality. Not merchant class at all, then.

"You're a noble?" I ask.

Bowie's smile indicates he's pleased I've parsed this out. "Was a noble," he says. "Technically, I'm dead."

I wave this off. "Your family is noble, and you're clearly not dead. I don't know what makes a vampire a vampire, but you're as alive as I am."

"Ah." A mournful sigh accompanies the utterance. "Put your hand on my chest, and you may change your mind, dear Andras."

Does he really want me to touch him, or is the suggestion rhetorical? I decide not to reach out, though now I'm imagining it. Laying my palm on his chest, feeling...what exactly? "Your heart doesn't beat?"

"Not anymore. And my flesh is cold as graves." The melancholy notes in his tone make me sad for him.

"Perhaps, but you're still very much alive." Maybe a compliment would cheer him up. "Dead people don't have sparkling eyes like yours."

The aforementioned eyes connect with mine. "Have you seen many dead people?"

"A few." Images come to mind. I push them aside.

"You think my eyes sparkle?"

Is he fishing for more compliments? "You know they do."

His dips his chin and looks at me through his lashes. "But you noticed."

"Hard not to."

He takes a deliberate breath. "Yours are like golden nuggets straight from the earth." His hands form a cup in front of him as if holding something precious.

I laugh. My eyes are mostly brown; the flecks of gold come from the wolf. "What's that supposed to mean?"

Playfully offended, he declares, "They've raw beauty, like a jewel before man polishes all the unique qualities away." His voice has turned to honey. "A treasure. Two of them, actually."

My neck warms. This conversation has gotten out of hand. Weren't we supposed to be talking about the villagers? "Are you avoiding my question?"

"What question? I've forgotten." Bowie's grin throws me off-kilter.

"The missing girls. The villagers. Why are you helping them?"

"Oh, right. Well, because they need my help. Isn't that enough?"

I wonder if he's intentionally missing the point. Not that I disagree; he's right, of course. Because they need help is a fine reason. "But you're a vampire. Humans and vampires are enemies, aren't they?"

"I don't see why we should be, but historically, yes." His expression darkens. "Quite a lot of blood spilled on both sides."

"You're not afraid they'll find out what you are? Turn on you?"

"I won't be working closely with the humans, Andras. I'll be working with you. You're not going to turn on me, are you?"

I certainly don't plan on it, but if Bowie turns out to be a bad person, I can't promise not to change my mind.

"Are you?" he repeats a little bit louder and a lot more incredulous.

"Of course not," I hurry to assure him. "As long as you've been honest with me and remain so. But I'd be a fool to trust you this soon."

He gives a slow nod. "Wise of you. And not surprising when I think about it. Your pack doesn't treat you well, do they?"

I don't want to talk about this. "I have Ava."

Bowie doesn't push. I appreciate him for it. "Ava is an absolute delight. I could have listened to her stories all night."

"She's full of them." I've lost control of the conversation again. How does he do that? And with such ease, it's already happened by the time I've noticed.

"Is she your grandmother?"

"No." Ava is my grandmother's cousin. I don't know what that makes us, but my grandmother died before I was born, and my mother left me to the pack as an infant. I don't remember her. Ava is all I have.

When I offer no further information, Bowie continues as if he'd never dragged the conversation sideways. "The first rumors of missing girls began years ago in communities farther afield. I didn't know because the concerns never fell on the right ears. It wasn't until the kidnappings hit closer to home that we realized we might have a problem on our hands."

"Who is we?"

"My sister and me." A flick of his hand. "And my brother-in-law, Jakob, too, of course. We manage the estate together. When the peasants began to panic, we knew something was wrong."

"When was this?"

"Three weeks ago. My sister, Catherine, is well liked in the community, so she began speaking with the people to gather information. That's when we learned that the surrounding towns had been affected first and just how long ago the mystery had begun. I traveled to Zilah in search of answers, but distrust of nobility kept the peasants from speaking with me. And the Báthory family, which owns those lands, is tight-lipped. It behooves them to deny atrocity rather than seek remedy. By then, the trail had gone cold. I returned with little more information than I'd left with."

"That must be frustrating."

"Indeed, it is." He claps his hands. "Until the thought occurred to me that a talented werewolf might still be able to follow the scent."

"I'll certainly try. I've never been to Zilah." I've never been anywhere beyond the towns and villages that border pack territory, but I don't tell him that.

"It's much the same—hilly, beautiful, covered in trees. Though the Ottomans have yet to make it that far, and the Protestant locals are under constant threat by the Habsburgs." Bowie shrugs as if this matters not to him, but I find myself curious.

"Protestant locals? Protesting what?"

His brows arch nearly to his forehead. "The Catholic Church."

I only vaguely know what he means. Human religion eludes me. Wolves don't worship anything, though we honor the earth, the sun, and especially the moon. My face must reflect my ignorance.

"We are sandwiched between warring nations here in the Kingdom of Hungary," says Bowie, indicating as much with precise fingers drawing shapes in the air for me. "The Habsburgs to the north and west would have our lands. They do, in fact, already control a vast portion. And they're rivaled only by the Ottoman Empire to the south and east. Mostly Islamic people who would also have our lands and do, in fact, already control a vast portion. There isn't much left that belongs to the actual Magyars."

This is all fascinating, but I'm a bit lost. He must realize because his hand lands on my shoulder, and warmth tinges his voice when he speaks. "If you're curious, I'll teach you the history of these lands you call home, but for the time being, it's enough to say turmoil reigns. The desires of greedy men cloud the future, but these girls? I have to believe we can save these girls."

On this, we agree, though my curiosity has now wandered again to the world beyond pack territory and the potential it might hold. I'm glad to be in a position to learn something new from a teacher like Bowie, whose understanding so obviously eclipses my own.

A scent catches my attention, recent death, perhaps a fox. My ears perk up, listening for the sounds of scavengers. An easy opportunity to catch a vulture or maybe a raccoon. I take Bowie's elbow, silently directing him to stop.

"What is it?" he whispers.

"Shh." I touch my ear.

He stays quiet and listens with me.

Sure enough, other animals scurry around the carrion. Little do they know one of them will be my supper.

"I'll be quick." I take off my satchel, then yank my shirt over my shoulders. My shoes and pants I'll easily leap out of as I shift, but the shirt could tangle me up. I stuff it into the satchel. Bowie watches. I hand him the bag. "Collect my things for me?"

A smooth nod. "Of course."

"No need to wait. I'll catch up."

"All right. Good luck. Happy killing." He says this jokingly. I think.

I roll my neck and let the animal surge to the fore. With hardly any effort, as the full moon is on my side, I grant the wolf control over my limbs. The shift ripples through me from toes to snout, a change so natural I ease into the fur and fury with joyous anticipation. The forest calls to my soul with each screech of an owl, every creak of a tree branch, and all the crunching of dried leaves beneath my paws as I leave Bowie behind and race to my dinner.

I think of the vampire neatly folding the clothes I've left crumpled on the ground and hope he doesn't snoop in my bag. A grown wolf explaining a child's rag doll isn't something I look forward to. I can already see the amusement in his glittering gaze.

We've only just met, but I like Bowie. I like the way he speaks to me as if I'm his equal and he respects my time. I like the warm tingling feeling I get in my stomach when his eyes are on me. And I like the way his hands move as if he isn't thinking of them at all, yet they're perfectly in tune, communicating his thoughts alongside his words.

What am I thinking? He's dangerous, and I don't actually know him. With a full-body shake, ruffling my fur into place, I focus on my prey.

Definitely a raccoon that's found an easy meal, and now I've found him. I sit low on my haunches, ready for the attack, muscles coiled and eager to pounce. The scent of fresh blood in the air whets my appetite. Saliva fills my jowls. A feast at last. My feast.

I leap.

CHAPTER 4

I trot back to Bowie with a full stomach and clean fur. I've taken a dip in a chilly creek not far from our path. Though my coat's wet, underneath, my skin remains dry. When I shift, only my hair will stay damp.

Approaching from behind, I can tell when Bowie senses my presence. His stance is more casual when he thinks he's alone. When observed, his body snaps to attention, straightening, shoulders back—not tense, exactly, but not relaxed either.

I don't hurry to. Rather I enjoy the slight sway in his hips, the arch in his spine under his tightly fitted frock, the way his hair hangs in waves down his back. He's nice to look at.

"I know you're back there," Bowie croons, his rich tenor quiet but clear.

I give a little yip in response. I'm not ready to shift yet. It feels too good being a wolf with the moon's glow on my back and the cool night air drying my fur. I catch up and walk at his side.

"Have any luck?" he asks, though he must know the answer. He'd have heard the raccoon's squeal just before I broke its neck.

I flick my chin to indicate yes, I was successful at dinner, thank you. He grins as if he's heard the words from my mind. I wonder if he's hungry and how he eats if he doesn't kill. A question for later. One nice thing about being a wolf is that I can't be expected to hold a conversation, and sometimes, it's nice to have that break.

The road has widened again, joined with another coming up from the south. Trees line either side and reach across the divide, nearly forming a tunnel of leafy branches.

It must be midnight by now. I'm curious where we're headed and how we'll go about gathering information when most humans will be asleep by this hour.

We're close to the pasturelands and villager settlements that dot the landscape before reaching Varad proper. I've been here before, though Farkas forbids it. What he doesn't know won't hurt me. I would simply tuck my tail into my pants and pull my woolen hat over my flattened ears to blend in. Though not comfortable, it always does the trick. As long as I'm careful, no one is the wiser, and I'm usually able to find some companionship, however brief, among strangers.

Bowie is watching me again. I feel his gaze like the fizzling of the air as a summer storm approaches, tingling and warm. I glance up.

"Shall I fill you in on the plan for tonight?"

I huff-snort, and his grin returns.

"We're going to my sister's estate. Catherine is expecting me, and she'll be waiting up. You're safe with them if you'd prefer your human form, or this one is fine, but it's up to you. Don't pay any heed to what I said to Farkas. I'll not dictate your choices."

That's a relief, though I'd expected as much. Bowie isn't the controlling type. I'm overly familiar with assholes, and Bowie just isn't one.

"Catherine will know you're a werewolf, by the way, regardless of which form you take. Jakob too. And Istvan, the steward." He looks a bit sheepish. "I told them my plan to speak with the local pack and ask for help. They want to save the missing girls as much as I do."

Farkas would be furious. He guards our identities like he guards his power—with brute force and gnashing teeth. I understand the importance of secrecy more than most, but Bowie doesn't seem concerned beyond possibly offending me. His nonchalance on the matter is much different from what I'm used to.

"I'm sorry if that bothers you," says Bowie. "When I thought to seek assistance, it didn't occur to me I should keep it a secret. I consult Catherine on everything, but don't worry. She's discreet."

It will be interesting to meet humans who know what I am. I wonder if Bowie's sister lives in the giant stone mansion on the hill overlooking the town. They're noble after all. It could be their house. I've only ever seen it from a distance, its looming enormity a mystery reserved for the richest of men and not the likes of me or the peasants I interact with. We're headed that way.

Sniffing the air, I smell smoke from fireplaces and the earthy tang of farm animals along with the waste such creatures leave behind. If I'm going to shift, I'd better do it now before I completely lose cover. I look to Bowie and whine. When I've caught his attention, I stare at the satchel.

Bowie catches on immediately. "Shifting, then, are you?" He swings the satchel off his shoulder, folds the strap inside, and kneels to offer it to me.

I take it between my teeth and scamper off into the woods. When I'm dressed again, I toss the bag over my shoulder and join him.

"You're certain this is okay?" I ask. I've got on my disguise, which is really only a hat. Anyone who looks too closely will realize there's something off about my backside where my tail is tucked, but most people are too polite to mention it. Except children; they'll say anything.

"Of course." His hand flutters in front of him. "Why wouldn't it be?"

"Well, look at you." I flutter my hand to match his. "Then look at me." My shoulders hunch. "You're dressed so nice, and even in my best clothes, I still resemble the poorest of farmers."

"Frocks and stockings don't make a man, Andras. Character does, and yours is fine as any." He offers his arm with a crook of his elbow and a pointed glance.

I take it, still feeling self-conscious. We walk at a brisk pace. I suppose he doesn't want to keep his sister waiting. I understand, so I match his stride. Sure enough, we march directly through the farmland, then uphill to the most massive house I've ever laid eyes on. Never did I think I'd be welcome inside. My stomach flips, and the jitters set in. Next to me, Bowie is relaxed, and that helps.

The mansion appears even larger up close, with its giant white limestone bricks. Two attached towers stand on either side, wide and rounded, their charcoal-gray roofs like little hats, almost as if this were not a grand estate but an actual castle.

We pass through meticulously manicured grounds, gardens line a bricked courtyard, all of which smacks of wealth and resources unfathomable to me. As we climb the stairs to the tall set of wooden doors, one swings open, and a friendly servant appears.

The man smiles and bows. "Master Bowie."

I drop Bowie's arm as he nods to the man. "Istvan, good evening."

"Shall I take your coats?" Istvan looks from Bowie to me, realizes I'm not wearing one, and corrects himself. "Coat, sir?"

"No, I've got it, thank you." Bowie gestures to me. "This is

Andras, my guest. Please let the staff know to make him comfortable."

"Yes, sir." Istvan then bows to me, which I find utterly bizarre. "Master Andras. Should you need anything during your stay, I'm at your service."

I mutter an uncomfortable thank you and follow Bowie inside. Istvan closes the door behind us with a gentle click.

Bowie's confident stride takes us down a hall lit one either side with oil lamps and through another set of double doors into a sitting room. The pleasant scent of beeswax candles fills my nose. Inside, a tall woman of middling age rises to greet us. Her dress is shining emerald-green satin, bright even in the dim light.

"Bowie." Her voice is strong and warm. She smiles and reaches for him with both hands.

He takes them into his own. They resemble one another, with the same dark hair, high cheekbones, and lean frames, though she's much older than him. Older than I'd imagined a sister of his could be. Perhaps forty, whereas Bowie looks my age, twenty.

"Catherine, dear. So good of you to stay up for us." He kisses her cheek, then turns for me. Since he's stretched out a hand toward me, I come close enough to take it. He tugs me in farther. "This is Andras. He's the pack's best tracker and has generously agreed to help us."

Catherine graces me with a smile. If she's worried about me being a werewolf, it doesn't show. This close, I see her jewel-like green eyes match her dress the same way Bowie's match his coat. In an instant, her hands are in mine, and she's leaning forward. On instinct, I kiss her cheek, as Bowie had done, though surely not as gracefully, and hold my breath until she lets me go.

With a wave of her hand that reminds me of her brother, she

gestures to a chair. "You've come a long way. Take a seat. Would you care for a drink?"

Istvan remains at the entrance, waiting, I assume, to serve us. I decline with a shake of my head and try to disappear into the cushioned chair. Though everyone has been kind, I feel as if I don't belong.

Bowie takes over. Bless him. "Have you any news?"

A cloud passes over Catherine's pretty features. "Nothing good, I'm afraid. Rumors of another girl gone, though this one before the others. If it's true, she's been missing since early summer."

Seeing as it's late summer, that tells me she's been gone nearly three months. She must be very homesick...if she's still alive. The sobering thought brings with it a frown. I focus on the golden embroidered brocade of my chair, rubbing my fingers along the raised edges. It makes listening easier.

"From where?" asks Bowie.

"Debrecen, nearly a day's travel to the north. Whoever is responsible for stealing these girls has broadened their reach, coming this far south."

"Too many missing from one place would leave a clearer trail. This scattershot approach provides better cover. Little do they know we now have a tracker with the nose of a mighty wolf on our side."

I glance up because I know Bowie's looking at me. His confidence is well placed. I'm an excellent tracker, but I find their attention unsettling. I manage a smile and hope I don't look silly.

"Andras, dear, are you sure I can't get you a drink?" asks Catherine. "Brandy perhaps or port? Just because Bowie can't partake doesn't mean you shouldn't."

Catherine seems awfully comfortable with the notion that her brother is a vampire. Remarkable woman. I shake my head.

"No, thank you." I've never had spirits, and this would be a terrible time to find out whether I'm an easy drunk.

"We'll begin our hunt tomorrow at dusk," says Bowie. "I'll speak first with the families of the missing girls, which should give Andras an opportunity to catch their scents. Instinct tells me the trail will lead north. If you could gather the details of each missing girl to the north, we'll visit their families along the way."

"Already done. Istvan's left a packet of papers in your room with maps, locations, and the names of each victim—"

Catherine is cut off as a young girl clad in flowing layers of yellow silk bursts into the room, past a startled Istvan, and heads straight for Bowie. "Uncle!" Her gaze passes over me next. "And you've brought a friend!"

"Cecily," Catherine snaps. "What are you doing out of bed at this hour? In your nightclothes in front of company, really?"

Cecily, who is perhaps twelve or thirteen years old, looks not one whit ashamed. Her blonde curls bounce defiantly as if to punctuate her words. "I haven't seen Uncle Bowie in an age, Mama. I didn't know he'd brought a guest. Sorry." She lifts her skirts a fraction. "I did put on a dress," she offers in the most insincere apology I've ever heard.

"You didn't bother to lace it." Catherine rolls her eyes, but when they land again upon her daughter, her expression loses its annoyance and grows fond.

Flouncing onto Bowie's lap, Cecily sweeps up her curls to expose her back and the trailing laces. "Will you, Uncle?"

I don't know much about what is and isn't appropriate for a young noble lady to wear, but Cecily is thoroughly covered from head to toe. It seems to me she's thrown a dress over her nightclothes, all in various shades of yellow, and just wasn't able to affix the laces herself. To have clothes so fancy you need help to put them on is unfathomable.

She looks me over with wide eyes as Bowie obediently ties

up her laces. Though I must be quite the eyesore in her charmed life, with my shaggy hair and shabby clothes, her gaze holds the same kindness as her mother's and uncle's.

Cecily must resemble her father. Her face is quite different from theirs, oval-shaped with plump pink cheeks, strawberry-bright lips that grin like a naughty child who's gotten away with stealing sweets, and crystal-clear blue eyes of a shade much lighter than Bowie's stormy-sky irises. She smells so strongly of mint she must have a sprig of it on her person somewhere.

"Who are you?" she asks casually, causing her mother to tut.

"Manners, Cecily, please."

"Sorry, Mama," says Cecily with her eyes still trained on me. "Who are you, please?"

Behind her, Bowie laughs, finishes with the laces, and pats her back. She lets down her hair but doesn't leave her spot in his lap. Bowie tolerates this with the patience I've come to suspect is in his nature.

I swallow. "I'm Andras. Pleased to meet you." Somehow my name seems inadequate here. Like I should be Andras of so and so from such and such, but none of that exists for me. I'm just Andras, just a mongrel.

"My pleasure, Andras." Cecily's excitement spills over to her voice, lending it a high musicality as she speaks. "I am Cecily, Bowie's niece. Are you his beau?"

I can only blink.

"Cecily!" Catherine rises from her chair, takes the girl's arm, and gently pulls her from the relative safety of Bowie's lap.

"What? He's handsome. I thought—"

"Questions like that are inappropriate," Catherine chides. "But surely you already know as much. Besides, they've only just met."

"So? It could have been love at first sight!" Cecily claps a hand over her heart and swoons in a dramatic fashion. "How romantic." She catches her uncle's gaze. "Was it love at first sight?"

Catherine pats the girl on the bottom while shooing her from the room. "Go to bed, you horrible pest. To say such things to our guest! Have I not raised you better than this?"

Though the words alone could be harsh, their tone is soft, and Catherine is obviously holding back laughter.

"But my gown is now laced," Cecily whines as Istvan takes over, calmly leading her away. "And my maid is long since asleep. How am I to undress?"

"That's your problem, my darling. Should have thought of that before interrupting the adults in the middle of the night."

Cecily huffs, and as she disappears around the corner, calls out, "Good night, Uncle Bowie. Good night, Andras, Uncle Bowie's suitor!"

My cheeks flush with heat.

"That child is a nuisance." Catherine has a hand on each hip, somehow managing both a formidable glower and an amused smirk at once. "Andras, you must accept my sincere apologies for my youngest child. I'm afraid I've been far too indulgent in her rearing. She's become quite the little devil as a result. Her brothers never gave me this kind of trouble."

Bowie is enjoying a fit of laughter at his sister's expense. I'm not sure what to say, but a chuckle escapes my throat in spite of myself. I slam a hand over my mouth.

"No, no. Go ahead and laugh, my dear. I deserve it." Catherine plops back onto her lounge with a flustered sigh. "That girl will be the death of me."

I take her at her word and laugh along with Bowie. This family. The sister knows he's a vampire, the niece knows he fancies other men, the housekeeper knows I'm a werewolf, and all seem perfectly at peace with those details.

My life has been shrouded in secrets and hiding since before I even understood what those words meant, so this sort of openness comes as a delight. Against all odds, I find myself relaxing in their company. I enjoy watching them together, brother and sister, each with obvious affection for the other. They tease but with kindness. They're more likely to laugh at themselves than at the expense of another. I admire that.

They chat the rest of the night away, and I join in. Shy at first but with more confidence as time drifts by until I forget to worry that what I say might sound dumb. When Catherine starts to yawn, Bowie insists she get to bed. I can't believe how late we've kept her up. I can't believe how my night has turned out.

I can't believe I'm free of the pack and out of their territory.

CHAPTER 5

As late night turns to early morning, Bowie leads me up a flight of stairs to where a guest room has been prepared.

"My suite is here," says Bowie with a wave of his hand to indicate an open door revealing a dark blue interior and the pleasant scent of lavender and rosewater. We sweep past it. "And this"—another dramatic flick of his wrist to accompany the pause—"is Seashore."

Of course it has a name. I've never slept in a room so fancy as to be properly named, and suspect I'd be more comfortable outside under the shade of a willow tree.

I enter a sea-foam green palatial space big enough to fit all four rooms of Ava's cottage. I've never seen a bed so large. It stands like an island fortress among the other finery, covered with quilts in shades of aqua and white fluffy furs I'm instantly afraid to touch for fear of soiling their pristine beauty. Four towering posts rise, one from each corner of the bed, and over them hangs a drapery of green-and-blue silk.

As the name would suggest, seashells of every type decorate the space. Paintings of oceanside views adorn the walls.

I can't touch anything in this room. I'm pondering shifting to my wolf form and sleeping *under* the bed when Bowie pipes up.

"Or you could stay with me?"

My gaze darts to meet his in an effort to interpret his meaning. I'm not opposed to *sleeping* sleeping with Bowie, but in his sister's house? And so soon? What if it makes working together awkward?

But his face is open in a vulnerable way, not a flirtatious manner. He rushes to fill the silence. "Just to sleep, of course. I don't know much about werewolves, but I did some research. I know you're pack animals and prefer not to sleep alone. We could watch each other's backs?"

I relax. Take a breath. Of course he didn't mean...what I thought he meant. Just because Bowie favors men doesn't mean he favors me. I'm still a freak, and he's a handsome nobleman. A handsome *vampire* nobleman who surely could have his pick among men. I didn't want to sleep with him anyway. So why am I suddenly disappointed?

Bowie's correct about most werewolves not sleeping alone, but I've had to get used to it.

With a glance back to the gaping space, I know my answer at once. I don't want to be alone in this room, however nice it is. "You're sure you don't mind?"

"Not at all." The smile I'm coming to enjoy dances across his face, lips curling at the sides. "Come."

I follow him into his suite, which is actually several rooms. A sitting room as one enters, a space with a table, desk, and chairs, then the bedchamber. As big as Seashore but somehow less intimidating. The deep blue of the walls makes the space seem smaller, cozier, and though his room is clean, it's not untouchably pristine. It looks lived in, with possessions scattered around. Books, clothes, shoes, scarves—the normal stuff of life —clutter the surfaces.

Yes, I'd rather sleep here.

"Make yourself at home," says Bowie. "I've kept you up all night long. You must be exhausted."

I'm not, but I don't reply. The full moon would have kept me up anyway, and though I'm ready to sleep, I wouldn't say I'm exhausted.

Bowie is removing his blue coat, button by button. "I must ask a favor, a small one. Should you wake during the day, please don't peek out the windows. The drapes block out the light for a reason. The sun will burn my skin quite quickly."

The drapes are a thick velvet, also blue, with silver embroidery. They cover the windows so completely I hadn't known they were there. "I won't."

After folding his coat over the back of a chair, Bowie sits to take off his boots. "You're welcome to roam the grounds if you like. Catherine's staff will have food prepared when you're hungry. Her husband Jakob is a pleasant man. I'm sure he'll offer you a ride if you fancy horses. He has a stable full of the majestic beasts. Big ones, fast ones, fluffy ones. You name it, Jakob has it."

I like horses just fine, but they generally spook around me. I wouldn't want to scare them.

Bowie rolls his stockings down shapely calves, then rises and blows out the nearest lamp. "I fear I'm stuck in this room until sundown, but please don't let me keep you when you wake."

Nodding, I realize I've been staring at him and turn my back. I kick off my shoes, take off my hat, and pull my shirt over my shoulders, but the pants I leave on. I have nothing underneath, and I don't want to assume it's okay to sleep naked.

When I turn around, he's in some sort of cotton under-clothes, his bare chest revealing lean muscles, flushed nipples, and no hair to speak of. He folds the bedding down and slides in.

His bed is just as large as the one in Seashore, but it's not an island unto itself. Little tables stand on either side, each with a pile of books. There's no great draping tent above to make one feel trapped. The bedclothes match the room, dark blue silks with fawn-brown furs atop. Bowie gestures to where I should come to rest.

"Could you snuff the last lamp, please?" asks Bowie.

I admire him in the glowing orange light before fulfilling the request. His hair looks nearly black, loose around his shoulders in pretty waves, much like his sister's. His features are relaxed, not feigning respect like with Farkas or genuine amusement like with Ava or affection like with Cecily. He just looks tired and maybe a little nervous. Just as I am.

I snuff out the light and join him in bed. My eyes adjust quickly.

His unmistakable presence is impossible to ignore, so near to my side as I settle on my back. The pillow is like the fluffiest cloud, clean and cool under my head. The mattress too. It must be stuffed with fine feathers; it's so luxurious. I imagine this is the sort of bed angels must sleep on—heavenly.

"You can touch me," says Bowie, his voice low. "If you like."

My ears flick to attention. I swallow. Touch him how? Does he want to cuddle, or is he asking for more?

When I don't respond or move, he continues, "I mean, if that's what you're used to. I'm sorry. I've never had a sleepover with a werewolf before. I'm trying to be considerate, not... however that came out."

A breath passes through my lips. Touch Bowie. Hold him as we sleep. I want to now that the option is there. It would feel natural, but somehow it also feels dishonest because what might be true for other werewolves has never been true for me.

"The others kicked me out from their beds when we were still cubs," I explain. "What you've learned of wolves is correct for most. They're communal sleepers, but I usually sleep alone."

"Usually?"

"Well, I have Ava. I was still a child when I first moved in, and she coddled me until I was strong enough to be by myself." I hesitate, unsure whether revealing this next part will make me seem weak. I don't care. "But if I'm sick or have a nightmare, I can still curl up to her. Back to back so I know I'm safe."

"Ah, we should all be so lucky," says Bowie, making me glad I chose to share. "Well, the offer stands. I promise not to bite."

I laugh. "The vampire promises not to bite."

"Unless you ask nicely."

"And if I ask meanly?"

"Then I shall withhold my sharp kisses until you learn some manners." Bowie shifts under the covers, rolling onto his side to face me. "I cannot be seen to reward bad behavior. Then what would you think of me?"

"I've no idea what to think of you," I say to the ceiling. "You aren't anything like what I would have expected."

"What did you expect?"

I consider that. Vampires were the subject of scary stories passed from the older cubs to frighten the younger ones. "I thought vampires were monsters. Killers in the night, stealing human blood and leaving a trail of corpses in their wake. But you..."

"But me?"

"You tease your sister and dote on your niece. You live in their house, not in a coffin, and you invite mongrel werewolves into your bed, then worry if you've offended them."

"Just the one," he quips.

"I stand corrected."

"Are there others like you?"

"Mongrels? I don't think so." I look at him in the darkness. Even in shadow, his features are attractive. He has a hand curled under his cheek. "I suppose there could be, but I've never seen another."

"If I may be so bold as to ask, how did you come to be, Andras? I've never seen another either."

No one has ever asked me this part because everyone in my life already knows my worst secrets. They spurn me because of them. Will Bowie?

I don't ever want Bowie to view me the way Farkas does, but Bowie is a better man. I decide to risk it. For the first time in a long time, I think I could make a real friend.

But since I've never told this story, I'm unsure where to begin. I open my mouth, but the words don't come.

"You don't have to tell me if you don't want to," says Bowie in a soft voice. "I didn't mean to pry."

A laugh huffs from my throat. "Yes, you did."

An answering chuckle comes from Bowie. I feel the puff of breath on my shoulder. "Only a little."

"I'll tell you. I just don't usually talk so much. I'm not used to it."

"Take your time."

I collect my thoughts. I suppose it would make the most sense to start with my mother. Though I never knew her, Ava has since filled in the details. "Before I was born, my mother got into some trouble. Farkas's uncle, Vuk, was the alpha then, and she disobeyed the rules. She left him no choice but to punish her."

Sighing a breath, I tell the next bit faster, hoping that maybe if I rush through it, this time the story won't be as painful. "She fell in love so deeply with a human villager that she chose to reveal her true nature to him. He didn't take it well, told others, and panicked the town. Vuk was forced to take drastic measures to calm the rumors, for a while going so far as to relocate the entire pack. My mother was banished for her crime, driven east into the Carpathians to die or go feral, whichever came first."

Bowie's hand closes gently around my wrist. His cool touch is an unexpected comfort. He says nothing, so I go on. "Well, she didn't die, at least not right away, but she must have succumbed to her wolf entirely because nothing else explains what happened next."

I dread this part. "One winter's night some years later, she crept into camp, naked and emaciated in her human form—holding me, a sick, wailing infant she couldn't care for."

When I pause, unsure how to spell the next bit out, Bowie's whisper breaks the silence. "She must have loved you very much to let you go."

I've never really seen it this way, but I suppose he could be right. Ava has explained my mother was too far gone to raise a son and that it was a miracle she managed to shift long enough to bring me to safety.

"She left me at the home of a girlhood friend of hers. A wolf with three cubs of her own and no time for another. I suppose the woman felt obligated to take me in, even though I was the obvious product of a forbidden union."

"Your father is a real wolf, then, an animal?" Bowie guesses the truth of it. Or he already knew and says as much so I don't have to. Either way, I'm grateful.

"Yes." The word comes out like a weight falling from my shoulders. A confession. A burden from my very soul.

"What a remarkable woman your mother must be to go on living when she could easily have given up. And you, my dear"—he squeezes my wrist—"you are unique among millions."

No one has ever interpreted the story this way before. Stunned, I flip my hand in order to take his, but immediately I worry mine is too hot or too sweaty or too gross to touch. If he thinks so, I can't tell because he only gives another tender squeeze, then interlaces our fingers.

"You're magnificent, Andras," Bowie says with a confidence I wish I had. "The real crime in this tragic tale is that Ava seems to be the only one smart enough to know it."

My heart thumps so forcefully I wonder if it's trying to escape my chest. My whole life, I've been hated, an outsider, a freak, and in one night, Bowie has made me feel like I could be special. I'm used to people being mean to me; what I'm not prepared for is someone being nice.

My eyes water with unshed tears. I'm glad for the thick curtains and the enveloping darkness of the bedchamber. I don't want him to see I'm crying, though I have a feeling his night vision rivals my own.

"Come, let me hold you," says Bowie.

My body accepts the invitation before my mind can pose an objection. He shifts to his back, and I roll to my side to settle against him, my hot skin against the coolness of his. His arm circles my waist. Mine lies heavy on his chest, the other tucked beneath me. I curl into him as if we are lovers, and he accepts the embrace with that natural ease he has in all that he does.

"Sleep now," Bowie whispers against my hair. "You are safe here."

This is an entirely new experience for me. I've had lovers, mostly human, but I've never had anything like this. Never truth. Never acceptance. I feel whole in a way I hadn't known was possible. Pressing my nose to his skin to better scent the sweet attar rose oil, I take a deep breath and relax my muscles. Already sleep nudges heavily at my senses.

Bowie's hand caresses my back from the fur along my spine to the skin at my flanks. I think I let out a sigh; I'm not sure because I'm floating.

I close my eyes, wondering if this is what peace feels like and hoping I can keep it forever.

CHAPTER 6

I don't get up to explore the estate or seek out a fancy breakfast or meet the stable's horses because nothing short of a tornado could convince me to leave my place against Bowie in this bed. Even a tornado would warrant serious consideration, perhaps a list of merits and flaws, before I consent to budge a single inch.

We're tangled together beneath the soft silken bedsheets. I can't tell where I end and Bowie begins. The slightest shift brings blissful awareness of all the places we touch: foot to foot, thigh to thigh, cheek to chest. My head rises with each inhale he takes and falls with each exhale. Though his heart doesn't beat, mine pounds loud enough for two.

Is this what it's like for the other wolves? The ones who aren't excluded? Wolves who find their mate? Because I've never slept so well in my life.

Bowie stirs, a subtle movement that begins in his hips and ends with a quiet yawn. I stay perfectly still because I'm not ready to unwind from this warm cocoon we've spun. My hand rests on the round curve of his shoulder. The muscles beneath my fingertips tense and release as he stretches.

Inklings of fear prickle in my chest. I squeeze my eyes tight. What if he's changed his mind? Doesn't want me in his bed anymore? Am I about to be rejected?

His hand firms and comes alive against my skin. He rubs my spine from nape to lower back, ruffling the fur there. I want to arch into the touch, to ask for more, but the anxiety isn't gone, just paused, waiting for what he'll do next.

He nuzzles into my hair. "G'morning, Andras." His voice is rough. I feel his breath along my scalp as he clears his throat. "I trust you slept well?"

Like the dead, but I don't say that because I know Bowie is sensitive about the dead thing; I remember from our walk to Varad. "Yes. You?"

"Very well." He scratches his nails through the fur between my shoulder blades.

If I were a cat, I'd purr. Thank the moon I'm not a cat.

"You're like my own personal furnace."

My eyebrows knit together. "Is that bad?"

"Course not." More scratching. "I love it."

How is he real?

His hand trails to skin, causing chill bumps. "I never got used to being cold."

I like the coolness of his body against mine, though I have no easy words to tell him so in the way he's just reassured me. Words come readily for Bowie. I can, however, return the caress. I slide my fingers from his shoulder to his collar bone and notice a section of raised flesh, gnarled and thicker than the rest.

As I lift my head to see what I'm feeling, he explains, "Would you believe I was almost staked *before* I became a vampire?"

It's an impressive scar, above his heart but too close for comfort, perhaps three inches long and one inch wide. The flesh is marbled pink and white next to the creamy pale healthy skin around it. "What do you mean, staked?"

Bowie arches his brows. "Don't you know how to kill a vampire?"

"I know how to kill a lot of things. Are you special?"

His laughter brings a smile to my lips. He's handsome like this, freshly woken, head haloed by his wavy brown hair on the pillow.

"Special? Probably not, no. However, I can survive a great many abuses mortal men cannot. But a stake through the heart? That would surely finish me."

"That would finish anyone." I press my fingertips to the scar. "What happened?"

"Nearly a stake through the heart. Luckily, I missed." His mood seems awfully light for the topic at hand.

I'm confused. "*You* missed?"

"Indeed, my fault. I was in a hurry and dared to jump my favorite gelding over a fence to make it home before my father noticed I'd gone. I wasn't supposed to leave, you see. Something spooked the horse at the last minute. He refused the jump but sent me sailing forward to crash into the fence."

I wince. "Oh my. Impaled by a fence pole? That must have been agony."

"I nearly died. And when I failed to die, my father nearly killed me himself." Bowie's expression darkens. He shakes it off. "Butter was unharmed, and that's what mattered to me."

I wonder at that fleeting expression but dismiss it. "Butter?"

"The horse, silly." Bowie taps my nose with his finger. "Keep up."

I swat the digit away. "Who names their horse Butter?"

Bowie pulls a faux-offended face. "He was an absolute pearl of a pony with a shining coat the color of freshly churned butter. It was a perfectly sensible name for such a good boy."

I should have known. "So *you* picked the name."

His playful gaze holds no shame. He grins, flashing gleaming white teeth. "Guilty."

"Well, I'm glad you didn't die. What would your tombstone have read?" I give it a try.

"HERE LIES Bowie of Varad
   a man with no common sense
   who spooked his Butter
   and it was death by a fence."

MY SILLY RHYME is rewarded by the mellifluous sound of Bowie's laughter, and I vow to myself then and there to become a poet henceforth.

"It would have served me right," he says between chuckles.

I hover over him, watching him regain his breath. Our gazes meet. I savor the fond expression he gives me. Then I worry that staring at him like this might be off-putting or even a little desperate. I roll away from him and sit up.

Bowie laughs again, only this time, I don't know why. My stomach clenches, muscles tensing. I don't like being laughed at.

"Your hair." He chokes out the words. "You must look at yourself in the glass. It's sticking up taller than your ears."

Oh. Well, that's not so bad. My ears twitch as I relax and comb through the tangles with my fingers. His silky tresses fall over his shoulders as he sits up, looking perfect, of course.

I shuffle to the garderobe to take care of business and stop at the water basin to wet my unruly hair. A silver comb with intricate engraved filigree along the handle lies on a shelf, but it looks too nice to use. My fingers will do.

When I return, Bowie is dressing. Cream stockings and shirt with black knee-length pants and another blue doublet. Blue must be his color. It suits him well, but so would a burlap sack. I shrug my arm into the same shirt from last night. Bowie stops me with a hand to my elbow.

"May I offer an alternative?"

I look at the tattered shirt, worn thin from use, and though it's clean, the fabric holds old stains that refuse to wash out.

Bowie rushes to fill the silence. "Not that there's anything wrong with your clothes. Only, I have so much, and we are near to the same size. I'd love to see you in black." His tongue darts out to wet his bottom lip. "Or maybe red."

Heat creeps steadily up the back of my neck. Before it can make it to my cheeks, I surprise myself by accepting. "Black."

He smiles, having gotten his way, and pulls from the wardrobe a soft black shirt nicer than anything I've ever worn. The fabric feels like rose petals in my hand, velvet smooth and light against my skin as I put it on.

Though he's a bit taller, he's correct. We're of similar size. However, Bowie is obviously accustomed to garments tailored to fit him, while I'm not. So the shirt feels tight simply because it sits closer than my usual clothes. I stretch my arms wide, throw them over my head, and twist. It's not bad; the shirt moves with me well enough. I could get used to this.

Bowie watches with the amused expression I could also get used to, his eyes glittering. "Very nice. Would you also like a coat?"

I shake my head. That would be too much. I don't get cold easily, and the weather has only begun to turn. I pull my hat over my ears, flattening them to my head. It muffles my hearing, but hiding them is a necessity regardless.

"Shall we get you some breakfast?" asks Bowie.

A twinge of worry clouds my appetite as I think of the massive house I'm in, of the servants, and the room they'd prepared for me that I didn't use.

"Will your staff be upset when they realize Seashore hasn't been slept in?"

"No, they will not." Bowie pauses. "Or if they are, the staff know better than to say as much. And my family certainly won't mind, I assure you. No need to worry."

I take him at his word, for I have no other choice. If he isn't concerned, then I won't be either. "All right, then. Breakfast."

We head downstairs, where we find Catherine's had the cook prepare an enormous meal the likes of which I've never imagined. As my eyes feast upon the extravagant display running the length of a polished wooden table that must seat a dozen, I try not to drool. My stomach betrays my enthusiasm with a gurgling rumble.

"Good morning," says Bowie to his sister, who's already seated at the head of the table.

"It's evening," she corrects with a flutter of her lashes to accompany her eye roll.

"Not to me, it isn't." Bowie sweeps around the table to greet her with a kiss on her cheek and gestures to a seat. "Come along, Andras, help yourself."

I've frozen, watching the two of them interact with each other. They're so alike, even decades apart in age. Or—a thought occurs to me—perhaps Bowie hasn't actually aged since he was…bitten? Turned? I must ask him later.

As I make my way to the table, my gaze drifts over the options. Smoked meats, fried potatoes and beets, hard breads, an assortment of cheeses, and dried fruits present a colorful array of choices. I spot candied figs and wish Ava were here to enjoy this with me.

"Did you sleep well?" asks Catherine.

I'm momentarily embarrassed because I slept wonderfully— with her brother—and I've no idea if that information has reached her ears yet or not. I mumble, "Yes, thank you," while keeping my focus on the food.

"You'll have to excuse Jakob," she says with a fond smile. "He's out on an errand but sends his regards to our guest."

Bowie hands me a plate, and I'm immediately glad to have

something to do with my hands. I serve myself some of every-thing and sit next to him. The place setting before him is empty, of course, and makes me all the more curious about his meal schedule and how that must work.

Breakfast, or supper really, is uneventful except for the whirlwind of yellow skirts and golden curls as Cecily bursts in to say good evening. She then dramatically apologizes for having kept us waiting (I hadn't realized we'd been waiting, and by the looks of it, neither had Catherine or Bowie.) and apologizes further for having to leave right away on urgent business.

As I'm wondering just what nature of urgent business a twelve-year-old girl could possibly have, she explains, though no one has asked.

"Lilith has got a new racing hound, you see. A puppy! She's calling him Imre. But that is a silly name for a dog, don't you think? I'd rather she call him Fire Feet or Lightning Strike, but she won't listen. Anyway, we're teaching Imre to fetch, so I really must be off."

Cecily grabs a handful of mint candies from a glass dish on the table and stuffs them into her dress pocket.

"Be careful, darling. Don't rush," says Catherine. "Be home before bedtime, or I'll send your father after you."

I get the impression this isn't the threat her mother thinks it is by the jovial expression on Cecily's face as she races from the room. "Yes, Mother!"

I turn to Bowie. "I see she has the same knack for naming animals as you do."

He swats my arm. "There's nothing wrong with the name I chose."

"Did he tell you about Toast and Butter?" Catherine asks with a chuckle.

I grin and side-eye him. "You had a horse called Toast as well?"

"Um-hmm," Catherine answers before Bowie can defend

himself. "Butter's younger sister. Together they were Buttered Toast."

Bowie leans back in his chair and gives an impish shrug. "She was the perfect shade of brown to be called Toast. Was I supposed to resist?"

"You could have." His sister flashes an indulgent smile. "But you never do."

CHAPTER 7

We're on our way to visit the homes of the missing girls from the surrounding villages. Bowie carries my satchel, and I walk as a wolf on all fours by his side. I won't have to worry about being exposed as a werewolf if I'm simply a wolf. A *trained wolf*, as Bowie suggested—his pet. That's the story we're going with. I'll get the most scent information in this form anyway.

"May I pet you on occasion?" asks Bowie as we approach a small log hut. "For verisimilitude, of course."

I rub my cheek against his leg and huff, secretly enjoying the fact he smells like me.

He reaches down and strokes my fur. "My goodness, you're soft."

Oh, that feels nice. I tip my head up for more, and he offers it with a smile. If this is what being a pet wolf is like, sign me up.

We walk side by side to the front door, and Bowie knocks. Inside, I hear shuffling and voices. It's not too late, but it's an odd hour for visitors nonetheless.

The door swings open to reveal a harried-looking man of middling years, his face gaunt with worry. His anxious expression shifts to full-blown concern upon seeing me, though I'm seated just behind Bowie, trying my best to look docile.

"Apologies, good sir, if you'll be so kind as to pardon me for calling unannounced." Bowie bends gracefully at the hip, bowing to the peasant as if this man were the nobility and Bowie just an average farmer.

"That's all right," says the man. His dark eyes, though haunted, look kind, and he keeps them on me with caution. "What can I do for ye?"

"I'm Lady Catherine's nephew, Beauregard. I'm here on her behalf. She thought perhaps we"—Bowie steps to the side and gestures to me—"could be of some use to help find your daughter."

The man's face falls at the mention of his missing daughter. My heart goes out to him. I didn't miss the fact Bowie called himself Catherine's nephew. Is that because the brother should be closer to her in age?

"S'that a wolf?" he asks, though surely it's obvious.

I don't blame him for his trepidation. Tame wolves are uncommon, and though I may be small for a man, I'm quite large for a wolf.

Bowie strokes my forehead. "Only part wolf. The other part is hound." The lie slips from his lips with ease. "No need to fear him. He's a gentle giant."

I see the jut of the man's Adam's apple as he swallows. "As you say." He offers Bowie his hand. "Name's Albert."

Bowie clutches the man's wrist. "I wish we'd met under more pleasant circumstances, Albert. May we come in?"

Albert's gaze lands on me. "Can he really find my Bethie?"

"I can't make any promises, but we're going to try."

Pushing the door wide, Albert steps aside to allow us to enter. "Thank you."

It's a humble dwelling. The inside smells of damp earth, cheap tallow candles, and the sweat of working people. A woman sits in a low chair, her sewing abandoned in her lap, watching. With hunched shoulders and eyes red and puffy from tears, she is the picture of a grieving mother. Beside her, a young girl, perhaps seven or eight, has fallen asleep upon a rug on the floor.

"My wife, Rahel," says Albert. "And please pardon Esther. She won't stay in her bed since her sister…" At this, he trails off sadly.

Bowie gently fills the silence. "Greetings, madam. I won't trouble you for long. My wolfhound needs to pick up your older daughter's scent in order to follow the trail, and I have but a few questions."

"Of course, thank you," says Rahel, her voice strained as Albert drags an extra chair from behind a modest table and gestures for Bowie to sit.

If there are any useful details to be had from the grief-stricken parents, I trust Bowie to uncover them. Meanwhile, I patter away to the only other room in this house.

A small adjoining bedchamber makes up the back half of the home. One straw mattress rests upon the floor covered in brown woolen blankets. A second is shoved upright against a wall to make room for a child's puzzle game on the floor. A tall chest with crooked cabinet doors stands between.

I imagine two sisters playing in the room, perhaps arguing, but still enjoying each other's company. At night the other bed would be tugged to the floor, and the girls would sleep soundly across from their parents, knowing they were safe. What happened to the poor elder sister?

I dip my nose to the creaky wooden floorboards and gather all the information available to me. This family smells of farm work, earth, and the animals they care for. Simple foods, vegetables and poultry cooked without any of the fancy spices found at Bowie's table. Minerals from the water used to rinse and cleanse their clothes. Good smells. Normal smells.

Following instinct, I make my way to the first bed, and it's all very much the same. A familial scent with four slight variations, one for each member of the household. The upright bed holds the scent of the missing girl more strongly than the one on the floor. I close my eyes and concentrate, committing her smell to memory so I can follow her trail.

Pausing, I take in the game left sprawled across a tattered blanket. Round pebbles about the size of olives on one side, flatter rocks on another, the whole thing divided by four sticks. It isn't a game I know, and I wonder how to play.

Saddened, I take a final whiff and head back to the others. Bowie sits straight, his ankles crossed, hands in his lap as if he's purposely trying not to wave them about as he speaks. The younger girl, Esther, is awake now and in her father's lap. She sees me first and lets loose a delighted squeal.

"It's a doggy!" Her grin spreads wide, and she starts to scramble from Albert's lap.

He stops her leaving with a quick arm about the waist. "No, no, Es. That's a wolf. You must be careful."

Her face falls. "I want to pet him."

As Albert begins to console her, Bowie catches my gaze and raises his brows. It's obvious he wants me to let the child approach, but he's not rude enough to offer without my permission. I slink to his side and dip my chin. I'd happily do anything to make the girl forget her troubles, if only for a moment.

"Albert," says Bowie. "So long as it's all right with you, she's welcome to pet him. He's really quite docile and accustomed to people."

Albert looks nervous but Esther has already perked up. She aims her big brown eyes directly at her father and croons, "Please, Papa? Please?"

He gives in, as would I, as would anyone with half a soul under such a sweet, charming stare. "Go on then, but be gentle. That wolf is a noble creature, and you must be kind."

"Yes, Papa." Esther's on me in a heartbeat, tiny hands in the long fur of my ruff, giving my neck a very nice scratch indeed.

Oh I like her.

My tail wags like it has a mind of its own. It likes her too.

She kneels in front of me and tells me I'm handsome. I would tell her how pretty she is if I could. I try to let her know with my eyes. She giggles and sits back on her heels. The moment her hand drops, I nudge my snout against it and put my chin in her palm. When she scratches there too, I melt. I love that spot.

"What's your name, boy?" she asks me directly as if she absolutely knows I could answer her if I wished to.

I glance to Bowie, who for once is at a loss for words. He can't rightly call me Andras. It isn't a name used for dogs. And I know he won't say Mongrel, though it really wouldn't bother me in this situation.

Both the parents and the girl clearly expect him to say something. All eyes are on him, including mine.

"It's really quite silly," says Bowie, and I think he's just stalling for time until I see the mischievous sparkle dancing in his eyes. "His name is Beans."

Esther giggles. Even Rahel cracks a small smile.

"Beans?" asks Albert. "Heavens, why?"

I'm thankful wolves can't fall over laughing because surely that's what I'd do in my other form. *Buttered Toast and Beans.* Bowie really is ridiculous. I wonder to which level of hell Dante would condemn him for this atrocity of naming.

Bowie's grin is careful, but present. He doesn't show his teeth, but he's no doubt amused with himself. "He likes to eat them. Learned that the hard way when he stole more than one of my dinners as a pup."

"Such a handsome boy, Beans," says Esther, her little hands like magic running through my coat. She asks Bowie, "Does he know any tricks?"

Now I'm in for it because there's no way he'll let that one slide. And really, I don't want him to. This family deserves a moment of levity, even if it must come at my expense.

"Does he know tricks?" says Bowie, as if the question is preposterous. "Well of course he does, fair Lady Esther. He knows dozens. What would you see him do?"

Esther squirms with barely contained enthusiasm. "Can he shake hands?"

"Indeed, he can. You must stand in front of him, hold out your hand and say, 'How do you do?'"

Esther hesitates, suddenly shy. She glances back to her mother.

"Go on," says Rahel. "Ask how Beans is doing."

She climbs to her feet and follows Bowie's instructions to the letter. I wait for her to stick out her hand, then reach out my paw to meet it. Her laughter is a treasure to my ears, tinkling with the sort of delight only young children possess.

"Now," says Bowie. "Ask him to dance for you. Move your hand like this." He elegantly flails one pointer finger in little twirling circles.

"Dance, Beans." Esther copies his movement.

I'm not entirely sure what they want me to do, but I spin in a tight circle and hope that's enough. The joy on her face tells me it is. Bowie looks positively gleeful.

"All right," says Albert. "Very good, Esther. Very good, Beans. But we should let the wolf rest now, don't you think?"

Esther happily goes back to petting my forehead. I collapse at her bare feet, completely content to let her pet me the rest of the night.

But Bowie's not quite done with his show. "One more," he says, and I glare from my spot on the floor. "Esther, give him a good scratch just behind his right ear."

Oh no.

Esther shifts her hand to obey.

"Yes, that one," Bowie encourages. "Right there."

Oh no. Oh no. Oh no!

"Just a wee bit harder."

Esther hits my absolute favorite spot. I have no control over myself when someone scratches behind that ear. It's just so good!

I lose it. My leg jitters and flails, as if possessed by a throng of itchy gremlins. It thumps the floor wildly. My tail flails and my tongue lolls from my mouth. I am a puddle of bliss at Esther's feet, and I hope she never stops. *So good, so good, so good.*

Bowie's laughter is the first thing I hear as I come back to my senses.

Albert rises to collect little Esther, giving my head a nice pat. "Very good wolf," he says and scoops her into his arms. "And you, small miss, must be to bed. Say good night to your new friend."

"Good night, Beans," says Esther. I miss her already.

I'm still recovering from the delirium as Bowie stands from his chair and thanks them for speaking with him.

"We're off to follow the trail right away," he says. "Don't give up hope."

I stumble somewhat drunkenly to his side. His hand lands on my head. I lean into the touch. I can't help it. I'm quickly coming to adore him even though he just unabashedly exploited my greatest weakness.

"Thank you," says Rahel, the sadness returning to her voice.

I shake off the lingering effects of Esther's affection and sober up. Bowie and I have an important job ahead of us. I glance once more around the humble home, its missing member a hole in the very heart of this sweet family.

We must bring Beth home to her little sister. To Albert and Rahel. I know I can find her. I just hope she'll be all right when I do.

"Oh, my dear Andras," says Bowie as we leave the last of the missing girls' houses. "I cannot believe my luck in finding the most tolerant, the most kind, and the most clever werewolf in the land!"

I snuffle-snort next to him. He's had me put on the Beans performance twice more tonight, and I can't find it in myself to be bothered, even though I do feel rather silly when I entirely lose my mind in front of strangers.

But that spot! It's magical.

"You're not mad, are you?" he asks, though his face holds its usual mirth. He already knows I'm not mad.

I snarl because it's fun. And because we need all the levity we can get in these circumstances, which if I dwell on them, are overwhelmingly depressing. I can't sink that low, or I'll be useless to the girls. So I don't dwell on it. Instead, I nip Bowie on his rump, then make a break for the tree line.

"Ouch!" He races after me, faster than I knew he could go, and overtakes me with ease. Suddenly, he's in my path, and I must swerve to avoid running straight into him.

Bowie lunges, tackling me from the side, knocking us both

to the ground. In the grassy field, he rolls me to my flank and triumphantly pins me with an arm around my furry ruff. His laughter is a delight.

"Didn't know I could do that, hmm?"

I didn't. He's faster than me. A lot faster. What else can he do?

"That's what you get for biting my ass, you wild creature."

He deserved it. I roll out from under his arm, stand, and stretch. My fur is all wrong, so I give a vigorous shake to right it. Meanwhile, Bowie stays lying in the long grass, flopped onto his back, staring up at me with those shining blue eyes of his.

It's been a difficult night. Seeing families in anguish over missing daughters is an experience I wouldn't wish on anyone. Bowie treated each grieving family member with tenderness as I stalked around their homes, making sure to commit each unique scent to memory. The task was hard on us both.

I couldn't help but notice how he tempers himself around strangers. He loses the hint of flamboyance I've come to associate with him and becomes more proper, more reserved. I wonder at that, but it's not my place to ask.

"Do you feel like shifting and telling me what you've learned?" He slides his arm beneath his head and crosses his ankles as if lying in this field was actually our end goal for tonight. "You don't have to, of course. I'm just curious what you're thinking."

We do need to talk. I don't know what he's learned either; I was too busy tuning him out and concentrating on the smells to keep up with his conversations with the families. But what I actually want to do right now is lick him. One big slurp, maybe two, right across those chiseled cheeks of his.

I pad forward, intending to retrieve my satchel. His free arm comes up to pat my neck.

"You were really something," he murmurs in a low voice, "with Esther. You made her happy. Thank you."

Luckily, I can't blush in this form. I give in to temptation and lick a broad stripe from chin to ear. When this earns me a grin, I do it again. Then I nose at the satchel, grasp it with my teeth, and give a tug.

"Oh, right." He sits up, takes the bag from around his shoulder, and hands it over. "There you go."

I wander off into the forest. I'm not sure why privacy beckons; it just does. When I'm far enough into the trees to feel like I'm alone, I roll my neck and coax my body to change. With a rush of sensation that feels a lot like the moment you jump into cool water, my flesh obeys the command. Bones morph and reform, fur becomes skin, and my snout flattens to the familiar shape of my human face. Of course, the ears, tail, and ridge of fur that connects them remain as always, ensuring I can never blend in with other werewolves or humans, but I've accepted this.

And now I have Bowie. I find myself hoping that once we've solved the mystery of the missing girls, perhaps we can remain friends. I would like that.

I dig through the satchel and pull out the black shirt Bowie loaned me as well as my pants and leather shoes. My hand lingers on the soft, worn cloth of my rag doll, Marta, and I relax. Silly that a child's toy still brings such comfort, but I'm glad I brought her. She deserves an adventure as much as I do.

After dressing, I swing the satchel into place and take a few deep breaths of sweet-smelling forest air. Pine trees mix with deciduous, and their needles coat the ground as their scent permeates everything around us. This would be a good spot for a nap, but I've got scent trails to follow. Being limited to the hours the sun doesn't shine will hinder our progress, so we need a good start before we rest.

Making my way back to Bowie, I see he hasn't budged from his spot among the greenery. His eyes are closed, though surely he hears my approach.

"I'm dressed," I say, feeling shy.

"Pity." His lips curl to a grin while his eyes remain closed. He pats the grass next to him.

I sit cross-legged and take the opportunity to stare at his face. Dark lashes fan in perfect crescents over his cheeks, and his upper lip juts out ever so slightly over his fangs. That reminds me...

"Bowie, you haven't eaten." Or at least I haven't seen him eat. "Have you?"

He shakes his head. His eyes flutter open, revealing stormy skies. "Not in a while, no."

"Aren't you hungry?"

"I am."

My brain has trouble putting those facts together in a way that makes sense. "Then why don't you eat?"

"It's complicated." He must see my confusion because he continues, "It's not always easy for me to feed. I don't condone killing, and there aren't many humans I can trust with the truth. So to feed from them, I must lie, coerce, and nudge their very memories aside to quench my thirst. It doesn't seem fair."

"Nudge their memories?" I'm glad I eat only prey animals, not humans. I can't imagine the guilt. "You can do that?"

"Not well and not always. Some minds are too strong for my manipulations. So I must be careful."

"How long can you go without eating?"

"Well, it's drinking, really, and sixteen nights is the most I've ever made it."

Sixteen nights without a meal sounds like living torture. "How long have you gone now?"

"Not long."

"How long, Bowie?"

"Four nights." His hand settles on my knee. "Don't worry about it. I'll manage."

Now that I think on it, four nights without a meal also

sounds like living torture, but I take him at his word. "Did you learn anything useful?"

Bowie's lips part on a sigh. "Not particularly. Three girls gone, all near to the same age, twelve to fourteen, none who knew each other, all missing for nearly three weeks. Whoever took them has a good head start on us."

He sounds defeated already. My thoughts drift to the worst of the unspoken possibilities, and I can't decide whether or not to voice it. Instead, I study Bowie's hand on my knee. Slim. Pale skin. Long, graceful fingers and perfectly buffed nails. I decide to speak up. "You know, it may already be too late."

His gaze intensifies and becomes desperate. "I have to believe they're alive. I have to."

I do too. "I didn't smell any unusual amount of blood at any of the houses, nothing like that."

"Thank god. Tell me what you did learn. Will you be able to follow their scents?"

"Yes, to a point. Scents fade over time, so we should hurry." I don't want to give him bad news, but I must. "There's a problem. I could be wrong. I won't know for sure until we begin following the trails, but the paths diverge. Tonight's three scents led in two different directions."

Bowie's eyes widen. "What?"

"With any luck, they'll converge."

"I've been operating under the assumption the girls are being stolen away to the same place. If that's not the case..."

"I know." I place my hand over his, warming the cool flesh with mine. "This complicates matters."

"It could be a nomadic band. Stealing them and selling them into slavery. In which case, there could be dozens of trails to follow."

I can think of only one piece of good news. "We're in luck that at least it hasn't rained."

Bowie's face crumples. "Rain! I didn't think of that. How hard is it to track a scent after a rain?"

Well, I thought it had been good news, but Bowie's right. It's only a matter of time before weather inevitably interferes. "Much slower. Not impossible."

"We must hope for no rain then and move quickly. What's the plan?"

My jaw drops. I'm to come up with the plan? I feel inadequate to the task. Following Bowie's instructions I can do, but making decisions for both of us? My heart begins to pound. What if I'm wrong? The consequences could be dire. Panic rises in my chest. Those families are counting on us. On me. If I fail—

"Andras." Bowie sits up, bringing himself directly in front of me. He drops my hand to put both of his on my cheeks. "Just breathe."

I blink and suck in a gulp of air. My palms are sweaty.

"There, that's good." He keeps his voice low and soothing. "You're all right."

I wrap my hands around his wrists to keep them in place. They're cool against the rushing heat of my cheeks. The back of my throat is tight like a vise, and I can't think.

"Look at me, Andras. We're all right. Can you tell me what's happening?"

I'm not sure I can, but I will try. "Scared," I mutter.

He nods, eyes locked on mine. "This is frightening, isn't it? I'm scared too."

That's hard to believe. He seems so unflappable. "You are?"

"Yes."

Somehow, that helps. It becomes easier to control my breath. I close my eyes and just feel his hands on me. Slowly, my racing heart finishes its sprint and returns to normal. We sit together in the field as the sound of crickets chirping filters back into my consciousness. I think on the scent of each girl, how two went north and the other east. I have an idea.

My lids flutter open to find a concerned expression on Bowie's face, his forehead wrinkled, brows drawn tight. He gives me a sweet, closed mouthed smile.

"How long until sunrise?" I ask.

Bowie glances at the sky. "About six hours."

"Then we spend three following the trail that goes east, then three back here to the safety of your home. Tomorrow we follow the other trail north and hope to discover they converge." This next part is hard to say. I don't like abandoning either trail. "If not, we continue on the trail of two girls rather than the trail of one."

"That's wise. I agree."

A huff of relief escapes my lips. Though not perfect, it's good to have a plan. A place to begin.

"How are you?" he asks.

"Better now. I'm sorry. I don't know what happened."

Bowie shakes his head. "You've nothing to apologize for." He draws me in, plants a soft kiss on my forehead, and releases my cheeks.

I could swoon. I don't.

"Ready?" he asks.

I suppose I am. I want to cover as much ground as possible in the next six hours. The more information we can collect, the better chance we have of solving this mystery and bringing the girls home alive.

I nod. "Let's go."

THIS TIME no one has waited up for us as we return, exhausted, to Bowie's mansion on the hill. I'm glad about it. I don't want to disturb anyone, nor do I have much to say. It will be our last night here. Tomorrow, we follow the second trail, which leads north, toward Debrecen where yet more girls have gone missing. I will play Beans again to collect their scents. Then with luck, their trails will converge into a singular direction. I don't want to think of what could happen without luck.

I feel defeated. Following a scent, only to have to turn around when the trail keeps going, is agonizing. So many girls and precious little time.

Bowie leads us on silent feet up to his room. I try to match his effortless quiet, but my steps are clumsy in comparison. Still, I'm careful not to wake anyone as we make our way to the inner chamber of his bedroom.

"We'll have to say our goodbyes early and head straight out at sundown," says Bowie, beginning to strip off tonight's set of clothes.

I nod in agreement and find myself watching him again. I don't mean to stare, but his every movement is as graceful as dancing. He's mesmerizing.

He notices my attention, and I look away, embarrassed. I undress to my pants, which I leave on, and hurry to bed. My eyelids are heavy, my body is drained, but my mind stays restless. The missing girls, these new places, a handsome vampire, and a maze of faint scents keep me on edge.

Bowie douses the lights. The bed shifts to accommodate his weight. He shuffles rather close but doesn't touch me.

"Tonight was hard," he whispers. "How are you feeling?"

Questions like this often stump me, but this time an answer comes straightaway. "Muddled. Overwhelmed." I rub my hands over my face, trying to wipe away the memory that arises. "Like when I was a cub, under the full moon. We'd all shift to play hide and seek. But when I hid, no one looked for me."

"How awful. That breaks my heart," says Bowie with the sincerity of the sort of person who'd never condone that kind of cruelty.

"I knew I should do something, but I didn't know what. So I

just stayed there in my hiding spot, frozen, wondering where everyone else had gone. Pathetic."

"Not pathetic. Not at all. What a nasty thing for the other children to do. You must know it's not your fault."

"Everything feels like it's your fault when you're young." I'm not sure when sadness became anger or when anger turned to apathy, only that the apathy is easier to live with. I consider it an improvement.

"Mmm. Isn't that the truth?" Bowie sounds as if he's never moved beyond the sadness. He hasn't spoken about his youth, and I'm hesitant to pry.

I tell him the truth behind my fears. "I'm afraid it will happen again. I'll freeze, and I won't know what to do. Only this time, it won't be me who suffers. It will be innocent young girls."

The bed dips with Bowie's movement as he shifts to press against my side. His arm comes around my waist, and his chin lands on my shoulder. "Don't be afraid, Andras. We have each other to lean on. I won't let you freeze."

I turn into him and let him draw me into a tight embrace. How did I live so long without this simple comfort? He feels good against me, so natural and safe. Whether it's wise of me or not, I trust Bowie to keep his word.

"I'm sorry to ask so much of you," he murmurs. His breath wisps across my collarbone. "I knew this plight would be taxing. I couldn't do it alone. Thank you for volunteering to help."

His thanks mean a great deal to me. I want to tell him not to apologize. That I'm glad to be here. That our mission is important, and I understand the urgency. But what comes out is:

"Ozor wouldn't have been nearly as snuggly."

That earns me a laugh from Bowie. He pushes his nose into my neck and sniffs. "He wouldn't smell as nice either."

"I smell like a wet dog."

"You most certainly do not." He takes another whiff. "You

smell of the grasses we traversed, of fresh spring water straight from the earth, and of the spicy nectar of blood pumping just beneath your skin. Together it's intoxicating."

His snuffling tickles my throat. I squirm to press him closer, for a firmer touch, more real and less teasing. Stupid of me because as his lips make contact with my flesh, I'm forced to suppress a moan.

A vampire who's just told me my blood smells intoxicating is mouthing at my throat, yet my only worry is not to let on how much I like it for fear he might stop.

Bowie doesn't stop. He licks my neck, one broad stripe, like another wolf, not a lover. "You taste nice too." His breath is cool over the wet patch he's left behind.

I shiver.

He rises to catch my gaze. "You did lick me first." It's dark, but somehow I know his eyes are sparkling. "It's only fair."

He's teasing, and I like it. But a part of me also wishes he were serious. A part that longs for Bowie to look at me with desire rather than the fondness of blooming friendship. I'm quiet, watching him watch me, enjoying his closeness.

Bowie's smile fades. He lays his head back down beside mine and gives my waist a squeeze. "Good night, my dear. Sleep well."

I return the embrace, determined to be content just to have him in my arms. It's more than I've ever had before, and I won't take the intimacy for granted.

"Night, Bowie. Sweet dreams."

As soon as Bowie is safely able, we rise, collect our things for the journey, and head downstairs so I can eat before we say goodbye. I'll miss waking to an extravagant breakfast. Catherine insists I eat my fill, and when I stop after one serving, she loads another plate herself and sets it in front of me with a pleased expression.

"You're a growing young man. Eat up," she orders.

I won't argue with Bowie's sister, and the extra portion of roasted fowl spiced to perfection slides down without protest. Bowie grins as he watches me eat.

Jakob joins us, and I meet him for the first time with my mouth stuffed full of vegetable stew. He's all smiles and laughter, so I don't feel bad. His plate is piled as high as mine, and he's nearly twice my size. A gentle giant, who greets his wife with a kiss to her lips that makes her blush, and his daughter with a gentle pluck of her curls so they bounce out of place.

"Father, really," Cecily tuts, grooming her hair back into submission.

Jakob winks, and her put-on little scowl lifts to a grin.

Bowie brought the packet of maps and information Istvan

curated for our journey, but we can't go over them with Cecily present. The subject might frighten her. He chatters away while the rest of us eat. If it bothers him that he can't partake, he does an excellent job of hiding it behind words.

"If Lilith dashed in front of a stampeding horse, would you do so as well?" he asks Cecily after she pleaded for a new puppy of her own because if Lilith could have one, why couldn't she?

"Well, of course not, Uncle. That's silly," Cecily huffs.

"Might it also be just a smidgeon"—he lingers on the word, holding two fingers pinched close together—"silly to have a puppy only because your friend does?"

But Jakob shrugs. "I don't see what it would hurt."

Her eyes light up. "Really, Papa?"

Catherine casts a pointed glance at her husband. "Then that's you caring for the pup when Cecily bores of it because we can't ask Istvan to take on yet another task around this place. The staff is burdened enough as it is."

"I shall take care of him myself," Cecily promises. "Cross my heart." Her gaze lands on me. "Have you ever had a puppy, Andras?"

Surprised by the question, I open my mouth to say that I haven't when Bowie's expression turns amused. He jumps in to answer in my stead. "Litters and litters full of them. Some of them still behave like pups, though they are grown. I saw a few when we met."

"What kind?" asks Cecily. "Racing hounds like the one I will have?"

"No, dear. They're more like wolves." Bowie wrinkles his nose. "Smelly ones called Ozor and Jolan and one particularly nasty one called Farkas."

I try and fail to conceal my laughter.

"You must be kind to your pup so he grows up to be kind himself," Bowie says to Cecily, but his sparkling eyes are on me as I chuckle.

"Of course I'll be kind."

"Don't you have something to do?" Catherine says pointedly. "The adults need to speak alone, and since you've gotten your way, *again*, I should think you'd like to tell Lilith."

"I have plenty to do, but none of it is more interesting than watching Uncle Bowie fawn over Andras."

Jakob sputters, barely managing to swallow his wine, and returns the goblet to the table with a *thunk*. "Young lady, you mustn't embarrass our guest."

"I'm not trying to embarrass Andras. I'm after Bowie. You did hear him suggest I jump in front of a stampeding pony?"

Jakob tips his head. "That's not *precisely* what he said."

She may not have been trying to embarrass me, but my cheeks are hot, and I fear they're pink as rosebuds. Bowie still stares unabashedly, though under the table, his hand finds my knee in a calming touch.

"Just you wait, Cecily," says Bowie. "Someday, you will fancy a boy, and on that day and forevermore, I shall tease you without mercy, for you show me none."

Cecily raises her blonde brows. "You won't."

"Shall we wager—"

"All right," says Catherine. "No gambling with children, brother. Cecily, off with you. And don't bother Istvan either."

Cecily mocks a pout but leaves without argument, surely eager to visit her friend.

Catherine shakes her head. "Andras, I must apologize again for our casual manners. We're really quite uncivilized."

I remember Bowie has already told them what I am, but it still feels delightfully forbidden to say it aloud. "Well, I was raised by werewolves, so you may rest assured I don't judge."

Bowie is the first to laugh. When Catherine and Jakob see that it's okay, they join in.

The next hour is filled with studying maps and plotting the locations from which girls are rumored to have gone missing.

Our intention remains the same—we follow the scent trail. But if our quest leads us close enough to speak with the families so I can catch additional scents, all the better.

Jakob folds and stacks the papers to put them into Bowie's bag. My satchel is already in there. I feel bad he must carry everything for both of us, though he insists it's no trouble. Catherine offers to have the cook pack food for me, but I decline. I can catch my own dinner, and that will be less weight in our bag.

As we stand to leave, Jakob speaks up. "Bowie, oughtn't you?" He tilts his head to the side, revealing the long stretch of his neck. "Before you go?"

Bowie's usual fine posture wilts at the edges. Hardly noticeable, but I've taken to observing him closely. He shakes his head. "I'm fine, brother."

As Jakob's gaze narrows skeptically, I realize what he's offering.

Blood.

"You should," I say to Bowie. According to what he told me, this would make five nights of fasting. My stomach would riot in protest. Why wouldn't he want to eat? Er...drink rather. Jakob is a huge man; surely he can spare a few mouthfuls. I wonder if Bowie would drink from me if I offered. What would that feel like? It must hurt.

Bowie gives a resigned nod and follows Jakob from the room. I stare after them with curiosity nagging at my mind like an itch I long to scratch. How does Bowie feed? Is it as simple as a bite? How much blood does he take, and how many nights will it suffice?

Catherine clears her throat, and I whirl to face her, caught woolgathering. "They won't be long, dear. Are you sure there's nothing I can pack for your journey? Some bread and cheese maybe? Or those figs you nearly drool over?"

I grin. The candied figs really are a treat. Something about the look on her face makes me give in. I know the feeling of wishing to provide for someone you care about, and though we've just met, her generous nature is obvious. "Well, maybe just a few figs. If you really don't mind."

Clasping her hands happily, she says, "Perfect!" and springs into action. The entire dish of figs is emptied onto a pristine cloth napkin and carefully wrapped. Catherine ties the little bundle with a piece of ribbon lacing she pilfers from her shirt-sleeves. She knots it with a dainty bow and smiles as she stuffs them into Bowie's bag.

"Thank you. I'm not sure what your cook does to make them so delectable, but it must be magic."

"Magic? Or cinnamon and honey? Same thing if you ask me." Catherine points a finger and gives it a little shake, not quite as dramatic as Bowie's hand-talking but similar. "I'll have our cook make her ginger-spiced cake when you return. If you have a sweet tooth like me, you're going to love it."

Everything about those words sounds like heaven. Ginger-spiced cake. And I'd be willing to bet they'll let me bring some home to Ava. "That's motivation to return promptly."

"Oh, dear." Her face falls. "I do hope it won't take long. Those poor girls. They must be terrified."

I nod my agreement, but I really can't think about it. I'm not strong enough. Anytime I veer close to seriously considering the magnitude of the kidnappings, I choke up inside. My gut churns, and my throat clenches as if I'll be physically sick. Best to just get on with the task rather than dwell on it.

Jakob returns with Bowie in tow. The big man looks no worse for wear. In fact, I can see no change in him at all. But if feeding a vampire causes no ill effects for the volunteer, why is Bowie so hesitant to partake?

The coppery hints of blood filter to my nose, not an unpleasant smell. If I hadn't just eaten enough for two wolves, the scent would probably make me hungry.

Bowie emerges from behind Jakob, his complexion pinker along the high ridges of his cheeks. His lips are blushed darker than usual. Blue glittering irises flash bright against their crystal-white background, like sapphire jewels set in quartz. If possible, he looks younger than before, though I've yet to ask his age. His beauty is striking. I can't take my eyes off him.

"Ready?" he asks, breaking my stupor.

I grunt an affirmative. I've lost the ability to speak.

Bowie parts from his sister and brother-in-law with hugs and kisses. Jakob's big arms swallow him up in his embrace. "Be careful," he says. "Take good care of Andras."

"I will." A playful smirk forms on Bowie's lips. "Good luck with *your* new puppy."

Jakob releases him from the bearhug and claps him on the shoulder. "I think you're wrong about that. Cecily is ready for the responsibility."

Bowie's laughter rings out. "If you say so, but I think you'll be cleaning puppy piss off your fancy rugs in no time."

Catherine takes my hands. Her warm gaze lands on mine with genuine concern. "Thank you for helping my brother. Be safe."

I don't know what to say, but I don't have to respond because Bowie takes my arm and says, "Not to worry, we'll be fine."

We leave Bowie's massive estate and hurry through the village to take the road north toward Debrecen. With any luck, the trail will lead straight to the city. Traveling on a maintained roadway will be much faster than combing through wooded paths.

It's a cool evening, with a gentle northerly wind caressing my skin. The moon hides behind a high layer of wispy clouds, and I thank the stars they aren't rain clouds. A quiet settles as we make our way past farmlands and pastures toward the forest.

Before I shift to better follow the scent, I want to ask at least a few of the dozen questions that linger on my tongue. With Bowie so vibrant beside me, I'm dying to know more about how he feeds and why he waits so long between meals.

We are alone aside from the animals and the chirping insects. I take off my hat and shake free my ears, flicking them this way and that to enjoy the bug chorus with clear hearing.

I'm not sure how to start the conversation, so, clumsily, a question barrels from my lips without much forethought.

"Does Jakob feed you often?"

Bowie peers at me from the sides of his eyes, brows raised. "Why do you ask?"

For such a chatty creature, he's oddly sensitive about this topic. "Because I want to know."

He blows a breath through his nostrils, maintaining his stride. I keep pace next to him and bite down the urge to apologize for the question. I've been honest in answering him; this seems only fair.

"Yes," says Bowie with no further explanation.

My brows knit together. "What's wrong?"

"Nothing," he lies.

I decide to press. It's hard to know where his boundaries lie with these uncharacteristic one-word answers. "Then why don't you want to talk about this?"

"Isn't it enough that I don't?" He doesn't sound angry, just sad.

He has a point, and an uncomfortable guilt coils in my gut. "Sorry," I mumble. Maybe I should shift now. Bowie clearly isn't in the mood for conversation, and I don't want to risk upsetting him further.

I untuck my shirt, Bowie's shirt really, from my pants and lift it over my head. As I'm folding it, he halts suddenly. I make it a few steps ahead of him before my body catches up to my mind and stops too.

"No, *I'm* sorry," says Bowie. He strides forward until he stands an arm's length in front of me. "I'm not upset with you for asking. My relationship with Jakob is complicated. I am…" His gaze drops to the ground. "Ashamed of my need for human blood. Remorseful for past crimes driven by this infernal craving. Jakob knows my sins and helps to prevent them with his selfless offerings. I don't know what I'd do without him."

I shouldn't have asked. I've made Bowie uncomfortable and pulled from him a reluctant confession.

"There is more," he continues. "But it's a long story, and I won't come off well in the telling."

I wish I hadn't upset him. A Bowie who's unable to meet my gaze—favoring the ground instead—isn't the Bowie I've grown accustomed to. "That's all right. You don't have to."

"I will," he says, voice soft. "I'll tell you."

I take the one step that exists between us and tuck myself into his space. Nuzzling my nose into the soft spot where jaw becomes throat, I breathe his delicious scent. I don't know how to calm using words, but touch comes naturally. I hold his waist and will him to feel better. To forget I asked.

His arms come around my back, and his muscles unclench. He tilts his chin to allow me more room. I use it to press my cheek to his neck, mixing my scent with his. I whisper into his ear, "Tell me when you're ready. Or don't. I understand."

He takes my cheeks gently in his cool hands and draws my face in front of his so he can look at me. His eyes have darkened, deep blue and storm filled. They shift from my eyes to my mouth.

For the span of a few heartbeats, I think he's going to kiss me, but the moment passes like dandelion seeds on the wind. Instead, he says, "Thank you. For being so patient with me."

I'm all warm and tingly. A nod is all I can manage.

He releases my face and steps back. "You're going to shift?"

Right, that was the plan. "I should. I'm faster as a wolf, and you've proven you can outpace me even when I'm on four feet."

Bowie winks. "Someday, we'll have to race."

"I'm not that dumb. I already know you'll win."

His finger lands on my lips. "You aren't dumb at all. Don't say that."

I smile behind his finger. He removes it. I thrust my folded shirt into his hand to put in our pack. "Let's see how fast we can make it to Debrecen."

He rolls his shoulders and cracks his knuckles. "You're on."

My eyes go wide. "Wait, I didn't mean a race."

"I'll give you a head start."

"No, we aren't racing."

"So, no head start?"

"Bowie!"

"Fine, fine. Onward, mighty Beans. I shall follow in your wake."

I roll my eyes and rouse the wolf. "Come along, then."

CHAPTER 10

My instinct proves correct as the scent trail follows the public road and leads straight to the city of Debrecen. Even better, the trail of the girl who was first taken east converged partway, meaning we're now on the scent of all three missing girls from Varad.

We've been traveling all night. It's early morning, and we have only an hour or so before sunrise. Since the hour is wildly inappropriate for us to call on the families who've lost girls from this area, we're forced to call it a night and find a place to sleep for the day.

I shift back to my human form, hiding my tail in my pants and my ears beneath a black hat so people won't be startled by a wolf roaming their city. I can't hear as well with my ears smushed flat, but the city is mostly quiet anyway. It's too early for birdsong or roosters, and most people are still asleep in their beds.

"Where will we hide?" I ask Bowie, wondering if we can walk into an inn at this hour.

"There is an establishment that caters to our kind near the heart of the city."

Our kind. What does he mean by that? Are there other were-wolves here? And do people know about them?

He continues, "A meeting place of sorts run by a"—here Bowie hesitates—"brother of mine called Ivaz. We can take a room for the day."

"You and Catherine have a brother?"

"Not Catherine." Bowie takes my elbow as dirt roads become cobbled streets and the buildings get closer together. "Ivaz is a vampire made by the same vampire who made me, Bettina. We aren't real brothers, but Bettina likes the familial terms. And I like to keep her happy."

I have so many questions, but the last time I tried asking one, it didn't go well. I'm hesitant to try again.

Already I can tell Debrecen is much larger than Varad. A proper city and vast, sprawling from one street to the next from a central hub like the legs of a spider. The smells here aren't pleasant. Too much incense and strong decorative aromas that try—but fail—to mask the scents of human waste, rotten food, rodents, and mold. Perhaps to a human nose, it's not so bad, but each competing odor will make it more difficult to follow the missing girls when it's time to distinguish by which road they left.

"This is your first experience with a city under Ottoman rule, yes?" asks Bowie.

I murmur an affirmative. My eyes are as busy as my nose, taking in the complexity of my surroundings.

"Debrecen is a sanjak of the Turks, but most of the villagers are Calvinists."

"Is there fighting?" I don't smell recent bloodshed.

"Not currently, but control of the area has been wrested back and forth between the Ottomans, the Voivode of Transylvania, and whichever Habsburg is ruling at the time for decades. Luckily for the people of Debrecen, this is a notable market town with a history of gifted local negotiators. All they need to know is who to pay their taxes to this week, and otherwise it's business as usual."

Humans are so complicated. "How do you know all of this?"

Bowie gives a lingering sigh. "As a young man, I was groomed to be a worthy heir to the family title and estates." His free hand joins the conversation, waving in front of him. "Before my father changed his mind and deemed me unworthy, I received a proper education. As a vampire, I was blessed with a learned, albeit often absent sire, and a veritable gaggle of her many wicked children to further my studies." His eyes catch mine. "And I'm naturally curious. Like you. So I took advantage."

It's clear he thinks of this as a compliment, so I smile. Ava often called me curious. Growing up, I was lucky to have access to all her books, but I read mostly stories and folktales, whereas Bowie must have studied everything. "Do you speak other languages?"

His fingers dance in an elegant flourish, *"Oui, monsieur, je parle aussi Francais, le langage de l'amour."*

The words roll off his tongue like caramel dribbled from a spoon onto a luscious dessert.

"That means I also speak French, the language of love."

My cheeks flush warm.

"My mother's side is French," he explains. "I can also read Latin and German, but I speak neither."

I could listen to him speak French all night, but he quiets as we walk.

We pass a dozen or so closed-up market stalls, their banners and signs hanging low, unreadable in the dark early hours before dawn. I wonder what they sell. I smell meats and spices and know I'm near food vendors. Mixed with the other scents, even food smells are unappealing. A wave of longing for the wide-open woods, the pine-fresh air of the forest, and the simple comfort of Ava's cottage churns beneath my skin.

I take a breath and focus on Bowie's cool presence at my side. I'm glad one of us knows what we're doing. He leads us through Debrecen as easily as he led us through his home village, like he knows these streets just as well. Again, I suspect he's older than he looks.

"Here we are." Bowie releases my arm and turns sharply down a narrow alley. He tugs open a heavy wooden door placed oddly between two buildings sharing a brick wall and stands back for me to enter. I peer into the dark cavern below. A stone staircase descends to a pit of black. Damp and stale, it gives me the creeps.

I hesitate at the threshold. "Are you sure?"

Bowie's hand lands on the small of my back. "Sorry, dear. Ivaz's place is somewhat spooky, isn't it? I promise it's better inside."

This helps me precisely none at all. "If you say so."

"Here, I'll go first." Bowie brushes past me, and I follow on his heels. The door closes behind us with a thud that makes me jump. My vision adjusts, but it doesn't help much. The dark is so complete my eyes pick up almost nothing. A narrow staircase ending at an equally narrow hall. Perhaps doors on either side, but I can't be certain.

"Can you see?" I whisper.

"Yes. You can't?"

"No."

Bowie reaches behind to take my hand. I grab it like a man drowning. The walls are closing in, and they're taking my lungs along for the ride. Shutting my eyes and concentrating solely on Bowie's solid presence in front of me helps. His hand is cool in mine, and he hurries us down another set of steps. We must be two stories under the earth now. I've never experienced anything like this. Our footsteps echo off the stone floor.

Bowie slows us to a stop and raps three times. I open my eyes as a door opens, and a warm orange glow spills into the hall. Now that I can see, I take the chance to peer back from where we came. The little hallway is built from dark stone. It's swept clean, and the passage is clear of any furniture or decoration. Just a tunnel—nothing to fear.

"Beauregard of Varad," says Bowie to a petite dark-haired woman at the entrance. "Brother to Haci Ivazzade Pasha. And I've brought a guest, Andras."

Again I notice the simplicity of my name next to others. At least Andras is better than Mongrel.

Music drifts out from within A stringed instrument, perhaps a cittern, plays a lilting melody. The woman speaks over the tune. "Welcome." She steps aside so we can enter. "I'm Anna. I'll fetch Ivaz for you. Will you need accommodations for the day?"

"Yes, thank you, Anna," says Bowie. "And a bath, please."

"Of course. One room or two?"

"One will suffice."

"Are you in need of a meal?"

"I am not."

"And your guest?"

Bowie glances to me. I panic. He answers, "Meat and cheese, dessert if you have it. Thank you."

I'm still clutching Bowie's hand as if I'll perish without it. I'm probably standing too close as well, but looking around at the sight only makes me more hesitant to leave his side.

Crackling wall torches light a scandalous scene in glowing golden light. It's the people I notice first, more than a dozen men and women, some of them near to naked as they lie sprawled against others. Vampires, but not all. Humans too. Their scents mingle, so I can't tell which is which, with the exception of a naked bear of a man with his head tilted awkwardly to make room for a vampire's sharp fangs.

Bowie releases my hand and wraps an arm tightly around my waist. I lean into him as the feeding vampire glances up and catches my eye. Quickly, I look away.

The room—or series of rooms rather because one leads through to the next via a wide archway—comes into focus. Low lounging furniture lines the walls in jewel-toned velvets. Purples, greens, and ruby reds don't so much blend together as fight for dominance within the opulent space. Intricately painted vases stand half as tall as a man, their scenes depicted in shining silvers and golds. Even the tables have a metallic sheen, copper and brass next to gleaming mahogany. It's easier to focus on the decor rather than the people.

The scent of sex and blood permeates every corner, floats in the air, overwhelms my nostrils. Bowie gives me a gentle squeeze. "Come, Andras. Let me pour you a glass of wine."

That sounds good. He steers me farther into the room, past sights I ignore, and to a tall bar stocked with dozens of bottles of wines and spirits. He opens a cabinet door as if he owns the place and plucks out a crystal goblet. I wish it were a sturdy wooden mug instead.

"With water or without?" he asks.

"With, please," I mumble.

Bowie pours a bitter-smelling burgundy wine into the glass, stops halfway, then tops it with water from a pitcher. "There you are. Don't fret. No one will harm you here." He keeps his voice low, and though no one reacts, I wonder how many can hear him.

I sip my drink and lean back into his side as his arm returns to my waist.

"Shall we sit?" Bowie glances around the room, unaffected by the various couples at play, searching for an empty couch.

I'm saved from touching any of the furniture as a newcomer glides into the room on silent feet. Though he makes no sound, heads turn as he enters. An imposing man of tall stature hides a bulky frame beneath a richly embroidered blood-red robe. A golden sash delineates a comparably narrow waist, and tight golden sleeves strain over bulging muscles.

"Ah," says Bowie. "Here's Ivaz now."

Of course this intimidating man is Ivaz.

He guides me toward the behemoth in silk, who's already spotted us.

Ivaz doesn't smile exactly, but his eyes flare with recognition. For a big man, he moves gracefully as he meets us halfway. He doesn't look unfriendly, but he has a serious air about him to which his dark hair, eyes, and eyebrows lend a menacing quality. He's much older than Bowie. I'm not sure how I know that; it's as though the knowledge is part of his presence, a feeling that runs bone deep.

"Bowie," he says in a rumbling baritone, one hand extended. "Welcome, brother."

Bowie takes his hand. "Ivaz, it is good to see you."

"And you've brought"—Ivaz's smooth gaze takes me in from head to toe.—"a lone werewolf?

I suppress a shiver and the urge to cling to Bowie with the tenacity of a parasite.

"My goodness, that's unexpected. Greetings." Ivaz extends his hand.

I take it. His flesh is cool like Bowie's. A firm grip, but not overpowering, though his hand is twice the size of mine. "Greetings."

"This is Andras," says Bowie. "He's helping me with a very important mission."

"Is that all he's helping you with?" Ivaz lifts his lips in an amused smirk.

Though I can't see Bowie's eyes, I know he's rolling them. His hold on my waist tightens. "Don't tease. Tell me, have you heard from Bettina? I could use her help as well."

"She's in Vienna sorting some snafu with the twins. Something to do with King Matyas. I don't expect her back anytime soon."

"The twins *again?*" Bowie frowns. "Could I send a letter anyway?"

"Of course. Is there anything I can do to assist?"

"Perhaps. At the very least, I'd like to speak to you about the matter. In private. But first, Andras needs to eat and get settled. And we'll both need to bathe."

"Anna should have all that prepared by now. Come, I'll have her fetch parchment and ink for your letter." Ivaz turns, and we follow him from the parlor rooms, through a hall, and to my horror, down yet another flight of steps.

I try not to think of just how far into the bowels of the earth we've traveled. Aside from the low ceilings and lack of windows, the interior could be that of a castle, for all I know. Stonework, paintings, oil lamps, fancy rugs—it's all rich and eye-catching. To think, an entire city is waking far above our heads as we walk.

With a sweep of his big hand, Ivaz gestures through an open door. "Here we are. The bath is still being filled."

This becomes evident as a servant with a bucket full of steaming water nods to us as he passes into the room.

"Generous as always, Ivaz," says Bowie. "Thank you."

Ivaz clasps his hands low and dips his head. "Anything for family. I'll be in my study. Come to me whenever you're ready." His gaze shifts to me. "Andras, if there's anything I can do to make your stay more hospitable, you must let me know."

I should thank him, but my mouth refuses to budge. I manage to nod.

Ivaz's stony face breaks into a smile as he chuckles. "I must know how you found this one," he says to Bowie. "Surely there's a story worth telling."

"Let Andras be," huffs Bowie. He escorts me into the room and closes the door on Ivaz's smirking face.

"Apologies for that." Bowie's hands drop to his hips. "I'm

realizing now I should have probably warned you vampires can be blazingly rude. Are you all right?"

I'm still gripping my wine glass. My knuckles have gone white. I force myself to relax my muscles. "I'm fine."

"Oh, dear." Bowie stands in front of me and studies my face. "You're really not, are you? Are you claustrophobic? I didn't think to ask. I'm so sorry."

Shaking my head, I recover my tongue. "I'm not. Or at least, I don't think I am, though I've never been this far underground to test the theory."

"Is there anything I can do?"

There isn't. In any case, it's better now that we're alone. I glance past him at the room. Hot water steams from a wooden bath barrel in the corner. I can't believe that's just for us. A large bed stands against the wall, overflowing with thick black furs. The same type of furs—bear, if my nose is to be trusted—covers the floors. An excess of lamps, perhaps a dozen, flicker about the room, lending it a brightness I wouldn't have expected in a vampire hostel.

"I'm all right," I say to reassure Bowie. It's mostly true. I'm growing accustomed to being overwhelmed at least. "Are there other werewolves here?"

"I don't know. I can ask. Would you like to meet others?"

Fear prickles. All my life, I've been told other packs would never tolerate me the way mine does. I'd be banished. Or worse. I took this at face value and believed it to my core, but now I wonder. What would another werewolf think of a mongrel? I recognize it would be useful to find out either way, but that does little to diminish my fear.

"Maybe," I say. "If you were with me."

Bowie smiles. "I'd be happy to accompany you."

A knock at the door interrupts us. I step farther into the room as Bowie opens it to reveal Anna with parchment and ink.

"Anything else I can fetch for you?" she asks.

"No, thank you, this is all."

Anna departs, and the door clicks shut. I'm gazing longingly at the enormous tub. A hot bath is a luxury to which I'm unaccustomed. I tug off my hat and shake my ears free. They twitch in appreciation.

Noticing a covered tray of shining silver upon a low wooden table, I suspect that's my dinner waiting for me.

Bowie takes off his coat and hangs it on a rack. He rolls his shirtsleeves up and takes the writing utensils to a desk on the other side of the room. He puts them down but doesn't sit.

"Andras, why don't I speak with Ivaz now? You can enjoy your meal and a bath in privacy, and I'll have a turn when you're finished?"

I don't want him to leave, but don't so. I nod instead.

He steps forward and peels the wine glass I've mostly ignored from my fingers. "I promise you'll be safe here. Try to relax." A dazzling smile. "The bath will help."

"Bowie, how old are you?" I blurt out of the blue.

His smile fades. "Forty-three."

"And how many years a vampire?"

"Twenty-three."

"And Ivaz?"

"Older."

"How much older?"

"I'm sorry. It's not my place to say. Shall I ask him if it's all right to tell you?"

"No." I don't want Bowie's intimidating brother to know I've asked about him.

"Andras, would you prefer I stay?"

Yes. "No, I'm all right. A bath will be good."

"And supper."

"Yes, that too."

"When you're done with your bath, pull that cord"—he indicates a gold rope hanging from the ceiling near the bed—"and staff will come to drain and refill the tub for me."

Such luxury. "I will."

"I won't be long," says Bowie. He sets my wine glass next to the silver tray and glides from the room, leaving me alone.

I kick off my shoes and peel away my clothes, wondering how old the vampire who made both Bowie and Ivaz might be. Bettina. Though Bowie would like her assistance, I can't help but be glad she isn't here. I'm not sure I want to meet a creature older than Ivaz.

As I climb into the tub, the heat encases my body like a forbidden embrace. Such luxury for the likes of a mongrel seems an illicit pleasure, one that might never happen again, so I might as well enjoy it now.

I stare at the ceiling as my muscles release their tension. A large archway of dark stone. I've no idea how such a thing was constructed so deep within the earth. It makes me glad to be a wolf and not a vampire. Wolves need no fancy dwelling. A pile of fresh pine needles and the shade of the tree from which they came is enough for their comfort.

I close my eyes and duck my entire head beneath the surface. Sound is muted to a dull ripple, lulling me to relax. I feel weightless, my body light, my mind, well, not tranquil exactly but less anxious.

My thoughts stray to Bowie, naked and wet, his dark hair soaked and clinging around his shoulders. Bowie smiling, his fangs on display. Bowie on one of those velvet couches, lounging with fresh blood on his lips from a recent meal, legs open so I could sit between them.

My cock plumps to hardness.

I'm alone. As if possessing a will of its own, my hand reaches down and strokes. A moment passes where I worry I shouldn't, but I dismiss the concern. No one will know. Bowie said himself the bath will be drained and refilled. And I haven't been alone for days. Nights. I need this.

As I drift toward bliss, I try not to think of Bowie. It seems wrong somehow to fantasize about him like this, in secret.

I try.

But I fail.

CHAPTER 11

When Bowie returns, I'm in bed under the thick covers, nearly asleep, dressed in a robe I found hanging by the bath. His face holds an uncharacteristic scowl.

I shake off sleep and sit up. "What's wrong?"

"Bad news." He rubs his shoulders, then rolls his neck. "You're not going to like it either, I'm afraid."

Worry patters its way across my mind. "What's happened?"

Bowie glances longingly at the waiting tub full of fresh, warm water. With a sigh, he trods over to the bed instead and sits next to me. "I sent word to Bettina requesting her help. Then I filled Ivaz in on what we know. I could tell by the look on his face it was no longer news to him."

I blink, stunned. "He knows about the missing girls?"

Bowie nods. "Whispered rumors have been circulating, though only recently has the matter become known among certain aristocracy, and thus, to Ivaz."

"Well, what does he say?"

His gaze darkens. "There are theories. Turkish slave traders, for one. But even more peculiar, there is a noble woman from a prestigious family who's thought to have left a trail of dead bodies in her wake across the whole of Hungary. Young maidens."

My jaw drops.

"Her name is Erzsébet Báthory, and if the rumors are true, she is a killer with an appetite so large as to require new victims from farther and farther abroad. Hence the insidious path of her *girl snatchers* to Varad."

I hear him, but I can't take it in. "How does Ivaz know?"

"Apparently, it's been going on for some time. First at her castle in Sarvaar, then at every location she traveled since, even so far as Vienna. All north of here. And now likely in Csejthe, where she's settled since the death of her husband, Ferenc Nadasdy. The killings have gotten worse since she was widowed."

My mind spins. "But if people know, why is it nobody's stopped her?"

Bowie pinches the bridge of his nose. "It's only in looking backward that the pattern became obvious. The early deaths were all peasants and explained away as outbreaks of plague or cholera. The bodies were burned or buried quickly to stem rising panic. No one would dare accuse a noble of such crimes, especially not a highborn lady. Her uncle was the King of Poland. Her cousin is Voivode and Prince of Transylvania. It's risking your own death to accuse one of such status."

"But the girls…" I can't finish my own sentence.

"Many may still be alive. She tortures them, Andras. A slow death." At this, Bowie stumbles on his words. "There's nothing to be done for the lives already lost, but we can still save the ones in her clutches now."

I'm at a loss for words.

Bowie continues, "King Matyas of Hungary has been made aware of her crimes. The legal process to stop her from further evil is underway, but it creeps at a snail's pace, held back by the interests of her powerful family and their many allies."

Reeling with this information, I'm having trouble processing all the pieces. "I don't understand."

"I'll try to explain," says Bowie patiently. "The crown owes the Báthory woman a vast sum of money. She's been funding them for decades, for she has more wealth than the entire fractured country. Believe me, King Matyas has every motivation to see her brought to justice. If she's found guilty, those debts are canceled. Furthermore, he can confiscate her lands and wealth."

This makes even less sense. "Then why don't they hurry?"

"It's complicated. The late Nadasdy appointed her guardian, Gyorgy Thurzo, to look after her best interests and those of her heirs. And Matyas directed him to see her face trial. Thurzo is between a rock and a hard place. The other noble families whisper their threats in his ear. They will fight against the setting of a precedent that the aristocracy can be punished the same as any peasant. Matyas can't take on the whole of the Transylvanian aristocracy. Thus the Báthory woman is well protected. For now."

"For now." But she doesn't know a vampire and a werewolf have sniffed out her crimes. "We have to find this woman."

"Yes. And we have a few likely destinations. West to Sarvaar, a residence of hers since her marriage. Possibly Buda or Pest, as she owns castles in both cities. Or northwest to the Little Carpathians where Csejthe Castle stands in the foothills. Erzsébet has a gynaeceum there, a finishing school for girls. Surely that's how she's gotten so many. She travels, so I can't be sure, but my instinct says that's our best bet. Though slave traders can't be ruled out either."

It's unfathomable to me that such a woman exists, that her crimes have been uncovered, and yet somehow, she remains unscathed. And slave traders? How horrible. Suddenly Farkas doesn't seem so bad. "Those poor girls."

A look of utter defeat is etched on Bowie's face that further breaks my heart.

"Don't worry," I assure him. "We will save them."

"Andras, there's more you should know." He hesitates. "I haven't been completely honest with you. I may as well give you all the bad news at once, and if you decide you'd rather be done with this and with me, I'll understand. I won't blame you."

My heart can't take much more. Bowie has been reluctant to speak of his past. I know he hides something that hurts him. But I haven't gotten the impression he's been dishonest. Not to me. "You lied?"

"Well, not lied exactly, no. I haven't done that. But I haven't told you the entire truth either."

I take a deep breath and let it out slowly.

He opens his mouth.

I stop him with a hand to his mouth and a shake of my head. "Whatever it is, it can wait. The bath water is cooling. You should get in while it's still warm. Let me think."

His lips stiffen beneath my fingers. I remove them. He nods and climbs off the bed.

I shuffle the pillows against the headboard so I can lean against them. My thoughts drift to Esther and her missing older sister, Bethie. I will save her and the others. If I have to kill this Báthory woman to do it, I will.

Bowie moves slowly, his body curving in on itself. Maybe I should have let him tell me whatever it is he needs to say to unburden himself. But I have so much to absorb. Can I handle his confession too?

Hugging one of the many decorative pillows to my chest, I watch Bowie undress. Because of course I do. Despite what I've learned and whatever else he might tell me, I can't take my eyes off him. His back's to me, so I can look without being seen.

My eyes follow the elegant arch of his spine, the rounded curves of his backside, the muscles of his thighs, his calves. His body is a work of art, but it's his mind I've grown to admire. His quick wit and clever chatter, his understanding and patience, most of all, the kindness he so easily showers upon me.

I can't imagine whatever he's hidden from me is going to change the way I feel about him. He already knows my secrets. Surely I can accept his.

Bowie sinks into the water with a titillating moan of pleasure. The sound bounces pleasantly around my ears, tingling my senses. His luscious raven hair hangs over the side of the wooden tub, begging to be touched.

My fingers trace the embroidery on the fancy pillowcase, over the tiny ridges and back, over and back. Curiosity swells. The thought occurs to me that it might be simpler this way—to learn whatever burden Bowie carries and for him to tell it— while we're apart, him with his back to me rather than face-to-face in bed.

"Bowie?"

"Hmm?"

"Do you think you could tell me now?"

When he doesn't answer right away, I start to feel silly. Perhaps it was a dumb idea. Maybe he wants to see my reaction for some reason, or maybe it's just weird to tell a story from a bathtub. I shouldn't have asked.

"Yes, I think that's a good idea." His voice, when it comes, is a relief. It's low and carries the stress of recent events with each word. "Trust you to have thought of it."

I feel better. Whatever he's about to tell me, I can handle it. "Whenever you're ready."

"Thank you." He's motionless in the water, the back of his head resting on the edge of the tub and tilting his chin upward so if his eyes are open, he's looking at the ceiling.

I take my eyes off him and look at the ceiling too.

"I didn't want to be a vampire," Bowie begins. "I still don't, but it's too late now."

This isn't new information, though this is the first time

Bowie's said as much so bluntly. It's obvious he's uncomfortable with himself.

I know what that feels like.

He continues, "My father turned me off as an unsuitable heir when he caught me on my hands and knees for the stable master." Bowie wags a finger in the air. "He didn't bother to turn off the stable master, mind you. 'Too hard to replace a man so good with horses,' he said. I was nineteen. Catherine would inherit, which was fine by me. I adore her, obviously, and she's smarter than I'll ever be, not to mention far better suited to run a noble estate."

He's selling himself short, but I don't interrupt to say so.

"She and Jakob were engaged at the time. She was sixteen, Jakob my age. I told her I was going to Debrecen but that I'd return for her wedding. If Father didn't like it, oh well. He wouldn't stop me from seeing her happily wed. It was a love match, you see, Catherine and Jakob. Luckily for both of them, the match was also advantageous for Father, as the union ensured no one would complain if the daughter inherited rather than the son."

Human laws have never made sense to me, but then again, neither have werewolf laws. I'd be lying if I said I had high hopes for vampire laws.

"Catherine cried as we parted and stuffed my pockets with her own jewels so I could start fresh in a new city. I can't say I did much of merit during my time in Debrecen before the wedding, but neither did I squander her gift. With a rented room and a job as an errand boy for several street vendors, I was all right. I was even beginning to make friends. Little did I know I'd caught the attention of a vampiress."

Something in the way he says this sends chills up my spine. Though I already know the inevitable conclusion to this tale—Bowie becomes a vampire—my muscles tense, and my chest tightens.

"Bettina was in town with another of her offspring, the two of them visiting Ivaz. Perhaps she stayed in this very room." His hands fling droplets of water around as he gestures at large to our temporary bedchamber. "Little gets past Ivaz. He heard rumors of a banished noble playing servant to the townsfolk. When you live for centuries, you must take your entertainment where you can find it, I suppose."

I'm hesitant to interrupt, but he pauses in a way that suggests he's struggling for words, a rare thing for Bowie. "Did you make it to the wedding?"

He shifts in the tub, bringing his knees to his chest and leaning over them. "I did. I shouldn't have, but I did."

Waiting through the silence for him to continue, I resist the urge to go to him. To place my hands on his back and assure him it will be all right, as he's done for me. But we are different people, and somehow, I think my coddling would make this even harder for him.

"Bettina took me one night. Scooped me into her arms as if I weighed nothing and carried me off the dirty streets, through the city, and out into the open farmland under the stars. I was dazed, shaking with fear, afraid for my life. Who was this terrifying woman? This monster with daggers for teeth and jewels for eyes?

"'Beauregard of Varad,' she said, looking me over from head to toe. I must have been a sight, trembling before her, frightened out of my wits. 'You should be heir to vast tracts of land, to the wealth of generations, and your sons heirs when you are gone. But instead, here you are flinging horse manure from the path so customers can more comfortably patron the merchant shops. All without complaint. No protest, no courts, no lawyers. Why do you not seek your birthright?'

"I couldn't answer. My panic was too great. We'd practically flown there, and my mind hadn't recovered from having experienced the impossible. Thoughts of my father and the estate seemed trivial in comparison." He pauses, drawing in a slow breath.

"I shall edit the story here, my dear, for it matters not our conversation when the end result is that I was made vampire before the dawn. I didn't consent, but neither did I protest when she presented her ultimatum. What was done is done."

I hope I don't meet this Bettina woman. Already I hate her for scaring Bowie and for her part in his sorrow.

"Here we come to my confession." Bowie lifts his head from his knees, straightens his back, and twists to face me. "I'd promised Catherine I'd attend her wedding, and I wasn't about to go back on my word. I wouldn't let my sister down. Such familial connections are against vampire law—for good reason I'd come to find out—but Bettina isn't restrained by such petty things as rules. She liked it when I stood up to her, when I demanded to go and wouldn't be denied. She granted her permission and even escorted me herself. Imagine my father's surprise when I showed up, appallingly late, and with a beautiful woman on my arm no less.

"We'd missed the ceremony, of course. It happened before sundown, but I'd warned Catherine in a letter that would be the case and begged her forgiveness in advance. We made it in time for the celebration feast afterward to see the happy couple all smiles and blushes. Bettina warned me not to get close. I should have listened. But when Catherine drew me aside, led me from her own party to the courtyard where we could speak in relative privacy, I was powerless to resist.

"I hadn't fed that night, being in such a rush, knowing I would be late regardless. A mistake I've regretted ever since. Catherine only wanted to know if I was all right, if I was happy in Debrecen. She brought a purse full of coin for me and a bag of my favorite candies as a treat. But when she embraced me, I caught the scent of the blood beneath her skin."

I hold my breath, afraid of what might come next.

"My wicked appetite roared to life. I pushed Catherine away, but it was too late. The monster was set free. One of Catherine's maidens, a childhood friend called Isobel" —at this he can no longer keep eye contact; his gaze shifts to the ground—"had accompanied us. I bumped into her in my rush to flee. She fell, and within the span of a heartbeat, I was on her. I couldn't stop myself."

Bowie holds the edge of the tub, fingers clenched. "Catherine cried out, grabbed fistfuls of my hair, and tried to pry me off her, but this infernal vampire strength withstood her desperate wrenching effortlessly. It was Bettina who tore me off Isobel."

I wince.

Bowie pauses.

The longer I wait to hear of Isobel's fate, the more the agony of this story dawns on me. I know Bowie killed the maiden without him having to say it. It's written in his posture, his caved chest, sagging shoulders, and bent neck. It's in his past reluctance to answer questions, his festering self-doubt, and certainly it's in this mission to rescue innocent young girls.

My heart aches for him. My palms itch to take him in hand and offer the same sort of comfort he always gives me. But he would reject the touch now. He wants to suffer. He hasn't finished the story, though he's visibly steeling himself to say the words.

"I'd nearly torn her throat out," Bowie admits with a guttural sob. "What little blood I hadn't consumed haloed around her head on the stones. Jakob appeared from nowhere and pulled Catherine away from Isobel, and more importantly, away from me. Bettina later told me he'd witnessed the attack, having come to collect his bride. I'll never forget the horror in their eyes, Isobel's blood on Catherine's wedding gown."

Bowie lifts his head and meets my gaze. His eyes are rimmed in pink. A reddish tear leaves a trail down his cheek.

I lean forward and press weight on my hands to shuffle out of bed, but he stops me with a raised hand and a vigorous shake of his head. I muster all the restraint I have left not to go to him.

He continues, "I don't know what happened after that beyond what Bettina has told me since. My anguish was all-encompassing. I ran from Varad with every intention of killing myself. Bettina handled all the havoc I'd left behind. She used her preternatural influence to manipulate Catherine and Jakob into silence, kept the other guests unaware, removed the evidence, and...disposed of the body. Of Isobel. I'd no comprehension of the power she could wield to keep me out of trouble, but I faced no legal consequences. I still haven't. I murdered that girl and got away totally free."

Bowie holds his head in his hands. Both cheeks have twin red trails from his tears. I simply can't let him relive this alone any longer. I leave the bed and drop to my knees in front of the tub. There are no words to make this right, certainly none that I know, but I won't abandon Bowie for a past mistake, even one as terrible as this.

He won't meet my gaze, but he lets me wipe the tears away with my thumbs. He doesn't shy away when I push his hair behind his ears and stroke the dampened length. When he speaks, his voice is low and broken.

"I couldn't kill myself. I tried, but I wasn't strong enough. And Bettina refused to help. Once I tried to simply meet the sun and let nature take its course, but my body refused. It dug itself, against my will, into the earth at the last second like a separate thing. Like my mind had no control. Eventually, I gave up trying. I accepted that my punishment was to live with what I'd done."

My eyes water, and my heart breaks for the pain he's endured. I hold him, the hard wooden tub between us, but my arms wrapped securely around him as he finishes.

Bowie drops his head to my shoulder. His back shakes as he

cries in silence. I'm here with him while he suffers, petting his hair.

The water grows cool. My knees begin to ache. His skin has pruned. But none of that matters. Sometimes pain insists on time, so time it shall have.

When he's ready, he lifts his head and meets my gaze. His eyes are all teary, pink and red and smelling of copper.

"You don't have to stay," he says in a voice so small it doesn't sound like my Bowie.

"Of course I'll stay." I reach for a cloth, wet it, and use it to wipe the blood tears from his face. "Come to bed."

Bowie's stare softens. He rises from the tub, water cascading down his torso, his hips, his legs. He takes the hand I've offered and steps over the rim. I fetch him a towel and wrap him up in it, then pluck another and dry him off.

He's quiet and malleable for this process, allowing himself to be moved this way and that until only his hair remains damp.

I pull him toward the bed, and he climbs in easily enough. Following, I tuck myself against his side and pull the covers over us. "Will you tell me the rest?"

"What more is there to say? I am a killer, a murderer, no better than the monster we're tracking."

"Bowie, stop that. You're entirely different. Do you need to hear it was an accident? That it wasn't your fault? You can't always tame instinct? That Bettina should have guided you better? Surely you know these things to be true, but will my saying so help you believe it?"

"Probably not," he mutters.

I'm so sad for him, that this tragedy happened, and that he's reliving it in the telling. But I think for both of us, he must finish the whole story. "Tell me how it came that you sleep in your family's house and sit at their table after such a terrible experience for you all."

"Ah, yes." He sighs. "My sister continued to write to me, so I continued to respond. At first, her letters were confused. Why hadn't I visited? Did something happen at the wedding? Had Father been unkind?"

"What did you say?"

"I was vague. Answered as best I could. Apologized for not coming around. But Bettina's power to influence isn't invincible. She'd warned me they'd remember, urged me to cut ties, to come with her to Vienna, anywhere, to forget. But I couldn't. I wrote back to Catherine as part of my penance. She'd lost a dear friend because of me, and though I didn't deserve her, I wouldn't let her lose her brother as well."

"It took years before we acknowledged it between us. That her memories had been tampered with, that the horror she'd witnessed had been real, why it happened and what I'd become. I've apologized a thousand times and would ten thousand more, but she ordered me to stop long ago. Somehow they forgave me, Catherine and Jakob both, though I've never dared to have asked them for it."

"You've never forgiven yourself."

"I never will." He sounds woefully final as he speaks.

"Well, if you want me to hold it against you, then you're asking too much. Besides, you've punished yourself far worse than I ever could."

Bowie turns to face me, takes me into his arms, and holds tight. I return the embrace with all my strength. If we could meld into each other, we would. I only relax again when he does.

I have one last question. "So you drink from Jakob?"

"Yes. Not only Jakob but often him. He's big, strong, and healthy. More importantly, he's willing, and I never have to lie to him."

"And now you don't have to lie to me."

Bowie gives a tired sigh. "No, I don't."

e wake to a sharp rapping at the door, which opens before either of us has time to say "Come in."

I startle away from Bowie and yank the sheets higher over us. I'm covered with a robe, but Bowie slept stark naked.

A harried-looking young woman bows as she speaks. "Ivaz has asked that you come to his study right away. A message has arrived from Varad."

"We'll be there shortly," says Bowie. The door clicks shut, leaving us alone. He turns to me. "From Varad. It could only be Catherine. She knows she can reach me at this address. That's worrisome."

The sinking sensation that this will be bad news roils in my stomach. Surely Bowie has had the same misgivings. We hurry to dress as an eerie foreboding settles between us.

I'm not looking forward to seeing Ivaz again, but leaving Bowie alone isn't an option, not when he's feeling so fragile.

We rush down the hall. Bowie leads us through an open door to reveal Ivaz sitting behind an enormous black desk, suitable for his huge frame, elbows on its shining surface, fingers steepled in front of him. Even seated, the man is intimidating. Behind him, a collection of weapons is mounted like artwork on the wood-paneled wall: an assortment of iron cudgels, battle-axes, swords, daggers, and crossbows—enough to kill a man in a variety of horrifying ways.

"Close it," he says.

I shut the door behind me. Side by side, we stand before him. That same pulsing sensation of power emanating from Ivaz has me on edge. It whispers of strength and age.

"Sit down."

Bowie shakes his head. "Just tell me. What's happened?"

"If you insist." Ivaz plucks a piece of parchment from his desk and offers it to Bowie, who takes it with trembling fingers.

"From your sister." Ivaz doesn't mince his words. "Cecily is missing."

Bowie clasps the letter to his chest. A pained cry escapes his throat. The revelation hits me like a punch to the gut, leaving me breathless and shaken. I take Bowie's arm, and he leans into my side.

Ivaz continues, "She was taken sometime last night. So her kidnappers have a head start. I'm sorry to be the bearer of such news," says Ivaz, his eyes on Bowie, who's gone quite still. "Cecily is your niece, is she not?"

Bowie wavers on his feet, stricken, Catherine's note dangling from shaking fingers. He doesn't respond and draws the note back up to read again.

Supporting him with an arm about his waist, I answer instead. "Yes, Cecily is his niece." I don't need to see the note Bowie is obsessively reading. Ivaz has already told us the worst of it. Combined with what we've learned of the wicked Báthory woman, we have much to fear.

"How?" Bowie chokes on the word. "She has guards. I don't understand."

"They don't know." Ivaz keeps his voice low and calm. "No one heard a thing."

I hold Bowie tight. "We'll find her. They only have a small head start. We can overtake them."

Bowie whirls to face me, his expression the picture of anguish. "We have to go back!"

"Go back?" I don't understand. "To Varad? But why?"

"Catherine will be out of her mind." His eyes are wild. "I must see her. Jakob is likely riding a horse into the ground this very minute in search." Bowie's words come faster and faster. "And you, Andras. We'll need you to find Cecily's scent trail immediately."

"I'll find it on our way. They might have already passed through this very city. Give me an hour to run the perimeter, and we'll leave from here."

"What if you don't find it?"

"Then they've taken another route, and we should still head west. The last two trails converged. Cecily's will too. We can't go back, or we'll widen their lead."

Bowie turns to Ivaz. "Can you send someone ahead to Báthory's residences in Buda, Pest, Sarvaar, and Csejthe? Janos perhaps? And Thomas? They can keep a lookout while I confirm it's not Turkish slave traders."

"Janos isn't here. He's working for me in Kiskoros," says Ivaz. "I'll send word right away."

"One vampire?" says Bowie. "That's not good enough!"

Ivaz leans forward, spreads his hands. "Beauregard, she's not been gone a full twenty-four hours. Your wolf will find her. Give him the chance."

Bowie crumples, nearly collapsing to his knees.

I keep him up. Barely.

"You then," says Bowie to Ivaz, desperation forcing his tone high. He pushes out of my hold and approaches the enormous desk.

"I cannot leave this moment," says Ivaz.

Bowie continues as if Ivaz hasn't spoken, his voice growing even more urgent. "Scout ahead to Csejthe, make sure Cecily's not taken inside the castle's gates while Andras and I go to Varad to follow the trail from the start."

Ivaz shakes his head. "I'm occupied this week. I'll come—"

"But, Ivaz! She's my fam—"

Ivaz thumps his fist on the desk, disturbing the inkwell but not tipping it. "My duties in Debrecen cannot be so easily terminated. I'll send word to Bettina. I'll send word to Janos. When I'm done here, I shall meet you in the pursuit myself. I'll arrange for wagons and men to help bring the girls home. In the meantime, I'll make arrangements for your lodging at The Twig and Berries in Pest. The proprietor is a friend of mine, and he'll take good care of you. And that will have to be enough, brother."

Silence.

The *thump thump* of my heart echoes in my ears. "Bowie…" I begin, but he doesn't look at me. He's staring daggers at Ivaz.

Ivaz gestures to me. "Listen to the wolf."

I can help, so I try to persuade him again. "Let me run the perimeter of the city. I'll know if she's come through and which way they're headed."

Pressing his fist to his chin, Bowie considers. He looks perfectly wretched, as if a feather could knock him over. "We're wasting time," he grits out between clenched teeth. "I'm going to pack."

Bowie storms from the room. I go to follow, hoping I can calm him enough to see reason when Ivaz calls me back.

"Andras, is it?" His voice softens. "Stay a moment, would you?"

Though it's phrased as a request, I feel an unnatural urge to obey. Testing it, I discover I can ignore the urge. I'm free to leave the room, but the odd sensation stirs fear.

"What are you doing to me?" I ask.

The urge recedes.

"Apologies," says Ivaz in his low rumble. His hands open in contrition. "Habit." He stands and comes around the desk to face me. He's at least a foot taller than I am and twice as wide. That, plus the invisible throbbing energy that radiates from him, has me backing up.

"I should check on Bowie," I mutter.

"And you will, but first." Ivaz cocks his head, studying me. "What are you?"

I hesitate. Revealing myself is a risk, but arguing will only take up more time we don't have. And I doubt this vampire is accustomed to much resistance. I don't want to provoke him. I tug off my hat and let my ears flick from my head.

"Nothing special," I say. "A mongrel. But I'm good at following scent trails."

His pupils dilate. His interest unnerves me. He looks like he wants to reach out and touch me but wisely holds himself back. "I bet you are." His gaze drifts lower, scrutinizing the fit of my pants. "Your tail remains even in your human form, doesn't it?"

I squirm as I answer. "It does."

His attention is a lot to weather. I glance past him to his trophy wall. My eyes land on a pistol. I've never seen one outside of a book before. The gun isn't as terrifying looking as the axes and cudgels surrounding it, but the peppery scent makes my nose itch.

Ivaz clears his throat, bringing my gaze back to his. "Bettina will be eager to meet a creature like yourself."

My hackles rise. If he notices the fur along my spine pushing at my shirt, he doesn't mention it. I don't want to meet Bowie's maker, and I don't want her knowing what I am.

Ivaz must sense my unease because he shifts topics. "Bowie has never brought a guest to my establishment. Everyone was pleasantly surprised to see you on his arm. It's good he's finally taken a lover."

Heat creeps to my cheeks. "We aren't...lovers," I stammer.

"You are," he insists, then reconsiders. "Perhaps not yet, but you will be."

This is none of his business, and I don't have time for it. "I'm going. He needs my help."

"Yes, he really does." The corners of Ivaz's lips rise. Whether it's a smile or a smirk, I can't say.

I hurry from the room with the feeling that I need another bath just to wash his gaze from my body.

* * *

BOWIE IS all action and no talk as he leads me out of the underground viper pit and through the streets of Debrecen. We're backtracking, which is fine for the moment, but once we reach the outer edges of the city, I need to run a perimeter. I fear his plan is still to race all the way back to Varad. He's assumed I'll concede to his judgment, but he's mistaken.

It would be easier to let him make the decisions, though I can't afford to let him make the wrong one, even if I'm hesitant to argue.

I'm practically running to keep up with him, scenting the air, hoping to catch a whiff of Cecily's minty smell. I don't. What I do catch is much worse.

The breeze carries with it the sweet, pungent smell of oncoming rain. The realization sits heavily on my shoulders. We really have no time to waste. I must change Bowie's mind. Our best chance at tracking down Cecily before she's in Báthory's clutches lies in forging ahead.

Steeling myself for conflict, I announce, "This is far enough."

Bowie doesn't slow his pace. "We're going back, Andras. We must."

"I don't think that's wise."

He ignores my statement. "Can you shift and run? We could cover ground much faster if you'd sprint. Can you do that?"

Not for long.

Wolves are best at short sprints, not endurance. "I can't. Bowie, listen. I need to circle Debrecen. Then we must forge ahead."

"No. We go back." The stubborn metal in his tone is new.

"But—"

"What if she was taken due south?" His voice is frantic with worry. "We can't risk missing such a clue."

He has a point, but it's still the weaker of our two choices. What could convince him? I recall each detail Bowie relayed to me of Ivaz's information on the matter until I hit on something relevant. "Aren't all of Báthory's castles north or west of here? Isn't that what Ivaz told you?"

"And if it's not Báthory? If it's Turkish slave traders? We don't have enough information to be certain."

My ignorance of history betrays me, but I wing it. "Wouldn't I have smelled that? Wouldn't Turkish foods smell different from what I'm used to? And do they really pluck noble girls to be sold into slavery? Isn't it more likely to be the woman? Báthory is being investigated by the king himself. It's her Bowie. We must go forward."

His breakneck pace doesn't waiver. We're alone as the rubble road becomes dirt and the outskirts of the city turn to pasture. The night sky is clouded and dark, the moon obscured.

Having this conversation while walk-running in the wrong direction has me winded. "Bowie, stop. Talk to me. Please."

He halts, tense reluctance evident in his posture. His voice is strained. "What must I say to convince you to listen?"

Words never come fast enough when I need them. I stand stupidly before him, my mouth hanging open.

"This is Cecily. Cecily!" He cries her name with utter misery.

I take his shoulders and squeeze. "I know. Bowie, listen. You aren't thinking clearly, and I don't blame you. Please trust me in this. Going back isn't going to help her. I know you're desperate to comfort Catherine, but we must do that by pressing ahead."

"I don't know." Bowie trembles in my grip. He shakes his head. "If Cecily was taken south, I'll never forgive myself. And I could never ask Catherine to forgive me after failing her for the second time."

"One night." I stare into stormy eyes, willing him to trust me. "Give me one night to pick up her scent from here." I don't tell him about the rain. There's nothing I can do to persuade mother nature to my side, but I must believe I can persuade Bowie.

He glances down the road ahead, then back toward the city. He's vacillating. It's clear in his expression.

I muster all the authority I can into the orders, "Get out the map. Let me see it." If I can get him to cooperate, he'll see reason. "Hurry."

Bowie shrugs our pack off his shoulder. I release a breath of relief. We spread the map between us, him holding one side, me the other.

I point to Debrecen. "We are here."

"Yes."

"Show me Báthory's lands. Point out her castles, ending in Csejthe."

His finger shakes as he guides me through her holdings.

"The king's investigation centers around Sarvaar, Pest, Ecsed, and Csejthe—where she's known to reside now."

My eyes pass over each destination in turn. Either due west or north and, most likely, northwest. My guess is our scent trail will lead us near or through Ecsed, to Pest and Buda, then out of the valley north into the Little Carpathians, where Csejthe sits nestled among a cluster of small villages. By the looks of it, perhaps four or five days of travel if we push my limits.

I don't need to circle the entire city after all; the western crescent should be enough. I see no reason for the kidnappers to have gone east. Which is lucky because omitting that side will save valuable time.

For my plan to work, three things need to happen. The trail must lead steadily toward Csejthe enough that the final destination is obvious. Cecily's scent needs to merge with those of the first three girls. And lastly, the rain must hold off until the first two requirements are met without a doubt.

If any item on this list doesn't come to fruition, Bowie is likely to return to Varad with or without me. He may be angry with me for the delay. But I'm certain my plan is our best chance to get to Cecily before any further harm comes to her. If I'm wrong, I'll never forgive myself for letting them down, and that will leave the both of us angry with ourselves forever.

My heart is racing. My throat is tight.

I look Bowie in the eyes. "I'm right about this. I need you to trust me."

His anguish bleeds from him in waves. I feel it in my soul. His pain becomes our pain.

"You're certain?" His eyes beg me for reassurance.

I force confidence into my voice. "As certain as I've ever been."

Bowie presses his lips to a tight line. Nods. Folds up the map and holds our pack open in front of me. "Then you should shift."

I tear off my shirt and stuff it into the satchel. Time to get to work.

"Andras?" he says as I'm about to transform.

"Yes?"

His gaze turns intense. "I do trust you."

I could cry. I want to hug him, but we don't have time for that.

By the moon, I hope I'm right.

CHAPTER 13

I've been running as fast as my four legs will carry me for hours. My lungs and paws are battered. My stomach grumbles in protest, hunger nagging with the persistence of a swarm of mosquitos. The wind has picked up. Branches wave overhead, leaves rustle, and night birds halt their songs.

If he hasn't already, Bowie will soon realize a storm approaches.

I have yet to find Cecily's scent. My time is running short.

We left Debrecen behind and traveled west toward Ecsed, but we've no hope of making the entire journey in one night. Especially not if we must stop early due to weather.

At least if we're forced to call a halt, the girl snatchers must do the same, though that's little comfort when I think about how scared Cecily must be.

My hopes of catching up with them tonight are dashed. They clearly haven't come this way. I'm thinking Cecily was taken straight through to Pest from Varad, which means the scent trails won't converge anytime soon. And the weather isn't getting any better.

Admitting defeat, I pause and glance back to Bowie. He catches up from where he's been following a few paces behind. We're alone on this narrow road between human settlements, a bit like the middle of nowhere.

"What is it, anything useful?" he asks.

We've devised a system. Look up for yes and down for no.

I look down.

His hope vanishes. "Cecily hasn't been through here?"

Down again.

When I glance back at him, his shoulders have canted inward, defeated. Wishing I had better news for him, I whine and rub against his leg.

He pets my ruff. "The other three, are we still on their scents?"

I look up. At least we have that.

The first roll of distant thunder rumbles low and ominous. Well, I needed to tell him about the storm, so I guess that covers that.

Bowie's face caves to misery. "Oh no, not rain! This is the worst possible timing."

We need to talk. I shift, slow and steady. Bowie's hand on my ruff remains in place while I gain height and lose fur. My bones morph and lengthen, as commanded, until I stand naked at his side, his hand on my nape.

Before I can say anything, Bowie has pressed himself against me. Though he's slightly taller, he seems to shrink in my arms as I hold him.

"This can't be happening," he says as another round of faraway booming sounds from the east.

Rubbing his back, I keep my voice calm. "It's going to be all right. If we must stop, so must they."

He listens as I share my thoughts that Cecily has probably been taken through Pest, which is our next destination after Ecsed. Surely we'll pick up her trail, then. I tell him not to fear. I make promises I hope I'll be able to keep. We'll find her, Bowie. She'll be all right, Bowie. Don't worry, Bowie.

His back shakes. He clutches my waist. I knew he'd been hovering on edge, but I didn't realize how close he was to stumbling over it.

"What now?" he asks against my neck.

I glance up at the sky. Fat-bellied clouds tumble along, readying to let loose their burden. "We'll need to take cover. Somewhere safe to pass the storm and for you for tomorrow during daylight."

"Right."

"Have you any ideas?"

Bowie sucks in a deep breath and pulls himself together. He stands back enough to look me in the eyes. "I can always go below ground in an emergency, but I imagine that wouldn't work well for you."

Just thinking about it makes me shiver. "I can curl up somewhere in wolf form if I must." Though in this weather and marshy landscape, it wouldn't be comfortable. I'm used to a higher elevation. We've been on a decline since we left Varad. This land is one muddy bog after another and makes me thankful for the decently maintained road we've been on.

"Let's see if our last resort options can be avoided." He scans the stunted trees and brush beyond the road.

We've passed several small villages and settlements, nothing so big as to have its own inn. And the terrain is such that I can't imagine we'd be lucky enough to find a natural shelter like a cave.

As I'm coming to terms with the idea of being quite wet for a long time, he speaks. "We're not far from a river crossing. The Tisza lies ahead. I'm actually much faster than you. Why don't I scout ahead while you take your time? I'll come back once I've found something suitable."

I don't like the idea of splitting up, but if his little show of chasing me down and catching me at a sprint back in Varad was any indication of his speed, then it shouldn't take him long at all.

I look up.

Bowie huffs. "Andras, use your words."

Oh right. "Erm, yes. Do that. Maybe I'll get lucky and find a meal while you're away."

His eyes widen, and his mouth opens in an *o*. "You're hungry! Oh, I'm sorry. I've been so selfish and forgotten your needs. Yes, you must eat. Please never let me stop you again."

"You didn't," I assure him. I was on a mission. Food could wait. Though if it waits much longer, I may fall over.

A flash of lightning streaks sideways, splintering across the otherwise black expanse of sky.

"We should hurry," says Bowie. "If you veer off the trail to hunt, just come back to it when you can, and I'll find you."

I nod.

"See you soon." He vanishes. There one moment, gone the next, so fast I don't even get to enjoy the view as he leaves. Stunned, I watch the road as if he'll magically reappear. How fast is he? My pace must be killing him.

Letting Bowie out of my sight makes me nervous, but his plan is infinitely better than mine, which is to curl up somewhere on the side of the road and be miserable for hours. Wherever we end up sleeping, it will be a hundred times better with a full belly. I shift back to my wolf form, flicking my ears for sounds of prey.

Along this road, I've scented a number of prey animals I'd be happy to call dinner, including beaver, a personal favorite, and an animal simpler to hunt alone than with a pack. I set my nose to the ground and get to tracking, heading through the scraggly bush and into the tall marshland grasses.

My paws sink into the ground, an unpleasant sensation and also a noisy one as I pull them from the muck. I seek higher ground to gain the element of surprise. Ambush is the best way to catch a beaver, but I don't know these lands, so I must rely on my nose, patience, and then a burst of speed.

I follow the scent trail, approaching from downwind. Beavers have terribly poor vision, so there's no need to stay out of sight, but I can't afford to warn them by giving away my scent.

A mound rises from the soft dirt just ahead, sticks and branches protecting the top. A beaver den, and my nose tells me they're at home, perhaps hiding from the same storm I also hope to hide from sooner rather than later.

If this were a normal hunt, I'd simply lie in wait until one of them ventured out. They're most active at night. But I'm in a hurry, so I grit my teeth and prepare to get dirty. Tonight I must dig for my supper and fast before they escape to the water.

Coiling my muscles, preparing to pounce, I focus on my target: the edge of the mound closest to the water. I leap and tear through the sticks and loose earth, pawing furiously into the den, eager to sink my teeth into my meal.

Beavers are all muscle and don't go down without a fight. I grab the first one that tries to flee, clamping its neck tight between my jaws. Its hind legs flail, claws trying to find purchase, ready to dig in. The heavy tail swings violently, nailing my left foreleg over and over—*thwack, thwack*—but I refuse to let go, even as pain radiates to my shoulder.

Rearing back, I fling my head to and fro with enough force to break the creature's neck. The others, for there were several in this den, have all made a swift watery exit. My prize dangles limply from my jowls, its struggle short but mighty if my throbbing foreleg is anything to go by. I drag it to higher ground to eat.

The delectable aroma of blood, flesh, muscle, and fat has me salivating. My stomach growls loud enough to compete with the echoing thunder. I tear into my meal with abandon, the satisfying crunch of bone music to my ears.

When my belly is stuffed full to bursting, I must fight the urge to sleep it off. My thoughts drift to Bowie, as they inevitably do. Would he cringe at the sight of me? My fur covered in mud, claws caked with dirt, mouth and snout dripping with blood. I huff, snorting, as I force myself up and pad over to the water for a wash. The wolf in me isn't in the mood, but my will overcomes its reluctance. I rinse as best I can, then make my way back to the road.

Would Bowie mind if I nap here while I wait? No, I shouldn't. Though my left front leg is aching, I force myself onward. If Bowie does find us a place to take cover, and it's still a ways ahead, I'll have to trek there eventually, so I may as well begin now. I hope he's found something, for him more than for me, because I can't imagine spending hours within the earth, covered in dirt. How uncomfortable it would be, especially since Bowie is fastidiously clean. I've never noticed a speck of dirt beneath his immaculate nails, so being covered in the stuff would be torturous for him.

I think about Ivaz and the things he said to me. The things he'd assumed. What would Bowie be like as a lover? It's not that the thought hasn't crossed my mind. In fact, it's arisen repeatedly lately, but I haven't allowed myself to dwell.

All my previous experiences were brief, secretive, and hurried, with strangers who didn't care that I wouldn't undress or even take off my hat. Desperate hurried groping, momentarily satisfying but ultimately unfulfilling.

Bowie wouldn't be like that. He isn't one to rush when something should be savored. Though Ivaz makes my skin crawl, I wonder if he's right. Does Bowie want me the way I want him? I think of his lips, pink and rosy, and the twin daggers they conceal, of his hands as they dance about when he speaks. I want them on me.

I give myself a violent shake, settling my fur and clearing my mind. I shouldn't be thinking of this. Even if Bowie might be interested, now isn't the time. Not with girls' lives on the line and Cecily in danger. What kind of terrible person am I to be thinking of myself in a time like this?

Lightning flashes, the landscape glowing brightly, then plunging back into darkness in an instant. The air sizzles with energy, and the sharp peppery scent of the storm magnifies tenfold. Soon we'll have no time to get to shelter. I hope Bowie returns before I'm forced to hunker down alone. I pick up my pace.

My wish is granted almost immediately as a new prickly sensation alerts me to his presence seconds before he appears in my path. I blink. That really is stunning. He walks toward me as if appearing from thin air is completely normal.

"My dear, I've found us a temporary refuge. It's not ideal, but beggars mustn't fuss or something like that." He stops in front of me and kneels. His nose scrunches. It's awfully cute. "You ate?"

I suppose he can smell it on me. I look up.

"Good." His hands land on my neck.

I lean into the touch.

"There's one issue." He pauses. Such a dramatic creature, my Bowie. "It's quite a ways away. At your pace, we'll be drenched in the storm long before we get there. Unless…"

He looks sheepish, an odd expression for Bowie. I nudge him with my snout, urging him to continue.

"You let me carry you."

What? I look down. That's ridiculous. I must be nearly as heavy as he is. He can't possibly carry me any real distance. Can he?

"Don't say no." He gently takes my chin and lifts my snout. "I know it's odd for one grown man to carry another. But I may as well put this infernal strength I've been granted to good use. Please?"

I resist, whining. I don't want to be picked up. I can't explain why; it's just a feeling of deep reluctance. The wolf and I agree on this.

"Please?" Bowie repeats, this time glancing at me through lowered lashes, his lower lip thrust forward enough that I take notice. "I don't want to go to ground, and you look as if you've already been soaked. Don't you want to dry off?"

I stare as his tongue darts out to moisten his lips. Then I force myself to look up. Fine. If we must.

He grins. "Oh good, thank you. Now how should we do this? As a wolf? On my back perhaps, or would you rather shift so you can hang on?"

All of these options sound terrible and embarrassing. I snort my displeasure.

"Come now. It's not so bad. I'll be fast about it. Promise." Bowie crosses his heart.

One last snort and I make up my mind. This would be better —still awful—but better if I could hold on. I step back from him, close my eyes, and force a quick shift. It hurts a bit when I rush, but with my arm already throbbing, I don't care so much.

I roll my head. My neck gives a loud crack. Ah. With another snort, less effective in this form but still perfectly ruffled at what comes next, I open my eyes to find Bowie staring.

Though I've gotten used to being naked around him—it just comes with the territory when you're a werewolf—he generally averts his eyes. His gaze has a weight to it that brings warmth to my throat and face.

"Are you sure about this?" I ask. "I've got to be as heavy as you."

He snaps out of whatever stupor he'd fallen into. "Yes, it's no problem. Did you want to dress first, or shall we go? There's no one around, and we'll be traveling too fast to be seen anyway."

I haven't even thought of that. I envision a farmer, perhaps up all night with a birthing cow or some such, peering out along the road and seeing to his utter shock one completely dressed man carrying one completely naked man in a mad rush for shelter. We'd scar him for life.

Thunder and lightning in a rapid burst, too close together for comfort and signaling an imminent deluge of rain, makes my decision for me. "Let's just go."

Bowie turns, goes down on one knee, and presents his back.

I can't believe I'm doing this.

CHAPTER 14

I climb on, gripping his shoulders. His muscles flex beneath my palms. As he stands, I wrap my legs around his slim waist, feeling ridiculous and far too heavy.

Bowie holds on to me underneath my knees. "Ready?"

I mumble an affirmative and cling to him as a flutter of anxiety floods my senses. I'm about to travel faster than the eye can see. I'm scared, but I trust Bowie, so I try to relax.

He must sense my trepidation. "Perhaps if you close your eyes, dear. I'll let you know when we arrive. Ten minutes at most."

I shut my eyes and nod. With my head pressed next to his, he must feel the motion because the sensation of the wind sweeping beneath us drops my stomach. I hold my breath and squeeze his hips between my thighs. I've never experienced anything like this. The speed. The pressure. Are we flying? Do birds feel this way when they take to the sky, soaring over clouds? Because I feel as if we're gliding on a wind current.

There's no left-right-left-right of a man's stride in these sensations. Only forward momentum so fast as to make me release my breath and gasp for another. My lungs accept the rush of hurtling pressure, my chest tight, as I clench my fingers against Bowie's flesh. I hope I'm not hurting him with my death grip, but I'm terrified to let go.

I don't open my eyes. I think about it, but I'm afraid of what I might see. I doubt my mind's ability to take in the sights, so I focus on smell instead. First the comforting scent of Bowie himself. His freshly washed hair, the soap from his skin, the blood beneath his veins. I take another rushing breath and tuck my face into his neck. He squeezes my legs in his grip—an attempt to comfort me, but I'm doing all right.

As good as a person can be doing when flying through a strange land on the back of a vampire you've only recently met and have half fallen in love with on the way to rescue girls from a terrifying lady murderer.

I'm fine.

Really.

I'd tell him so if I didn't think my voice would be lost to our speed.

By the time I've finally settled in, Bowie is slowing down. He walks at a regular pace. The familiar rhythm of an actual stride rather than the sweeping glory of flight is my cue to open my eyes.

"How are you? Still breathing?" asks Bowie, his voice perfectly normal. He isn't the least bit winded after such exertion.

Blinking, I collect my thoughts. "Can all vampires do that?"

"I don't know. Many can." He comes to a stop.

I unclench my thighs and peel myself off him to look around. We stand in front of a tumbledown abandoned farmhouse, its wooden beams crooked, the roof caved in. Just when I'm thinking this surely couldn't be the shelter Bowie meant for us, I notice a barn off to the side. It's in much better shape, a massive building, at one time painted white, but the paint is mostly cracked away and flaking. The roof remains intact, and I smell no signs of human or farm animal habitation.

Bowie interrupts my inspection. "Come along, before the rain."

Only then does it occur to me that we've outrun rain. We're yet again ahead of the advancing storm. Though if the thunder is any indication, we won't be for long.

I trudge behind him through overgrown plants and tall grasses. Thorny vines prickle and scratch my legs. I hiss, and Bowie spins.

"Oh, dear." He reaches for me. "I've set you down too soon. So sorry."

In the span of a heartbeat, he swoops me off my feet and into his arms. I hug his neck, feeling slightly less ridiculous the second time around. He walks us through the dense brush, shoves open a giant timbered door with his shoulder, and once we're safely inside, sets me down.

I lift the satchel from around Bowie's neck and pull on my clothes. He turns his back politely, which draws a chuckle from my throat. He's just carried me stark naked through a field, but now he shies away?

As I dress, I scan the barn. One side is entirely taken up by four giant mounds of spoiled barley, damp with rot. A set of horse stalls stand at the far end, and above us, a loft spans both sides and connects above the stalls, though I wouldn't trust the rickety staircase that leads to it. Decaying hay covers the loft and most of the ground. Not much is left in the way of tools and equipment, so whoever abandoned this barn must have taken their things with them.

But where will Bowie sleep? Though the barn is in decent shape, it's clearly not light-tight. Sun will pour in through the cracks between beams on all sides. I open my mouth to ask when he answers the question as if he's read my mind.

"There is a cellar in the forward half where the barn was

built into the earth. It's not in great shape and smells of rotten vegetables, but it will do. I wouldn't blame you if you preferred to sleep up here."

I doubt the smell on this level is any better, but I'll reserve judgment. Regardless, I want to sleep where Bowie sleeps.

A crack of thunder so strong I feel the boom in my chest startles me. Bowie is at my side in an instant.

"Are you afraid of storms?" he asks.

I shake my head. "No, but that was close. Should we head below?"

"You may regret it."

"Let's go anyway so I can find out."

He's not wrong about the smell. As we descend a stone ramp into the barn's bowels, the scent arises like mist after rain on a hot day. Sweltering to my nostrils, the aroma of spoiled apples, onions, potatoes, and beets, all mixed in a mockery of what vegetable stew should smell like.

I scrunch my nose.

Bowie grants me a look of sympathy. "I did warn you."

Above us, the rain finally hits, pounding the roof like a thousand fists banging to be let in. Perhaps the cellar will be fine after all. Glancing around, I don't see the piles of rotten food I expected, just a few remnants here and there. I suppose animals, then bugs made off with anything edible long ago.

Stone floor, stone walls, and a flat timber ceiling make up the cavernous space. Aside from some dirt and a few onions, it's empty.

Bowie sits on the hard ground, his back against the wall, legs stretched in front of him, hands clasped in his lap. "It's going to be a long day."

I nod my agreement. Compared to past accommodations, this is a dungeon. But I'm well and truly exhausted. My bones ache from shifting so frequently, my left arm is throbbing from where the beaver bashed me, and my spirit is battered from thinking of the girls and Cecily and how scared they must be. It's a lot to bear.

Sinking to the ground next to Bowie, I don't think I'll have any trouble sleeping. I want to lean into him, to take his arm and cling to it, but it's impossible not to second-guess these urges, so I remain still. If I'm having a hard time coping, Bowie must be too.

"How are you holding up?" I ask.

His answer comes by way of a long sigh and a slow turn of his head in my direction. He smiles, but it's a grim smile, not his charming grin. "I've been better. But I've also been worse." A small shrug. "I have hope."

"Me too."

"Tell me more about the consequences of this weather," he says with dull resignation. "What will the rain do to the scent trail?"

The last thing I want to do is bring down our depressed mood even further, but I must be honest. "Mostly, the trail will be washed away."

"Mostly?"

"I can still pick up stray whiffs, enough to know we're on track, but not enough to follow. We'll have to continue on our course and hope for the occasional affirmation it's still the correct one."

Bowie gives a slow nod.

"I expect to pick up Cecily's scent in Pest. We've every reason to believe they're there now and will leave from there after the rain, meaning her trail will be fresh."

"Let us hope that comes to pass, for if it doesn't, I'll be so distraught as to prove worthless."

"You won't be," I assure him and nudge our shoulders together. "We'll find her scent, but if we don't in Pest, then we'll keep searching until we do."

"You're right." His voice comes so low and quiet it's difficult to hear over the pouring rain.

We fall silent. I listen to the swirling tempest outside, the furious thunder and battering wind, thankful we're not in the middle of a forest where trees would surely be downed in a storm as strong as this one.

Absently, I rub my left forearm, trying to ease the throbbing. A healthy respect for beavers is a painful but worthwhile lesson.

"What's wrong with your arm?" asks Bowie.

"Only a bruise. I'm all right."

"Let me see."

I don't want to look at it. I find that visually confirming an injury always makes it hurt worse. But Bowie has gently taken my wrist in hand and is working up my sleeve to see for himself. I avert my eyes. Best I don't know how black and blue I really am.

Bowie's gasp alerts me to the severity. "Andras!" he scolds. "What's happened? Why didn't you tell me you were hurt?"

I guess it's rather bad after all. I risk a glance.

Yikes.

Should not have done that.

A fresh wave of pain makes me wince. Sure enough, my forearm has become a color palette suitable for painting midnight landscapes. I thought as much, but the confirmation is somewhat alarming. It's going to make our continued travels quite painful, to say the least.

"It's not that bad," I lie.

Bowie gently traces my skin with his fingers. "It's hot, Andras. And swollen. Tell me what happened."

"Beaver."

"A beaver did this to you?" He looks confused. Ordinarily, that expression on him would make me laugh, but I can feel my heartbeat in my arm, which is weird enough to have me worried.

"They're stronger than you think," I gripe.

Bowie doesn't hold in his little burst of laughter. "But you are a wolf!"

I smile despite myself. "Next time *you* can catch the beaver and then tell me just how simple it is. I dare you."

He lifts my injured arm until my fingers reach his mouth, and kisses the backs of my knuckles. "I shall leave the hunting to you, my dear. But let me heal this appalling wound. It looks terribly painful."

Reeling from his show of affection, I need a moment to interpret his words. My brows greet my hairline. "You can heal this?"

"My blood can," he says matter-of-factly. "If you'll allow it."

The wolf in me shows immediate interest in the form of a wave of longing swelling from the bottom of my soul. Do I want Bowie's blood? Yes. I can't help it. But I want more than that. An urge to sink my teeth into his shoulder and claim him as my own threatens to overwhelm my senses.

"You want it," whispers Bowie, his eyes darkening with interest as he studies me. "You *really* want it. My goodness, you should have told me. I'd have offered sooner."

My hurt arm is forgotten. The rotten vegetable smell vanishes. My world becomes the aroma of the blood beneath his veins. My mouth fills with saliva. I wrench my head around to stare at the floor instead of Bowie. I can't handle the intensity of his gaze or the depth of my desire.

He has no idea what I want or what he's offering.

It's not as simple as a craving for blood. The wolf desires ownership, but I am the master here. And I want Bowie to *choose* me. I don't want to possess or force him.

His fingers find my chin and direct my head to face him. "What's wrong?" he asks. "Tell me because I don't understand." Rather than draw back his hand, he reaches farther forward and clasps my nape. I wish he'd squeeze.

My mouth opens, but words elude me, as usual. I'm caught in the storm of his eyes. Thunder rumbles, shaking the ground beneath us, but nothing short of the apocalypse could break our connection in this moonstruck moment.

His gaze drops to my lips, his lashes a set of dark fans against his pale cheeks.

"I'm going to kiss you..." He meets my eyes again. "Unless you stop me."

I couldn't stop him if I wanted to, which I don't, because I need his kiss more than air.

My heart flutters wildly under this onslaught of anticipation and yearning, this revelation that *Bowie* wants to kiss *me*. His blue irises sparkle behind wide pupils; mine must be equally blown. I'm spinning with the force of my desire.

Waiting even a second longer is more than I can bear. I spring at him like an arrow shot from a bow and take his rose petal-pink lips with an urgency I hadn't known myself capable.

Bowie gasps against my mouth and fervently returns the kiss. His lips part for me. I take his face into my hands and hold him captive for my exploration. His mouth is pleasantly cool like the rest of him, a welcome contrast to my burning heat. Soft and supple as the delicate skin of a fresh nectarine and just as sweet.

I don't know which pounds louder: the rain against the barn or my heart in my chest.

Bowie rises from his spot without breaking the kiss, climbs over me, and straddles my thighs to sit in my lap. I tilt my face up for him as he takes over, his hand fisted in my hair. The delicious tug against my scalp sends a shuddering prickle down my spine.

I grab his waist to pull him closer, deliciously trapped between the wall at my back and his body at my front. His free hand strokes my ear, my hair, my throat until I feel as if I might vibrate out of my skin.

Running my tongue along the sharpened points of his fangs, I wonder how much pressure I'd need to exert to pierce it. Bowie pulls at my hair, a warning I heed only because he's given me his tongue to suck instead of his fangs, so I do that instead.

This feeling of being wanted—being desired—ignites a warm, tingling rush of sensation I have no control over. It passes through me, settles over me, and wraps me in an embrace I would linger in forever.

Bowie moans as he leans back—out of reach of my seeking lips—to study my face.

I must look desperate. Kiss swollen and pouty, wondering why we've stopped. He graces me with an alluring smile. His fingers find my lips. I open and suck one into my mouth, causing his eyelids to flutter and nearly close. He tips his chin, and I marvel at the chiseled line of his jaw, his high cheekbones, his delicate brows.

I like the weight of him in my lap, how solid he feels in my hands, the way he looks at me as if I were precious.

"Your arm," he says.

"My what?" I ask around his finger, which I do *not* wish to relinquish, but he pulls it from my mouth anyway.

"Your arm," he repeats. "Let me heal it."

Oh, that. I'd utterly forgotten. I feel no pain. "It's fine. Kiss me."

Bowie's amused grin is so lovely it begs to be painted and hung in a museum for all to admire. "It's most definitely not fine. It's quite injured, in fact. And if I ever meet the beaver who did it, I shall have strong words for the creature."

"I ate him."

He blinks. "Oh. Well, I suppose your solution proved a more fitting punishment than mine would have been. Beavers probably care not for harsh words."

"Bowie."

"Hmm?"

"Kiss me."

"It would be my pleasure—" He stops me from leaning in with a firm hand on my chest. "After we've taken care of your arm."

Seeing as he isn't likely to be swayed, I relent. "How?"

"A little blood, not much. Is that all right?"

"I think you know it is."

Bowie's smirk sends a pool of warmth to my core. My cock is hard between my thighs. His squirming on my lap feeds my ardor. I wonder if he's hard too. The way he's sitting, I can't quite feel that part of him.

"Shall I open a vein myself, or would you prefer to bite me?"

Oh, moon and stars above, I fear I might pass out from the rush of exhilaration his words inspire. "You'd let me bite you?"

"Gladly." He arches his elegant neck, tilts his head to allow more access, and leans in.

Ah. There's his cock, hard as steel against my abdomen. I want to put my mouth on it, but his throat beckons first.

Bowie has my biceps in his tight grip. Wrapping my arms around him, I slide my hands up his curved back. My mouth waters as I take his flesh between my teeth.

I hesitate. I don't want to hurt him. Animals squeal when bitten, but I only want to give Bowie pleasure.

He reads my mind. "Don't worry," he murmurs. "I'll like it."

I trust him and sink my incisors through his skin into muscle. He quivers against me. I hold him tighter until he settles with a needy groan. Blood hits my tongue, both familiar and altogether different. A spicy burst of copper, salty and thick, trickles down my throat and along with it an infusion of power zings through my veins, tensing my muscles and rushing to my head.

My body is on fire, and all I want to do is burn. Bowie gently pulls his flesh from my mouth and replaces it with his lips. He licks his blood from my teeth and feeds it back to me with his tongue.

Thunder roars, reverberating around us. The air is fizzy and charged. We feed off it, rife with energy, passing vitality back and forth with each deepening kiss. It's almost unreal, making me feel drugged or drunk; I don't know which, as I've experienced neither.

Bowie clings to me, speaks into my ear, "The blood affects people differently. I've got you."

Never let me go. I meant to say it aloud, but I don't think I managed. My lips are tingling like they'll go numb. Feels amazing when he kisses me again.

I grow lightheaded, my mind dizzy with pleasure, with the possibilities between us. My limbs feel heavy. I'm buzzing. The world grays and turns black at the edges.

Bowie strokes my face. "There, there, that's good. Don't fight it."

Don't fight what? I'm not fighting anything. I'm loving you.

"Go to sleep. I'll be here when you wake."

Sleep? No—I want...

CHAPTER 15

*L*eaving dreams of passion and kisses behind, I come aware gradually. If I squeeze my eyes shut, perhaps dream-Bowie will continue his tender caresses. But it's too late. I'm awake, and the real Bowie feels just as nice, pressed against my back, his arm slung over my waist.

That's the only nice thing, though. The ground is hard, my hip is sore, and this cellar stinks of damp onion. I roll over to find he's already awake.

"Good evening," he says with a warm smile.

In lieu of words, I take his lips instead. Gentle kisses, which he accepts with a pleased sigh. I slip my hand into his hair, relishing its silken softness against my palm, and push it behind his ear, then follow the length of it down his back. Such beautiful hair and never a tangle. I can't believe I'm allowed to touch it.

The urge to deepen the kiss and explore him further is hard to resist. But the sun is nearly down, and we have a mission to complete. I lean back to look at him, needing to know what happened before we slept. One moment, I was so high on his touch I feared I might come from kissing alone, and the next, I passed out.

"How are you?" He returns the favor and strokes my mess of wild hair away from my face. My ears twitch, seeking his touch. Somehow, Bowie knows this and scratches them for me. His nails on my scalp work little miracles with each pass.

Before answering, I take stock of my body. I'm a little stiff from sleeping on the stone ground, but the exhaustion from the distance we traveled is entirely gone. My feet and hands feel fine. My bruised arm isn't the least bit sore. Apparently, Bowie works large miracles as well.

"I feel good." Stretching against the length of him, I continue my assessment. "Like new. How did you do that?"

"It wasn't me. Just the blood." He wraps an arm around me and draws me in. Our legs tangle to make this position work.

"Well, it's *your* blood. I'd say that counts. But why did I faint?"

He gives a hint of a shrug, his fingers still combing through my hair, gently unknotting as he goes. "That's a common side effect when the recipient is as exhausted as you were. You were on the verge of passing out before I gave you the blood. You're just good at hiding it."

That makes sense, I suppose. Traveling vast distances four nights in a row was beginning to take its toll. The damned beaver didn't help. "My arm feels as if it never happened."

"Mmm," Bowie murmurs, "it would. Bruises and such heal almost immediately."

"Does that always happen? If you share blood?"

His lips curl to a grin. "It's not something I do often, my dear. In fact, I can count all the occasions with my fingers and have a few left to spare. But no, it won't always be like that. Your body took a lot of wear and tear from the road. It wasn't only your arm that needed repair. If I were to give you blood when you had nothing for it to heal, you'd get the opposite effect. Energized and full of vigor."

Let's do that, I think, but I know this isn't the time. We must pull ourselves together and get back to our mission. See what kind of damage the storm has wrought both to the road and the scent trail.

Bowie squints his eyes shut and frowns. He must be so worried. I touch his face. "We'll find her."

He lays his hand over mine. "I know."

When his eyes open, I kiss him again, putting all the comfort I can into the gesture. "Are you all right?"

"Yes, just worried. I will be until she's safe in my arms."

"We should go, then."

He sighs. "It's still too light out. Soon."

That's got to be so frustrating, though he never complains about the limitation.

I can't resist another kiss. Not when Bowie is right there and his mouth offers such alluring, succulent lips. I could kiss him for hours, but I force myself away. I sit with a groan, my back protesting.

Bowie watches as I stand and stretch out all the kinks. He has a curious look on his face I can't quite make out.

He bites his bottom lip with one fang in an expression so adorable I nearly sink back to the ground to kiss him again. "What?"

He flutters his lashes. "Can I see your tail?"

I suppress an urge to squirm. I've been bullied about my tail all my life, but I know Bowie won't tease me. "But...you've seen it."

"Not really. Not in this form."

That's true. He's always been polite about my nudity. Not taken advantage. I trust him. And even though I'm probably not supposed to like my tail, I do. It's part of me, and it's hard to imagine my body without it.

"All right." I pull my tail free from where it's tucked in my pants. I can never leave it loose like this. Pants aren't made to fit below my tail, and having the waistband there feels awkward at best. It's a blend of black, gray, and white, like the rest of me, fluffy and soft.

"It's lovely." He sits up and gathers his knees to his chest.

I don't mind showing Bowie if he's curious. I spin for him.

"Why don't you wear it loose when we're alone?"

I explain the fit problem.

"Hmm, I wonder if we couldn't have pants tailored to accommodate it either way. Perhaps a covered hole"—he mimes this by circling his hands in the air—"so you could wear the tail inside or outside the flap, depending on company."

That sounds amazing, but I don't exactly know any tailors. And the wolves from my pack who can sew won't be eager to do me any favors.

"I could arrange it," Bowie offers. "When this is over, and everyone is safe. I'd like to see you comfortable."

The confidence is back in his voice. I'm relieved to hear it. Seeing him shaken and panicked after learning Cecily had been taken was awful. He sounds more like himself now, a vampire on a mission, believing he'll succeed.

I consider his offer. Pants fitted for my tail would be convenient, and Bowie has such a generous nature, he makes it seem simple to accept. "Thank you. I would like that."

Offering my hand, I reach down to haul him up. He takes it, stands, then leans into me for a proper hug. "Are you ready for more of the same?"

"Yes." With my body damn near rejuvenated, I feel as if I could run all night. "Let's see how far we can get."

He reaches around me with both hands to pet my tail. I feel his chuckle where his chest is pressed against mine. "It really is lovely. So furry."

Suppressing a shiver along with a wave of desire, I give it a wag for him. He grins.

"All right, that's enough." I step back and tuck my tail into my pants for now. "Time to return to work."

THE GIRLS' scents have been properly annihilated. I expected as much, but still, it's disappointing. Once the enhanced smells of damp earth, wet grass, and muddy bogs have faded to normal, I should still be able to pick up lingering traces here and there, but for tonight, we must continue on the assumption they traveled through to Pest.

After three hours of walking, we stop only briefly in Ecsed.

Bowie insists on buying me a proper plate of food. "For the sake of beavers everywhere," he says as he leaves me seated at a low table in the corner of a near-to-empty tavern. There's only one other pair of men here, on the opposite side, so deep in their cups they don't register our arrival.

The pub is rather dim, quiet at this hour, and smells of ale, smoke, and plain, unspiced foods. Giant wood timbers span the low ceiling. A fireplace and hearth stand along the far wall, but it's not lit; the air is still warm enough without it.

Returning with a plate in one hand, a mug in the other, and an utterly delighted smile on his face, Bowie fails to hold in a snicker. He sets before me a meal of buttered toast and beans.

His laughter tickles my ears. I love seeing him so amused with himself.

I join in. "You didn't."

"I did!" Chortling, he hands me an ale. "Drink up. I'm going to make a quick round through the village while you eat. I won't be long."

Shaking my head, I can't help but smile.

He warned me we'd have to be careful asking questions in Ecsed. The Báthory family owns these lands, and Erzsébet was born and raised here. Though she hasn't lived in Ecsed for decades, she's been known to visit on occasion, and that's what Bowie will try to discover with his snooping.

He doesn't need my help with this. He's faster without me, and conversation comes far more naturally for him. I would only get in his way.

So I watch his pretty silhouette as he leaves, take a sip of my ale, and settle into my buttered toast and beans.

* * *

"Anything useful?" I ask as we make our way back to the road toward Pest. It's pleasant to walk along beside him in my human form so we can chat. But I'll need to shift soon if we're to keep up our pace.

He shoves his hands into his pockets and shrugs. "Not particularly. I'm not sure what to make of the information. I've never been good with persuasion. Not like Ivaz or Bettina. They are masters."

"Tell me what you mean." He's mentioned this power before, calling it a nudge. I'm curious about the details.

"Persuasion is a skill some vampires develop," he explains. "It enhances with age, though I'm perfectly happy if my skill never improves. I find the tactic rather uncomfortable. Imagine being able to nudge a person's thoughts in the direction you wish or to tell them to forget, and they do."

Suppressing a shiver, I remember Ivaz asking me to stay and speak to him and the overwhelming urge I had to obey that felt unnatural. Bowie can do that?

"Anyway." He pulls his hands out of his pockets and flails them around as he talks. "I have the rudimentary ability. I went to the Báthory estate and nudged a stableman in an effort to determine whether Lady Báthory had been in attendance recently. *No*, he said. Had there been any young peasant girls brought here? *No.* Had anyone come through in the last three weeks? *Yes, a merchant wagon selling cloth and beads.* And was the wagon headed for Pest? *Yes.*"

"That could have been them."

"That's what I thought too, but the groom didn't know. If the wagon hid girls, it hid them well. I couldn't risk approaching the estate to inquire further. The fewer people that know we're asking questions, the better."

"But did you make him forget?"

"I did my best, which isn't very reliable."

"It's more than we knew when we arrived. We know to keep an eye out for suspicious merchant wagons now."

"True." He loops his arm through mine. "How was your dinner?"

"Toasty. Buttery. Beany."

Laughing, he tugs me closer. We are alone under the stars, as we often are. There aren't many other travelers at night in general, and tonight there are none at all. The road is far too dangerous for night passage; it would be easy for horse, cart, or man alike to veer off into a muddy bog and get hopelessly stuck.

The storm's damage will keep travelers from a quick passage for days. The debris in the road will have to be cleared before wagons can safely pass this section again. Perhaps that will help us catch up, as the detritus won't slow down a vampire and a werewolf like it would a horse and cart.

As much as I enjoy the feel of him next to me, tonight we must strive for distance. I give his arm a squeeze before letting go and tugging off my hat and shirt.

"I do love this part," says Bowie.

My cheeks warm. Even after he kissed me senseless, his attention still makes me bashful.

He takes my shirt and folds it, then packs it and my hat neatly into our bag. At this point, he'd often turn or avert his eyes, or at the very least, pretend he wasn't staring. Tonight he stares brazenly, eyes roaming my torso with a flare of hunger. Or thirst.

My nipples harden under his loaded gaze.

He's fed me; it's only fair I offer to feed him. That's what I tell myself when I step into his space and arch my neck.

Bowie staggers backward as if pushed. "Oh," he says, his hand flying to cover his mouth. "Oh my. I can't."

"Of course you can." My brows knit together. "You're hungry. So eat."

"It's not so simple."

"Why not?"

His tongue darts out to wet his lips. "What if I can't stop?"

His fear is tangible, hovering in the air between us like fog. I want to squash it. "How often does that happen?"

Crickets chirp, filling the silence as Bowie's expression turns sorrowful.

"Only once." The words sound haunted as they roll off his tongue.

I suppose once was enough to fuel his terror for a lifetime. But there's something I don't understand. "Why would you be afraid of hurting me, but not Jakob?"

Bowie hugs himself and takes another step back as I step forward, shaking his head. "I don't crave Jakob like I crave you, Andras. Please."

Halting, I consider this. Bowie craves me? It seems too good to be true, and though I've had evidence of his desire, it's still hard for me to believe. I want to help him with this block he has around feeding, but pushing anymore tonight feels overbearing. He'll need time to trust himself as I trust him.

"All right, I understand. I'll shift so we can be on our way, but, Bowie, when you're ready, my offer stands."

The effort he makes to nod is painfully obvious.

Melancholy stirs in me as I rouse the wolf. My poor Bowie must be hungry all the time. I'm resolved to help, but I get the feeling he won't make it easy.

That's all right. I don't need easy; I just need Bowie.

CHAPTER 16

The next two nights are spent traveling to Pest. I pick up whiffs of the old scent trail on occasion, mostly where the girl snatchers stopped to relieve themselves, and the smells are strong enough to let me know we remain on the correct path.

I've become better at setting a quick pace, one I can maintain for hours without injury. Bowie insists on checking me over after each hunt and has forbidden me from tackling beavers, which is fine with me. I prefer rabbits anyway, and they have far less muscle with which to fight back.

There's been no trace of Cecily's scent, but I hadn't expected it. I still think we'll pick up her trail somewhere in Pest, and from there, either north to Csejthe or west to Sarvaar. Barring another drenching rain, determining the direction should only take a few hours.

We descend toward Pest. The walled city sits on the bank of the Danube River. A fog has settled over the land, and mist rises from the water in wisps and coils. On the far side, across a floating bridge, lies Buda, which makes Pest look small in comparison. A castle stands in the distance. We'll journey over the bridge to Buda tomorrow night. Ivaz offered to arrange lodging for us in Pest at an inn called The Twig and Berries, so that's where we're headed—and in a hurry because it's far too close to dawn for comfort.

Bowie leads us to a gated entrance in the city wall, unguarded and left open in times of peace. We walk straight through, unbothered.

I continue to sniff for Cecily's telltale minty scent, but it's not here. There's a southern entrance as well, and I pin my hopes on that instead. I'll check it first after we've slept.

"Do you know where we're going?" I'm eager to sleep in a bed again after one too many days in dank, abandoned cellars. At least Bowie hasn't had to resort to sleeping within the earth. I hope we can continue to avoid that.

"Yes. I've accompanied Bettina to The Twig in years prior." We walk briskly past one stone building after another, all in varying shades of cream and red, their occupants just beginning to stir. "I fear you won't like it."

"Why not?"

"It's run by incubi," he says matter-of-factly as if I know what that means.

"Incubi?"

He catches my gaze, my raised brows, and obvious ignorance.

The more I see of the world on this quest, the more I realize how little I know. Werewolves keep to their own, isolated in communal packs, each guarding their territory with little knowledge of what lies beyond their borders. I'm beginning to understand how much more there is to learn and experience beyond the pack lands. My isolation has been thorough. I wonder what Ava would think of a big city. Of a vampire hostel? Of incubi...whatever they are.

Bowie's sparkling gaze narrows. "You're unfamiliar I take it?"

I nod. "I'm unfamiliar with a lot of things, aren't I?" Admitting my lack of worldly knowledge would be difficult with anyone else. But I trust in Bowie, in his patience as much as his gentle way of teaching.

He takes my arm, a habit of his I secretly love. "You're a fast learner, my dear, so it matters not what you don't know. What matters is that you care to learn."

He makes me feel all warm inside. My lips creep to a smile. "Teach me of incubi, then."

"Where to begin?" he muses with laughter in his voice. "They're a race of demons, but don't let that scare you. Demons, like people, werewolves, and vampires, come in all types—good and bad, saintly and evil. Most are some mix of both, just like us. Well, me at least. I'm not convinced you have a bad bone at all in you, not even in your smallest toe."

"Tell that to the beaver I ate."

Bowie chortles and squeezes my arm. "All right, I'll grant you the smallest bit of evil. Anyway, incubi are highly sexual creatures, demons who draw their energy and sustenance from the lust and pleasure of others. As such, they're well adept at inspiring that lust and giving that pleasure. Even just one incubus can lure a slew of humans into an orgy on a whim."

Inspiring how? I gape at him. "Will they try to feed from us?"

"Depends on what we get up to," he teases, then grows serious. "But no, not overtly, and not when we're only there to sleep. But you won't be unaffected. There's a certain enticing nature to the atmosphere, a tempting haze that's difficult to ignore. It's not ill-intentioned on their part. They simply can't help it. And the inn we're going to isn't so much an inn exactly as it is a brothel. The demons cater mostly to humans who aren't aware of their supernatural nature."

Stunned, I let that sink in. So we're headed straight for a den of sex demons who feed off the lust of their oblivious human customers. Right. Nothing to worry about then except for the small fact I spend every waking hour and at least half of the sleeping ones pining for my handsome, clever companion. Perfect. Not that Bowie doesn't seem to be agreeable, just that we're on a mission—an extremely time-sensitive mission—and we've had no opportunity for such diversions.

"You've tensed," Bowie observes. "Please don't worry. I'll handle them. They can be perfectly reasonable when told no. Plus, we've all the coin we need to keep them happily away from us during our stay."

That's not really what I'm worried about, but I don't say so.

The beginning of dawn's golden light peeks from above the rise to the east. Bowie hisses and takes off at a trot, tugging me along with him.

"I really ought to pay better attention," he says rather flippantly, given the circumstances.

"Are you all right? You can run ahead if you need to."

"And leave you lost? Never. I'm fine. The light is still indirect. It just burns a little. We're nearly there."

We keep close to the darker shadows of buildings, hurrying down one side road, then a narrow street, and finally to an alley. If I expected a grand building with outward displays of the decadence within, I'd have been wrong. We fly through the entrance of a nondescript wooden dwelling, not much larger than an ordinary house, and descend immediately down a flight of stairs. Again.

Because, of course a den of demons would be underground.

I can smell sex from here. Musk and sweat mixed with frilly oiled perfumes in an odor that is as succulent as it is repellent. I can't make up my mind which.

A man approaches as we flee the last traces of natural light into what looks like a wine cellar. Bottles are stacked on specially designed shelving from floor to ceiling, lit with oil lamps suspended from low timbers.

"Cutting it close, vampire," scolds the stranger. He's petite, slender, with a swagger like a wild cat, not the sort of brute I'd choose for a guard, but something tells me he can hold his own despite appearances. Under his straight brown hair, his face holds a distinct lack of expression I find chilling. Is this an incubus? Instead of passion, he inspires revulsion. I'm eager to get past him.

"Names?" he asks.

Bowie, as always, is unbothered. "Beauregard of Varad, and his guest, Andras. I believe Haci Ivazzade Pasha made the arrangements."

It still feels novel to be introduced as Andras and not Mongrel.

"Yes. They're expecting you."

"Are there any messages for me?" asks Bowie. "From Janos, perhaps?"

"Not that I'm aware." He gestures to the wine bottles, and I notice his hands have claws instead of nails. I shiver. "You may enter."

I have only a moment to be confused—because he seems to be suggesting we walk through a wall—before the entire shelf of bottles opens out. A hidden door. The bottles rattle and jangle. A pungent scent of coupling wafts from inside, leaving me scrunching my nose. I can't imagine many wolves frequent this den. It's overpowering. Not that I'm prudish, but by the moon, that's a strong aroma.

We enter, and the giant door of wine closes entirely on its own. *Magic?* I'll have to ask when we're alone, though perhaps we are because I see no others. At this hour, I'm not surprised.

A lobby of sorts, half parlor and half bar, spreads before us. A large arched entrance leads to The Twig and Berries, and opposite, its twin opens to The Peach and Pearl as noted by ornately painted oval signs.

Following Bowie, I whisper, "Does every city have an underground labyrinth for vampires?"

His grin shows off his fangs. "Well, I certainly haven't been to *every* city, but it would appear so, wouldn't it?"

We pass beneath the elaborately carved arch into a cozier salon decorated in shades of emerald and gold. Plush lounging furniture is tucked into every nook and cranny. The uneven lines of the walls create semiprivate alcoves, each with an accompanying curtain, all of them drawn to the side as none are in use. A lush, thick carpet cushions our feet and brings warmth to this glorified basement.

Soft footsteps sound from an adjoining hallway.

Bowie and I turn as one to watch whoever approaches. Bowie steps closer and touches a hand to my lower back in a gesture I'd like to think means *mine*.

The creature that joins us stuns me with his beauty, his presence, and the massive serpentine horns sprouting from a mane of silver braids. His skin is a mottled lavender, oiled to a glistening luster.

My jaw drops stupidly. I can't help but stare.

To think, I worry about hiding my comparably tiny ears when this being—this incubus, I presume—possesses tusks upon his head the size of two dueling broadswords, if broadswords were curled like springs and made into a hat.

My gaze drifts downward. The horns aren't his only massive feature.

He's clad in nothing more than a sheer flowing skirt of shimmering blue fabric that does little to hide the impressive erection dangling between bulging thighs. Well then.

He must be at least seven feet tall from his toes to the tip of his horns and near as wide as Bowie and me combined. His naked chest is on display—his nipples pierced, the jewelry decorating them connected by a delicate golden chain that somehow complements his enormous muscles. A matching blue stone sparkles from his belly button. The whole of him presents an alluring combination of male and female the likes of which I've never beheld.

My cock twitches. I want to fuck him. No, I want him to fuck me. No, even better, I want him to fuck Bowie while I watch. Or—

Bowie nudges my side, snapping me out of my fantasies before my mind can gift me with even more creative options for the three of us. The wave of lust recedes. I give myself an extra shake to be thorough. I don't actually want this stranger at all, but for a moment, the idea possessed me like a…demon.

Oh right. Because he is one. I remember now.

Somehow Bowie's warning did little to prepare me for the reality of this creature.

"Hello, Dominus," says Bowie. His hand shifts from my back to my waist and tugs me closer against his side. "Sorry to keep you waiting."

"Don't be," Dominus purrs as he looks me over. "Not when you've brought such a fine specimen. A wolf? We don't get many of those."

How does he know?

"You don't have one now." Bowie clutches me tightly. "He's mine."

Just what I wanted to hear. I like the idea even more when Bowie says the words out loud. I lean into him.

Dominus just lifts a shoulder, shrugging off the rejection with elegance. "It's not like you to be so possessive." He's talking to Bowie, but he's still eyeing me, giving me the urge to squirm. When he circles us at a slow saunter, I shuffle even closer to Bowie.

I want to ask Dominus just what he thinks he's doing, but Bowie speaks up first. "We won't require your services today."

"No, I don't imagine you will." Whistling, Dominus lingers behind us, making me nervous. "Getting a piece of tail with an actual tail, Bowie? Nice."

How. Does. He. Know?

I tuck my tail as close to my body as it will go. It's hidden beneath my pants, but not so hidden that someone staring at my ass the way Dominus is won't notice the anomaly.

"I've brought coin. Which room are we in?" asks Bowie in a clipped tone.

Dominus returns to stand in front of us, hands on hips. "Are you certain I couldn't interest you in—"

"You can't. Which room?" Bowie's grip on my waist doesn't relent in the slightest.

"Worth a try." Dominus blows out an exaggerated sigh and spins. I'm surprised to notice he has a tail too. Different from mine, soft and leathery, whiplike with a heart-shaped nub at the tip. It sways with his hips as he walks. "Follow me."

We pass through a ramped hallway decorated with lavish draped silks hung at alternating angles from the ceiling. Dominus is so tall his horns sweep the fabric aside as he moves. Bowie and I walk beneath without touching the decor. The flowery scent of incense and smoke blends with the aroma of sex to create a heaviness in the air I find unpleasant.

Dominus pushes open a carved wooden door with the image of naked men engaged in fellatio. It's...quite realistic. "Here you are," he says with a flourish of ringed fingers. "Will there be anything else?"

Bowie hands over a purse of coin and shakes his head. "No, thank you. We'll leave at dusk."

Dominus bows low, giving me an indulgent look at his magnificent horns. "Do come again, but next time I insist you share." With one last leer in my direction, he leaves us alone, and we slip into the room, shutting the obscene door behind us.

"I apologize for being so possessive out there," says Bowie. "I'm well aware you're not *mine*. It's just that Dominus is rather pushy, and you're off-limits." He hesitates. "Unless you want to be...on-limits, in which case, you'll need to speak up because—"

"I don't."

"Good, good." Bowie nods. "He used his sway on you, didn't he?"

"If by 'sway' you mean I nearly lost my mind imagining him naked and frisky, then yes. He must have."

Bowie's brows arch. "Is Dominus your type?"

I take my time looking Bowie over. The room beyond him can wait because a vulnerable expression crosses his handsome face, and suddenly all I want is to reassure him.

He cuts a fine figure in the fitted blue coat that brings out his eyes. His shining hair fans over his shoulders, framing his pale face with its black glory. Pretty pink lips hang slightly parted, and if one looks close, which I most certainly do, twin protrusions give away the fangs behind them. He's perfect.

"You're my type." As the words leave my lips, I can't believe I've been so bold. But why stop here? I take Bowie's face in my hands and kiss him before he can respond. "I liked it when you called me yours," I growl against his lips.

He opens for me, returning the kiss with growing enthusiasm. Clutching my waist, he draws me close and presses us together so I feel his desire for me against my own. "Mine," he says.

And I want to be. I *really* want to be.

CHAPTER 17

"Wait," says Bowie against my mouth. "Are you certain about this?"

"Yes." Pushing him toward the bed, I break off our kiss long enough to make sure we don't trip on the lavish rugs.

This room has the same feel as the rest of the brothel. Seductive. Overly decorated.

Lush, brightly colored silk hangs on every wall and from the ceiling to drape over the bed. At least it smells better in here. Freshly laundered fabric and expensive soap, perfumed to smell of sandalwood and cedar. There's no hiding what this room is used for, but I don't care. Not when Bowie is wriggling in my arms.

His thighs hit the back of the bed, and he thumps to a sit. I press him back against the blue velvet bedcover, chasing his lips with mine.

"But—" Bowie turns his head to the side. I hover over him, waiting with heavy impatience. He feels divine beneath me. "How do you *know* you're certain and it's not their influence? Dominus did sway you back there."

When Bowie sucks his lower lip into his mouth and bites

down on it with one fang, I nearly explode with longing.

"I'm sure." I meet his gaze, and for once, the words come easy. "I've wanted you since that first night, when you wouldn't call me *Mongrel*, then more when I saw how loving you were with your family, and more still when you invented trained Beans tricks to make sad children happy. I wanted you when you made me feel safe among other vampires and when you told me the truths you'd rather keep hidden. I especially wanted you when you kissed me and gave me your blood. So please don't doubt me when I say I want you now."

"Andras," he breathes my name on a sigh, studying me with an intensity that steals my breath. "Kiss me."

I do. Immediately and with enthusiasm. He parts his legs and wraps them around my hips, making it simple to push him farther onto the bed. I drop my weight against his chest and moan. How can another person feel this good? Our connection is staggering in its immensity. I adore him and want only to worship him, to prove myself worthy of his passion.

In a burst of strength and speed, Bowie flips us over and pins me to the mattress with no more than a look. "Stay." He climbs off the bed. "I'll be right back."

Blood rushes from my brain to my cock at the command, warm and tingling with need. The urge to touch myself blooms, but I wait.

Anticipation is its own reward.

Bowie goes to the door and turns the lock I hadn't realized was there, then opens the top dresser drawer at the foot of the bed. He plucks from it a glass jar and tosses the little bottle next to me—oil. Its presence sends a barreling wave of expectation swelling to consume me. I want everything he'll let me have, starting with his gaze.

One button at a time, Bowie takes off his coat while watching me, his eyes dark and hungry.

I'm dizzy with desire, admiring him as he undresses, layer

after layer, until he's revealing his beautiful creamy skin. Peaked roseate nipples taunt me from out of my reach. My mouth yearns for them, watering. I swallow.

"Now you," says Bowie when he's gloriously nude. My eyes travel the length of him, lingering on his flushed, swollen cock, already eager for my touch.

I've seen him naked, but this is different. He is naked *for me.*

He crawls onto the bed and tugs off one of my leather shoes as I hurry to pull my shirt over my head. My skin tingles as it's exposed, longing for his. We work in tandem until I'm naked too. Finally, I tug him down on top of me.

If I thought he felt good before, I was mistaken because he feels amazing now. His cool body against my heat, flesh to flesh from toes to lips, his tongue seeking mine.

Groaning, I open for him, suck him into my mouth and savor. Bowie is ravenous, devouring me from mouth to jaw to throat. I wish he'd bite, but he won't. The scrape of his fangs against the column of my neck has my heart racing. My pulse thumps wildly in my ears.

Bowie lifts his hips to align our cocks. I widen my legs to make room for him and arch to meet his touch as he presses us together. With a leisurely rocking motion, he sends me from eager to desperate between breaths. I groan against his temple, trap him in my firm embrace, his soft skin beneath my palms a treasure of sensation.

Licking from my collarbone to my ear, Bowie rises to catch my gaze. "What do you like?" His voice is low, husky, and over-laid with desire, thick and sweet like honey. I'm in awe of him. To see him like this. To hear his bedroom voice. To know I inspired it.

"Everything. Anything. Whatever you want." My need to please him overcomes whatever preferences I might have. My preference is Bowie. I can't imagine anything we could do together that wouldn't feel wonderful. I could come from this, if only his lazy rocking sped up in the slightest. The slide and tug of his cock against mine already has me panting.

A naughty twinkle dances in his gaze. "We are in agreement, then, because I also want"—he leans down until his lips cover mine—"everything."

Kissing him, I explore his body with my hands and his mouth with my tongue, memorizing every curve, every line, every soft and hard space he has to offer. His silken hair caresses my cheeks, my throat, creating an ebony halo to encase us.

The slow press and retreat of his hips turn maddening.

I cradle his head and wrap my arm around his back, using my strength to flip us over. Positions reversed, I can bear down on him with as much pressure and speed as I like.

Bowie allows this with an indulgent grin, his mouth open, fangs glistening. He throws his head back against the velvet bedsheets as I thrust us together. Without oil, we're limited, or else pleasure would spike with pain.

Stopping for even a second requires all of my restraint.

I sit on his thighs and admire the view of Bowie laid out beneath me like an offering. My palms itch to hold him, to memorize more of him by touch, to learn all his favorite spots.

His stomach muscles quiver. His flushed, swollen cock is leaking. I take it in hand and swipe the fluid around his crown until it shines. Beautiful.

Wriggling, Bowie nearly lifts me as his hips thrust, driving his length into the circle of my fist. He looks positively shameless, fucking my hand like this. I burn the image into my mind to savor whenever I want. I'll picture it often.

"The oil," Bowie gasps, his pretty lashes fluttering. "And your cock against mine. Please."

The way he says "please," his wet lips pouty and lush, there's nothing I wouldn't do for him.

Bowie grips my thighs and squeezes while I uncap the little

jar and slick my hand. His whole body is in motion under me, writhing, sinuous, his muscles flexing and contracting. His nipples pebble to hard buds demanding to be teased.

I ignore his shaft and spread the oil on the twin nubs instead, flicking and massaging them between my fingers.

My reward is a breathtaking display as he arches his back and presses his chest out for more. And the noises he makes! Little sighs of pleasure, a deep moan, my name on his lips…I'm so worked up I will explode the moment he touches me.

But I want this to last. And I want us to fuck; I don't care how. Him in me, me in him. It makes no difference as long as we're joined, and soon.

I slide lower, pressing his legs aside to make room for myself between them, and suck one nipple into my mouth.

Bowie cries out. He gathers my hair in his fists and clenches, not pushing me away or holding me still, just squeezing like he can't help it. The tug on my scalp stirs fresh desire. I dig my cock into the bedsheets, thrusting because being still is impossible.

"Please, please," Bowie murmurs mindlessly.

"Anything," I breathe against his tender nipple, flushed nearly purple from my attentions.

"Fuck me." Bowie prods my belly with his dripping cock-head, slicking my skin and sending fire to my balls. "Come inside me. Please."

Oh, his words. His desperate words. I could listen to him talk for hours, but words like these? I'm out of my mind with lust. I've never needed anything as much as I need to be inside Bowie.

Sliding down his tantalizing body, I rush to obey the command. My mouth finds his cock and greedily laps its slippery gift.

Bowie makes a mewling noise. My ears twitch to hear more. He clutches my shoulders, fingers digging into muscle.

It feels so good to have him under me, to relish his desire for me. Sex has never been like this before—so intimate and personal—I could live in this moment forever. Bowie's cock in my mouth, the delight of sucking, my fingers exploring his entrance, caressing the ring of muscle, easing it loose.

The world folds and collapses to just this room, this bed, this man and his pleasure. I'm dizzy with joy, my body primed for union.

Bowie pulls his knees to his chest, totally exposing himself to my hungry gaze. I let his cock slip from my mouth so I can take in the vision he presents, all naked and open. Again the urge to claim him crashes through me, body and soul. My mouth waters. My cock twitches. My fingers prepare him to take me deep.

"Yes," he moans, turning the word into a sentence, and the sentence into a story. "Yes, please. I'm ready, Andras, please."

So polite, my Bowie, even squirming on my fingers and desperate he speaks so prettily.

I slick myself with more oil and climb over him. His embrace is swift and strong. I love the way his arms feel around me, his muscles flexing to hold me tighter. His thighs join the action, closing around my hips.

A desperate sound escapes my throat as I sink into his cool depths.

Bowie joins in harmony, both of us groaning our pleasure.

The tight grip as his body stretches to accommodate mine drives me wild. The need to thrust, to pound, to bite, and to claim wars with the need to take him slowly, to draw out every sweet second of this bliss.

I lose the battle. Or I win it. Both at once.

Bowie rocks into me and whines, "More."

I won't deny him. I give him all of me, hard and demanding. His answering cries of rapture urge me on. His eyes flutter closed. His lips, moist and reddened, are irresistible. I claim them too, dropping my mouth to his in a thrusting kiss that mimics our bodies.

He gives me more of his cries, his gasps, his desperate little noises. I want them all. I devour them with glee.

My balls draw tight, painfully so, ready to fill Bowie to the brim. I ride the edge, hovering at the peak of this cliff, but I don't want to leap alone. I need Bowie with me always. Shifting for a deeper angle, I seek his pleasure, commanding him to come with me.

He obeys.

A full-body shiver that begins in stuttering hips and bursts outward overcomes our rhythm.

Bowie clings to me, and I to him as we quake and tremble against each other, our bodies flying high, mine within his, his around mine. I shudder, holding him close, panting in his arms as my cock pulses and my mind shatters into a million triumphant pieces.

"Bowie, Bowie, Bowie," I chant against the soft shell of his ear. I kiss him there. And again because one kiss will never be enough. I nuzzle my nose into his silken hair, snuffle his neck, and suck on the skin of his throat.

Bowie moans, his legs keeping me hostage, but I will die a happy prisoner in this trap rather than seek my freedom.

"Andras." My name takes on new meaning when it springs from Bowie's lips. As if I am more me with him than without. "My dear Andras." He turns his head to catch my lips.

Kissing Bowie is the miracle of the journey and the destination at once, an end unto itself, and a new beginning that holds the promise of better still to come.

We twist and turn in each other's embrace without breaking the kiss until we settle on our sides, his legs tangled with mine.

He strokes my back, the skin sweaty from effort, the fur lying flat and soft as I relax. I love the way his nails feel as they card through my thick coat, then scratch over my sensitive skin, hovering over the place where man meets animal. Pressing into his touch, I sigh, sleepy and content.

Bowie kisses the tip of my nose. "You feel like a dream."

"Mmm," I murmur my agreement, snuggling into him and mixing our scents as much as I can. "Let's never wake up."

"I would agree." He matches my snuggles with one of his own, one that emphasizes the wet slick of his cum trapped between our bellies. "But we'll soon be sticky."

I chuckle. Trust Bowie to be fastidious about this as well. I don't mind. Everything about him is adorable.

I'd happily clean him with my tongue, but he's already sneaking out of my embrace and slips from the bed. Though he's gone for only the briefest of moments, I miss him all the same.

Taking the opportunity to tug the sheets free so we can settle beneath rather than on them, I stretch my muscles, finding them gloriously spent.

He returns with a wet cloth. I resist the urge to protest, loving the scent of our combined smells, but even as he wipes me down, I know the aroma won't vanish completely. I can still savor the traces. And his gentle strokes feel lovely against my overheated skin.

Tossing the cloth aside, Bowie climbs in next to me. We curl up together as close as two people can be. I settle the cover over us and give in to a big yawn. When I open my eyes, it's to see his charming grin.

"Rest now, my darling." He kisses me. "You've more than earned it."

"Have I?" I return his kiss. He's so beautiful, even more so now, freshly fucked and glowing with satisfaction.

"You know you have." He winks. "Next time it will be my turn."

My cock gives a valiant pulse at the thought. "I've never done it that way."

Bowie's brows arch. "Never?"

I shake my head.

"You don't want to?"

"Oh, I want to," I assure him. "With you. As soon as possible."

Bowie's ringing laughter makes me giddy. "It will be my pleasure, but can I ask why you haven't?"

I flick my tail over my thigh to whack his. "It's never been safe. I have to hide this."

"Ah, I see." He strokes my tail. It feels divine. "You'll hide nothing from me," he murmurs, so close his lips move over mine. "I shall take you from behind to observe your tail in all its glory."

I shiver against him. "Promise?"

"Cross my heart."

Delirious, we kiss until I pass out from the pleasure.

CHAPTER 18

As we leave The Twig and Berries through the parlor now crowded with incubi and their guests, I stay close to Bowie's side. There's an energy to the air that I can sense but not explain. My eyes roam from one being to the next, and somehow, I know which are human and which are incubi, though their horns and tails are entirely invisible. It's as if the magic itself has a presence within these walls—a living thing I could almost reach out and touch.

I spot Dominus, though he looks much different. Not so huge, his silver hair morphed to a golden blond, lavender skin now a sun-kissed tan. No horns, no tail. I'd say he passes for human, and certainly the humans seem to think so, but to me, he retains his otherworldly glow, even with these modifications. He flashes a flirty smirk in my direction.

I avert my gaze, cheeks heating.

Bowie chuckles. "You have an admirer."

I take his hand. "I'd better have two."

He squeezes. "You could have hundreds."

"I only want you," I whisper and lean into him. "Hey, how do they…"

He shakes his head. "No idea."

We pass through the arched exit, up and out of the brothel to a moonlit street. I suck in fresh air gratefully—well, as fresh as city air can be. At least the musk of sex is absent. I'm glad to be away from The Twig and Berries, above ground, and on the move, though peeling myself away from Bowie and out of bed this morning was a challenge. When this is all over, I want uninterrupted time with him, someplace peaceful, with a soft bed and no other people.

And plenty of oil.

Bowie leads us through a maze of alleys to the main street. We're headed to Pest's southern gate first to check for Cecily's scent, then west across the Danube River to Buda.

Pushing aside images of Bowie naked and writhing on blue velvet, I make myself focus. Around us, stone buildings line the streets, their awnings nearly creating a tunnel over the narrow roadways. Though it's evening, the hour isn't yet late, and people are out and about living their lives. I watch them with interest, all the while concentrating on the smells: smoke, roasted river fish, ripe fruit, urine, smelted metal, horse droppings, and so on. The scent of the masses congregated close together, both foul and fair, presents a cornucopia to be sorted and discarded as I search.

We emerge onto a market street as shops are closed or closing for the night. Before we've walked even ten full minutes, it hits me.

The blend of rosewater soap, fabric washed in lavender... and mint candy. The scent of Bowie's estate, his family scent, like pack, a faint but unmistakable aroma they share.

The smell of Cecily.

Stopping, I grab Bowie's wrist and spin him to face me.

His eyes go wide. "What?"

"I've got her. Bowie, I've got her! Cecily's been taken through here!"

His free hand clutches his chest, and his face goes perfectly still, almost as if he's afraid to believe it. "Really?"

I rush to reassure him. "Yes. I'm positive. This way." Dragging him with me, I hurry down the main street toward the river.

Bowie trots along next to me, and I'm so happy I want to hug him, pick him up, and twirl him around. I'd wag my tail if I could. The scent trail is fresh, only two days old, maybe three. Certainly, they came through after the storm.

This is the time for speed. We probably won't be able to overtake them, but surely we can follow and save her from Báthory's evil.

Buzzing with newfound energy, I follow the trail straight out of the walled city of Pest to the floating bridge that leads to Buda.

"Wait," says Bowie.

I pause beside him.

He digs into his inner coat pockets. "We'll need coin to cross, and we must blend in. No more galloping past people."

"Right." I'm impressed he can contain himself so well in spite of our long-awaited discovery. "Blend in." I tug my cap farther over my ears and take a deep breath.

A great stone gatehouse stands at the entrance to the bridge. There's a short line: a group of men walking as we are, a solo driver with a horse cart, then us. Bowie hands payment over to a gruff-looking attendant, and we're waved through.

The fish smell is much stronger here and fresher, like I could snap one up straight from the river and devour it whole.

Gazing at the water's great expanse, suddenly, I'm nervous.

I've never seen a bridge like this one, enormous and in constant motion with the rhythm of the mighty river it spans. Wooden planks line the surface, overlaid on top of a series of pontoons, dozens of them, perhaps forty or fifty in total. The inside lanes are for wagons and carts, wide enough two could pass without issue, and the outside lanes are for those on foot such as ourselves.

I clutch Bowie's arm.

He senses my nerves, as always, and wraps his arm about my waist. "Nothing to fear, my darling. I've crossed it before. Perfectly safe."

I appreciate the sentiment, but words don't vanquish anxiety. We press ahead on the heels of the other walkers. As I step from solid land onto the floating bridge, a flutter of nausea forms in my stomach. I force it down with a deep breath. I can do this. Bowie is with me, and that's all that matters.

"Concentrate on what lies on the other side, rather than what's beneath your feet," he advises.

Trying that, I lift my gaze to the far bank and take in the city of Buda.

It's much larger than Pest, perhaps three times the size, and as such, the whole of it isn't walled in. Only the castle and keep are walled, an impressive sight, even from far away. Its numerous towers pierce the sky with their green-roofed caps. As we draw closer, I make out a red stone staircase shining like polished marble that leads to a magnificent second-story entrance. Massive bronze gates remain closed, and a matching bronze statue of Hercules guards the courtyard.

Pest was flatter terrain in comparison. Buda is hilly throughout, and behind the city, even taller hills rise in the distance. We'll only be passing through, chasing Cecily's scent from inside the city to wherever it may lead. I wonder if we shall soon be exploring those far-off hills. I hope so because the forest calls like a beacon.

The planks we walk on lift and fall with the river currents. Nausea rises to my throat, but I ignore it as best I can, hoping it doesn't get the best of me.

Beside me, Bowie begins to chatter, and I focus on his voice. It helps.

"The bridge was constructed to allow four-way traffic," he explains. "A marvel of modern society. Not only can commerce pass from Buda to Pest and back, but the river remains passable for boats as well. When a ship needs to cross past the bridge, a larger section of the floating planks is simply moved—floated right out of the way to create a gap for the ship. Once it sails through, the bridge is floated back into place, locked, and people can cross again. Brilliant."

He's not wrong, but the idea that the bridge is so easily... portable doesn't exactly settle my stomach. A children's story flashes through my mind, a wooden bridge, a friendly troll called Arlo living beneath who liked to be paid with trinkets like shiny rocks and one-of-a-kind shells. It's been quite a long time since Ava read me that one. I suppose I'm too old for it now, but the thought is still comforting.

When we're nearly across, I'm shocked to discover we must pay on this side as well. But what do they do when travelers spend all their money on the first toll, not knowing the second one exists? I'm left to wonder as we arrive on solid earth, and I can finally breathe a sigh of grateful relief.

"You did well," says Bowie, releasing my waist to pat my cheek. From anyone else, it would seem condescending, but from Bowie, it's genuine affection and pride. "That is the only floating bridge I know of, so you can rest easy."

I won't take immovable ground beneath my feet for granted anytime soon.

I don't pay much attention to Buda as we make our way through on the main roads. The trail doesn't indicate Cecily was allowed to stop for any length of time in the city. Rather they traveled straight through, as we are doing. This close, my view of the castle is partially obstructed by its towering stone walls, though the tall spires can't be missed. The scene from the top must be magnificent, like what a bird sees when it soars above the entire landscape.

We pass from city to farmland, then farmland to forest. Our path ascends into the hills, narrowing from a maintained road to little more than a trail through trees. Horses could pass, but wagons and carts would find the terrain difficult, if not impossible.

Being within the woods' embrace has a certain homey feel to it, even though these aren't my woods. Thinking of Ava, I hope she doesn't miss me as much as I miss her.

I spend the rest of the night on four legs, my nose to Cecily's trail, covering as much ground as my body will let me. Making swift progress, I'm in deep concentration when Bowie's voice breaks my stride.

"Andras wait," he says from where he follows a few paces behind me. As I slow to a halt, he catches up quickly. "The view, turn and look."

The view? I hadn't even realized we'd crested a ridge line. Behind us stretches a wide valley with the Danube dividing it down the middle. The glowing torchlight above the guard towers reflects in ripples off the water. We're so far away the castle is a mere speck on the riverbank, its own torches like tiny stars, as distant as the sky itself.

I'm shocked at the distance we've traveled in just one night, and more so that my body is willing to press on. With Cecily's scent in my nostrils, my drive to find her eclipses my other needs. I should have known Bowie wouldn't allow that. It's the first thing from his lips.

"You must eat, and I thought you might like to see the city before we move on," he says.

I haven't been paying attention to prey smells. It seems a waste to spend time tracking down a meal. Remembering the sweet figs Catherine packed for me, I prepare to shift so I can eat them.

Bowie catches my gaze as I begin, and I'm struck anew by his exquisite beauty. Perhaps even more so now that I've had the chance to properly adore him, one gasp at a time.

We watch each other as I slowly transform from the wolf to the man. As it's happening, I realize I'm more tired than I thought. My feet are sore, so is my neck. I roll it, and a series of crackling *pops* relieve some of the tension.

Bowie steps into my space, and I welcome him with a nuzzle to his neck. Smelling myself on him, my scent mixed with his, brings a possessive growl to my throat. I hold it in. Growling in this form isn't sexy; it's weird. Bowie's hands on my skin turn me back toward the stunning view. We gaze across the starlit lands together, him pressed to my back.

Until my stomach decides I'll be growling after all.

"I *thought* you might be hungry," he says, humor laced in his soft tone.

"You're right, but I don't want to lose any time. Hand me the pack."

He swipes it off his shoulder, and I dig inside for the figs. They smell divine.

"You can't have only figs for dinner. Surely you need to catch something."

"There's plenty," I argue. Catherine has packed enough for a feast. I stuff two into my mouth and speak around them. "Then we'll be on our way."

"But they're just sweets, not a real meal."

I chuckle. "That's where you're wrong. Sweets should be the meal more often. Why eat potatoes when one could eat cake?" A memory stirs. "Better yet, potato cake."

Bowie unbuttons his coat and sits on a patch of wild grasses. "Is there such a thing?"

I join him, nodding and chewing. Moons, candied figs are delicious. "Of course. Potatoes, sugar, and butter are all you need."

His nose scrunches. "That doesn't sound very good."

"Well, it's not bloody."

"I do remember food, you know. From before. And it still doesn't sound very good."

Grinning, I polish off another handful of figs. "Suit yourself."

He rests a hand on my thigh as I eat, and we stare out over the horizon. It's quiet up here, with no breeze to speak of. Most of the animals are farther downhill where the tree cover is better, so there's no sound of scurrying feet.

Bowie has got to be hungry too.

I must confess the thought of him feeding from me is arousing. I want him to bite me, but it's such a sore subject. I'm not sure how to bring it up without upsetting him. And he's so peaceful in this moment. I don't want to disturb him. He knows the offer stands, so perhaps I shouldn't push.

When the last of the figs is gone and my belly is quite full, I get a second wind. Who says sugar isn't a proper meal?

Bowie takes our bag and slings it around his neck. "Are you sure you're all right to keep going? I don't want to wear you out. I'll need you strong when it's time to stage a rescue."

I nod. I'm feeling good. Cecily's scent is easy to follow, thanks to her own sweet tooth and those mint candies she favors. Even if she's eaten them, her dresses will smell of them until laundered. "I'm fine. Let's keep going. We're making good time."

"All right. I'll keep an eye out for a place to sleep as dawn approaches. Until then, I follow your lead."

He tucks his leg beneath him to stand, but before he can finish the movement, I grab him for a quick kiss. Just one before I shift. Or two.

Bowie makes it four before I pull away—reluctantly because he tastes even better than the figs—and call on my animal form once again. Shifting back and forth so often is making my bones ache, but I don't mind. It'll all be worth it when we succeed.

He leans down and gives my neck a scratch, whispering quietly, "Thank you, my dear. I love you."

The words come as such a surprise I find myself stunned. Warmth blooms in my chest. I rub my cheek on his thigh, glad that I'm not expected to answer as a wolf. I'm so overwhelmed and happy, I know I couldn't form words anyway.

* * *

WALK. *Sniff. Walk. Sniff. Walk. Sniff.*

The faster I go, the sooner we reach Cecily.

Walk. Sniff. Walk. Sniff. Walk. Sniff.

I've lost track of time, but nothing matters except this trail.

Walk. Sniff. Walk. Sniff. Walk. Sniff.

That is until Bowie calls a halt to my progress and insists I stop.

Stopping isn't pleasant. As long as I have momentum, I can keep going. But as soon as I stop, the pain creeps in. My joints, my pads, my spine, they're all achy and sore. I have no idea how far we traveled tonight, but it was a lot. *A lot*, a lot, and I want to keep going. We're getting closer to the end of my scent trail; I can sense it like the first frost or a spring rain.

"It's near to sunrise," says Bowie. "Look." He points to the right. Off our path is an old windmill, probably once used to grind grain and now quite derelict, its sails broken and useless. "The masonry appears to be intact. Let's go see."

He leads the way, and I follow on shaky legs across an overgrown field where the forest has already begun to creep onto old pastureland. Wondering how long ago this mill was built, I scan the area but see no other houses or huts.

We approach the base—broad, tall, and definitely still solid. The wooden cap has deteriorated, but this part, built from stone, was made to last.

Bowie shoulders open a rotten door, and we creep inside. It

smells damp, like wet stone, but not moldy, which is a relief. It's dark, which bodes well for the structure being light-tight enough to ensure Bowie's safety. The circular-shaped building houses old gears, wooden tools, and pieces of machinery my mind can't quite put together in a way that would grind anything, but perhaps it's not all here anymore. There's plenty of space on the ground for us to sleep.

"Yes, this will do nicely," says Bowie. He shoves the door shut and inspects it, I assume, for cracks.

With the door closed, I'm mostly lost. My other senses kick in, but my night vision is useless when there's no light at all. Bowie's at my side, his hand on my ruff, and I don't care that I can't see as long as he's here.

I drop to the ground with a huff, exhausted. The dirt floor is mostly dry. Not that it matters, and I curl up without another thought.

Bowie sits next to me and strokes my fur. "Are you all right, my darling? You've been an absolute warrior tonight, traveling this far."

Flopping my head into his lap to enjoy the kind words and gentle caress, I hope he doesn't mind if I don't shift. I'm going to fall asleep right away; it's inevitable.

"There, there," he croons, massaging my neck. It feels heavenly as if paradise had fingers and those fingers were Bowie's, and they were buried in the thick fur around my neck. With a sigh, I close my eyes.

On my next breath, I open them again. Because I smell blood. Bowie's blood. My heartbeat picks up. Is he hurt? I should shift.

I'm about to, when his wrist appears under my nose and he says to me, "Drink."

Oh. *Oh.* He's done this for me. Opened a vein to heal my body. He refuses to drink from me yet insists I drink from him.

Well, I'm certainly not going to turn it down, but tomorrow night, he must let me feed him. I won't take no for an answer.

As I lap the delectable blood from his skin with my tongue, tingles begin in my spine and work their way out to my aching limbs. Salt, copper, spice, and Bowie. So good sliding down my throat. So much pleasure I'm near to blacking out.

"Very good, just like that." Bowie's voice is low and soft, muffled as if I'm hearing him through a tunnel, but his free arm is heavy on my back, and his thigh is cool beneath my cheek.

I lick lazily until he takes his wrist away.

Then I sleep.

CHAPTER 19

*B*owie is curled around my back when I wake, one arm thrown over my middle, his breath ruffling the fur on my neck.

"Evening," he says and nuzzles his cheek against my ruff, somehow knowing I've woken. One of these nights, I'm going to wake first so I can watch him sleeping instead of the other way around.

The abandoned windmill sheltered us well. Dark, quiet, peaceful—definitely not as nice as a bed in an inn, but much better than a barn cellar that reeks of onions.

I roll onto my back, exposing my belly. Bowie takes the hint and rubs it. Bliss. My tongue lolls from my mouth as he scratches. I feel good. His blood has worked wonders on my sore muscles and aching joints. Tonight I aim to repay that favor.

But first I lick him from chin to forehead. Repeatedly. He squints his eyes shut and takes it like a champ. Only when I've licked so much he's having a hard time breathing do I relent.

Bowie smiles at me, chuckling, and wipes my slobber from his face. "Thank you for the bath."

I keep my eyes on him as I gently urge a shift, going easy on myself. Weirdly, I like that he's taken to watching this process. I feel as if I'm showing off. *Look what I can do.* Knowing he enjoys it makes me preen for him, stretching into his space, my furry belly turning to skin beneath his hand.

"Evening," I say when the change is complete. My legs are draped over his. He's had to uncurl himself to give me more space. "Don't stop."

I'm mostly kidding, but he rubs my belly anyway. His affection has a decidedly different quality to it in this form. My skin tingles under his soft, cool palm. My cock takes interest in the activity, and I realize, not without a hint of embarrassment, that I'll grow hard if he continues.

"Actually, maybe you *should* stop," I yield.

"You told me not to." He arches a brow. A mischievous glint sparkles in his sapphire gaze. His hand wanders lower. "Have I mentioned how much it pleases me to find you naked so often in my company?"

My cock twitches as if it heard that too.

I crave him. But we're on a mission, and if I cause a delay that impedes our success, the consequences could be dire. "Bowie…" I can't believe I'm about to protest. His fingers curl around my rapidly plumping cock, and I suck in a gasp. "What about the trail? What ab—"

"Ssh, relax." He gives an experimental tug that feels so incredible I squirm closer. I can't help it. "We can't leave now. The sun hasn't yet set."

I've never been so relieved for daylight.

Bowie props his head on one hand and strokes me with the other. He's on his side, fully clothed, while I'm on my back, completely nude. It makes me feel vulnerable, exposed, but not in a way I'm not enjoying. I'm safe with him, so the feeling is welcome. It's erotic. Makes me want to come for him, so he can watch that too.

I pinch my own nipple to see what he'll do.

His tongue darts out to wet his lips. I want to chase it with mine, but he sets a tantalizing rhythm with his fist around my shaft that makes it hard to move. Hard to do anything but lie here and enjoy his attentions.

Wasn't I supposed to be doing something? Not taking no for an answer. I groan out his name. "Bowie, please."

"Please what, my darling?" he purrs. "I'll give you anything."

He's going to regret saying that. "Bite me. Drink from me."

His hand stops. "Not that."

"You said anything." My hips thrust of their own accord, my hot flesh seeking more of his cool touch. "That's what I want."

"Andras, I can't."

Uh-oh. He sounds serious. And though he maintains his grip on my cock, he's not pumping anymore. I'm about to squirm out of my skin seeking more friction, but this is important. Bowie must be starving, and I've made myself a vow to help him overcome his unfortunate reluctance.

I want him to drink from me more than I want this orgasm. I roll over to face him, further disrupting *activities*.

"You can," I insist, studying his face. He looks a bit startled, a bit lost. My poor, sweet Bowie. "You can feed from me. I'm strong enough, and I want you to." I push my hair back to expose my neck.

His pupils widen. "I know you're strong. You're the strongest person I know. But I'm weak, and I cannot risk it."

I wrap my arm around him and shuffle close, pressing us together in all the places I can. He maneuvers his legs to accommodate me but doesn't lean in to drink. Stubborn vampire. I don't know what else to say. Wishing I had his gift with words, I mumble, "Don't make me beg."

Bowie's staring at my neck with an intensity that rivals a wolf with a bone. His lips part, but otherwise, he holds himself very still. His muscles are tense in my embrace.

"I will," I whisper. "If it will help."

He blinks, breaking his stare. "Will what?"

"Beg."

A whimper escapes his wet lips. "As delightful as that might prove in another context, I don't want you to beg. I promise I'm all right. I don't need blood yet."

He does, though. Need the blood. It's rather obvious in the quality of his attention on the veins in my throat. I swallow and arch my neck, trying to tempt him. He closes his eyes.

Huffing out a frustrated sigh, I admire his lashes as my mind whirs. What does he need to hear? What will help him through this? If it were me in his place, what would he say to help me along?

Taking a deep breath, I try my best. "Bowie, look at me."

He opens his eyes with a sad expression I'd like to wipe from his features forever.

"I trust you. Please, even if you don't trust yourself. Let my faith in you be enough for the both of us. We need this. Drink from me."

"Andras," he protests.

I stop him with my lips on his. A soft kiss, with all the meaning I can infuse in a meeting of mouths. Palming his cheek, I pull back enough to whisper, "Take what I offer. Let me do this for you as you've done so much for me."

Exposing my neck again, I arch to get closer to his mouth.

Bowie's breath caresses the sensitive skin on my throat. A soft puff of air. A pause. He's hovering, unsure.

"Go on," I murmur. "I'm for you."

He moans. His lips press a kiss to the juncture of my neck and shoulder. I stay still, letting him take all the time he needs.

Bowie licks a gentle path along my skin. I flush with heat. Ready. My anticipation spreads its wings and takes flight. He's going to do it. Finally.

Twin points of pressure send a jolt of arousal to my needy

cock. Bowie's fangs slide into my flesh, cool as ice. My blood rushes like fire from the vein to meet them, coppery scented and hot. His lips close over my neck. He sucks.

We're soaring.

I clutch him tightly to my body. He returns my desperate embrace with fervor. His strength dazzles me. Locked together in this glorious exchange, we rise to the stars.

Bowie's moan vibrates against my skin. My cock is a steel rod between us, eager for his touch. I thrust against his belly, tender skin rutting against the fine fabric of his coat. He takes pity on me and reaches between us to finish what we've started, curling his fingers around my shaft with a firm hold for me to push into. Perfect.

I press into his fangs, then his fist, the dueling points of pressure bringing me so high I could touch the moon. My heart races in my chest, my breath catches in my throat, and I'm hurtling over the threshold with Bowie in my arms.

Shuddering against him, my body quaking through its release, I let out a long cry of agonized pleasure. Ecstasy so deep, I feel it from my toes all the way to the place Bowie's teeth are buried in my neck.

I'm still trembling when he slides them from my flesh and licks the wound. His tongue brings another kind of bliss. A feeling of being cared for, cherished, protected. Like I'm special. Desirable. A host of emotions I thought I might never experience before Bowie came into my life well up inside me. I relish the moment, safe in his embrace, my panting breaths slowly evening out.

Bowie kisses my throat, my ear, my cheek. I turn to catch his lips. He tastes of my blood, a savory mix of salt and metal. I lick it from his mouth.

He's still holding my cock as it softens, which feels more intimate than all that's come before. Unbearably so, but I endure it because I want to give him everything.

I knew he could drink without hurting me, and now he knows it too.

He smiles against my lips, presses one more kiss, and draws back. "Thank you."

My heart is full to bursting. I don't say anything. No words would adequately express the depth of my affection for him.

Bowie lets go of my cock and brings his messy hand to his mouth. My eyes threaten to leap from my face as I watch him lick it clean. I don't think I've ever seen something so erotic as his pretty pink tongue lapping my cum off his fingers. I'm going to pass out if I don't remember how to breathe soon.

"You're delicious," he murmurs. "Every last part of you."

Another burst of pleasure sweeps through me at his words. My face burns. Our scents are mingled so thoroughly the wolf has decided Bowie belongs to us.

I could lie here all night, but reality comes creeping back. We have a job to do. Bowie must see it in my expression because his own clouds over. What will our future be once we find the girls and return them to safety? Will we always have this? I want to, but I also know better than to take one minute for granted. Nothing is guaranteed.

"I wish we'd met before...this," he says. "I feel like I've known you forever. My precious Andras."

Nodding my agreement, I stroke his cheek and jaw, running fingers along the bones beneath his skin. "You're warm," I note with a hint of surprise.

"You've warmed me. Your gift."

I'm staring into the great blue sea of his eyes when I realize I've come and he hasn't. "What about you? Let me—" I go to push him onto his back, but he resists.

"I've never been more satisfied. Truly. And though I wish I could keep you naked in my arms for hours on end, we must be going."

He's right. I know it. But it's still difficult to leave this cocoon of intimacy we've created.

Bowie pats my naked bottom. "Up you go. Four feet, my dear. And do not neglect your stomach this time. I insist you hunt when you have the opportunity. Promise?"

"Promise."

* * *

WE PASS another night of brisk travel north toward Csejthe. A young deer not swift enough to avoid my jaws ensures I keep my promise to Bowie.

The trail is so easy to follow even Ozor could have managed it. Thinking of my pack only makes me glad I left them. Except for Ava, of course. I miss her deeply. Oh, the stories I have to tell her when I return, though perhaps with some carefully crafted editing for decency's sake.

The hours tick along unmarked as my nose to the scent becomes my primary focus. My concentration is so deep I'm startled when another presence comes barreling out of nowhere to greet us. Hackles raised, I leap in front of Bowie without thinking, ready to defend him.

A man stands with both hands raised. Another vampire. He must be. The way he materialized was too fast for my eye to see.

"Whoa, easy there, wolfy." The vampire takes a backward step when I don't back down.

I snarl my displeasure, even as Bowie's hand lands on my ruff.

"This is Janos." Bowie gestures with a wave of his other hand. "I had Ivaz send for him. Remember?"

It's not easy to let go of my instinct to fight, to defend Bowie from this newcomer. Teeth still bared, I study him.

Janos is shorter than Bowie, but not by much. He's stockier, with a thick muscular build. Wide shoulders. A barrel of a chest.

Deep brown eyes the color of fallen acorns. Dressed to blend in, he wears peasant clothing, also in shades of brown, well fitted and clean.

"I'm going to put my hands down and say hello to Beauregard," says Janos, his eyes on mine. "Try not to attack me."

Huffing, I stand down but don't leave Bowie's side.

Janos opens his arms. "Brother." He leans in. His hand sits too low on Bowie's backside for my liking.

"Thank you for coming." Bowie returns the embrace.

Then Janos kisses him in a fashion entirely unsuited to simple brotherly affection.

A low snarl rises from my throat and emerges with a threatening rumble. Bowie has already turned his head from the kiss, but that doesn't stop me from wanting to tear out Janos's throat one crunchy vertebra at a time.

"Ooh." Janos watches me as if I amuse him, provoking me further. His gaze shifts to Bowie. "This one thinks you're his territory."

"I am." Bowie reaches for me.

I press against his thigh, controlling the urge to take out my competition. How many *brothers* does Bowie have? And how many has he slept with because that was a lover's greeting I just witnessed. Not that I'm jealous.

Brows raised to surprised arches, Janos stares at Bowie as if he's grown a second head. "You're what?"

"His territory," says Bowie with an air of finality that takes my breath away. "Janos, this is Andras. Andras, if you wouldn't mind pausing the constant growl, I promise Janos will behave himself. Won't you?"

Janos gives a reluctant nod and considers me. I don't like him, but I stop snarling because Bowie asked me to. I snort in Janos's general direction and position myself between them.

"Ivaz told me you were traveling with a werewolf, but I

didn't think he'd be boning you. He is, isn't he? Or have you branched out since we last rendezvoused?"

No. I don't like him. Not at all.

"Don't provoke Andras," orders Bowie. "We have more important things to discuss. Have you any news?"

Janos leans his weight onto one leg and crosses his arms. "You used to be more fun."

"News, Janos," prods Bowie.

With a put-upon sigh, Janos finally makes himself useful. "I scouted Sarvaar. The staff there says Báthory's in her castle at Csejthe. They seemed relieved by her absence. I've sent word to Ivaz. He'll be along soon, and he'll arrange wagons for transport. She's definitely killing girls. The gossip among the staff is too widespread to be mere rumor. There's truth to them, surely." At this, he turns serious, his expression softening. "I'm sorry about your niece."

Bowie glances down. "So am I."

I rub my cheek on his thigh and whine.

"Andras's on her scent trail now," says Bowie. "She's been taken through here recently. We're operating under the assumption the trail leads to Csejthe, but I don't want to run ahead and risk losing it. You go. With any luck, you can stop them before she's taken into the castle."

"How far ahead are they? And how will I know who she is?"

"Andras thinks several days, but we've been gaining on them, so two at the most. I fear it's too late to prevent Cecily's arrival, but fair to say you should stop any young girl from entering Báthory's lair. Run ahead, and we should only be a night behind."

"Come with me, and *Andras* can be a night behind."

I don't like the sound of that, but I don't want to stand in Bowie's way either if that's what he thinks is best.

Bowie shakes his head. "What if the scent trail veers from this road? Then what happens? Should Andras stop following it to retrieve me? Should he stage a rescue by himself? No, it must be this way. With us on the trail and you running ahead. We leave no stone unturned."

"As you wish," says Janos. "But we should bed down together for the day. I've traveled this route many times. Not too far ahead is an old church with an inner chamber suitable for our rest. That is, if your wolf promises not to make a snack of my juicy bits while I'm sleeping."

I glare at him.

Rolling his eyes, Bowie blows out a breath. "It's not Andras I'm worried about. Can you go an entire day without inciting violence?"

Janos's brown eyes glint with mischief. "Me? I'll be sweet as candy."

"You'd better be, or I'll let him bite you."

"Ooh, where?"

"No place good."

Janos clicks his tongue. "Yeah, you definitely used to be more fun."

CHAPTER 20

A small cruciform church stands amid a lush field of tall brushlike foliage and young trees fighting for dominance. The structure itself, built of stone and mortar, looks solid, but the thatched roof has seen better days. What's left of the surrounding dwellings—constructed of less sturdy wood and mud—has already been half-consumed by nature's relentless appetite.

I pad behind Janos and in front of Bowie up a rounded staircase to the deep-set covered entrance. Janos smells of sweetly scented smoke that lingers on his clothes, and of course, blood. He's kept quiet while bringing us here, and I hope he stays that way.

We step into the dank building single file. The gloomy interior reveals rows of rotten wood pews with a center aisle leading toward an altar. I'm unsure where we'll sleep, as patches of moonlight shine through cracks in the damaged roof. Water has long ago made itself at home; the planked floor is warped, and standing puddles appear throughout.

Janos strides down the aisle, past the altar, and to a flight of stairs. Because of course we'll be headed underground. At least I'm getting used to it. That or I'm just too tired to care.

I wish I could have Bowie to myself. Questions sit on my tongue, though whatever he and Janos are to each other is really none of my business. I wonder how many others of Bettina's brood have a claim on Bowie's affections.

Down we go into a dark hole of a chamber beneath the main church body. The scent of old death, of bones and dust, indicates a crypt. I'm glad to be in my animal form, as a shiver can be more easily disguised. At least this level is dry, and I spot a stack of woolen blankets that don't smell half bad.

"This will do nicely," says Bowie. "How did you know of this spot?"

"Ivaz has sent me on tasks in this direction before," Janos answers. "Over time, one comes to learn of any resting place more hospitable than the earth herself. A vampire called Laurence showed me this church long ago before the roof had sagged away."

"Be sure to thank Laurence for us when next you see him." Bowie strokes my shoulder and flank. His hand feels lovely in my fur. I'm almost tired enough to ignore Janos as he shakes open the blankets and puts together a makeshift bed. If he thinks we're sleeping next to him, he's mistaken.

With an annoyed huff, I grab one of the blankets with my teeth and drag it to Bowie.

"Are you shifting?" he asks.

I look down—our signal for no. Not only am I reluctant to shift in front of this stranger, but I'm well aware he could run circles around me with words. Remaining a wolf denies him that opportunity.

"I don't blame you," says Bowie. "If I had a fur coat as luxurious as yours, I'd never give it up." He spreads the blanket for us. Closer to Janos than I'd like, but in our own corner at least.

I pad in a tight circle and flop down on Janos's side but a few feet away, keeping myself in the middle and swallowing jealousy each time it bubbles up. It doesn't matter what's happened between them. Bowie has chosen me for now and made his choice clear. Hearing him confirm it pleases both wolf and man. I have no real claim on him, but that does little to assuage my longing for one.

Janos sits upon his blanket and pulls off his boots. He gestures between Bowie and me with waving fingers. "So this is new." His tone takes on a lyrical quality I find annoying.

Bowie acknowledges as much with a nod and redirects as he settles next to me. "It is. And what about you? Tell me. How have you been since last we met?"

I groom my sore paws as I listen to their conversation.

"Bored and boring compared to fucking a werewolf. I thought they were pack animals. How'd you hitch your wagon to a lone wolf?"

He won't drop the subject so easily.

"Andras isn't alone. He has a pack," says Bowie as I suppress an urge to cringe thinking of Farkas and the others. "Look, Janos, Andras has had to shift back and forth excessively to help me follow these scent trails. He's not used to endless nights of travel and needs to rest without an unnecessary shift. I'm not comfortable speaking for him as if he isn't here. You understand that, right?"

Bowie is so good with words. I admire his phrasing. Janos would have to be a real ass to continue pushing at this point.

Apparently, Janos is a real ass. He watches me lick my fur into submission with an interest I find slightly disturbing.

"He has a huge tongue. Does he use it on your—"

"Janos!" Bowie barks out the name like he's the werewolf in the room and not me. "Enough. Andras is not to be teased. If you value our friendship, I ask you to cease this line of questioning."

I rise. Staring directly at Janos, I give Bowie a long, possessive slurp of my tongue up his neck to his jaw and over his cheek, leaving a wet trail in my wake. *I licked him; he's mine,* I say to the asshole vampire snickering from his blankets. But inside, I worry. Will he remain mine when we return home? I can only hope as much.

"All right, all right, point taken, gentlemen," Janos finally relents. "I'll even turn my back so he can use his tongue however you like, but I can't promise not to listen."

I snuffle-snort into the soft place just behind Bowie's ear. He ruffles the thick fur around my neck.

Something tells me it's going to be a long day.

* * *

IT'S NOT A LONG DAY. Apparently, I can sleep just as well with an asshole snoring in the corner as I can without. Who knew?

Janos is less irritating come dusk, having taken Bowie's not-so-subtle hint to heart at last. He greets my wary stare with a polite "good evening," and I nod, hoping the truce will hold until we can be rid of him.

I notice the flap of our bag is open, and my dolly, Marta, is visible. I nose it shut with my snout. Janos grins at me, which I refuse to acknowledge.

Bowie and Janos rehash the details of the plan while we wait until it's safe to leave. I have the sinking feeling we're too late to prevent Cecily's arrival at the castle, but any information Janos can gather while we travel is potentially useful.

I stretch my muscles and assess every little ache and pain. All minor. That bodes well for tonight's pace.

"Right, then," says Janos as he gathers the blankets back to the pile. "I'll be on my way."

Bowie rises and goes to him. "Thank you, truly, for your help and for dropping whatever else you were doing to assist."

"Of course." Janos reaches for Bowie's hands, and it's all I can do to contain the possessive growl in my throat. "Anything for my brother." This time when he kisses Bowie, he's careful to stick to cheeks instead of lips, and though I don't want Janos's scent on any part of my man, this is easier to tolerate.

"Be careful," warns Bowie. "The Báthory woman is dangerous."

Janos scoffs. "She's human. How dangerous could she be?" He winks in my direction. "Au revoir, Andras, pleasure to have made your acquaintance."

I'm glad I don't have to say anything.

Janos leaves first. It's good to see the back of him.

Bowie turns to me. "I'm sorry about him, dear. Janos can be…let's call it *overbearing* to be polite."

I snort-sneeze as I approach him. Rising to hind legs, I balance myself with my paws on his chest.

Bowie laughs and holds my flanks. "What is it?"

Leaning in, I thoroughly lick his cheeks clean of Janos's scent and replace it with my own. Much better.

Bowie's expression turns serious. "I'm sorry I didn't tell you Janos and I have been lovers in the past. I wasn't thinking. It was never serious between us, merely convenient, but we share a certain affection. Lonely people being slightly less lonely together."

I understand and communicate as best I can with a look and a nuzzle. As always, Bowie seems to know just what I'm thinking.

"Good. I'm glad you aren't upset." He drops a sweet kiss to my snout before I push off him and return to all fours. "You're very attractive when you're snarling at my past lovers, by the way. Perhaps I should introduce you to more of them."

I grace Bowie with my attractive snarl before looking down. *No. Let's not.*

He chuckles. "That mean you don't want to meet Damon? Or Luther?"

I look down.

"Not Adony, Bela, or Vincse either?"

Growling, I knock into him so he stumbles.

Bowie catches himself gracefully, and we head up the stairs.

"Joking, joking, I swear!" He crosses his heart.

I bark-yip my displeasure.

"I made them all up. Well, except Adony. He's got a huge—"

I nip his ankles, forcing him to skip up the stairs two at a time.

"Sorry, sorry. It's just you're so sexy when you're being possessive."

Huffing, I trot in front of him down the aisle and soon come to an annoying pull-door I can't open because I don't have thumbs.

"Need a hand?" Bowie quirks. "How about two?" He takes my face between his cool palms and kisses my forehead.

I grumble.

"There's no one but you, my love," he whispers and pulls open the door.

I'm left all tingly as we step into the night to continue our mission.

CHAPTER 21

Csejthe Castle looms high on a hill overlooking the surrounding lands and villages. Stone towers bathed in moonlight reach for the stars. Encircled by tall defensive walls, the fortress will be difficult to access without the knowledge or permission of its wicked mistress. Men pace the battlements. More are stationed at the gates. If the early morning guard presence is anything to go by, a veritable army protects these grounds.

Bowie and I observe from below, both in quiet consideration. With no obvious point of entry and the gates under heavy guard, I'm unsure of the best approach, but the scent trail indicates Cecily is definitely here. We've yet to run into Janos. Perhaps he'll have some idea of how to sneak in, or maybe he's already inside.

Our time tonight is dwindling. We need to decide whether to risk making entry before dawn or to find a resting place nearby and plan our attempt for tomorrow night.

I stretch my back and huff.

Eager to shift now that we've reached our destination, I coax the wolf into letting go. Bones elongate. Flesh pulls taut as fur recedes. Rising from the ground, I roll my shoulders and catch Bowie's eyes.

We're alone at the tree line, having left the road toward the castle behind us to veer into the surrounding forest for cover. I've been the wolf long enough to feel awkward as a man again, even though this is Bowie, and I trust him.

His uncanny ability to comfort surfaces right away. "Welcome back, my darling." He cups my cheek and gives me a kiss in greeting. At once, I feel at home with him. "Would you like to dress?"

I nod.

He opens our satchel, hands me my things, and goes back to studying the castle. I'm unsure how he knows I need a moment to myself, but I appreciate it all the same. Pulling Bowie's borrowed black shirt over my shoulders, I take a breath and think on what we should do.

Since it will be impossible to scout the interior of the castle without being spotted, perhaps we should find someone with that knowledge who'd be willing to share. A vendor of some sort. Or a stable master perhaps. Bowie could convince them to speak with us using his vampire persuasion.

I sit to fasten my leather shoes, still pondering options when Bowie settles next to me.

"As much as I want to go storming through the gates, tear through the castle, and find Cecily this very second, I think we should wait," says Bowie.

That's a relief. I lean into his shoulder. "I agree. Csejthe is a fortress. And larger than I imagined." Large enough to easily get lost inside.

"I'm not sure what I imagined, but yes. This is much more complicated. Báthory could be keeping the girls anywhere. We need to find someone who has details about the gynaeceum, her so-called finishing school and likely where the girls are housed."

Nerves stir, unsettling my gut. "Bowie, what if you're

caught? Can a vampire be killed?" I realize I still don't know much about the species, despite having spent so much time at Bowie's side. Drinks blood, runs impossibly fast, and hides from the sun are the extent of my knowledge.

"Don't worry about me," he says. "It's you who must be cautious. I should be able to escape any would-be assassins by speed alone, but you don't have that luxury."

I wasn't worried for myself, but he's right. Of the two of us, I'm the weaker. Still, if he were caught and left within the sun's reach...I can't even think about it. "Bowie, tell me about vampires. What should I know?"

His hand drops to my knee. Sitting side by side on a blanket of pine needles, both of us staring at the intimidating walls of Csejthe, we lean into each other as the bugs chirp around us.

"We don't age after we're turned," Bowie begins. "Legend would have you believe we're immortal, but I've seen with my own eyes that's not the case."

I cover his hand with mine.

"We can be killed. A stake through the heart, as I've mentioned. Also beheading, fire, general dismemberment, and of course...the sun. I'm still quite young, in vampire terms, that is, and I was never good at fencing or combat."

He confirms my fears. Not that I thought vampires invulnerable, but he's more vulnerable than I'd thought.

"My edge will be speed," he continues. "I'm much faster than humans, so the risk of being caught is minimal."

I disagree. We're severely outnumbered. A large contingent of men is guarding the castle gates, and more march along the walls. We'll need more than speed to be successful without incident. A stealthy entrance will be our best bet. I'll need to think on it.

"Your turn," says Bowie. "Tell me about werewolves."

There isn't much to tell. "Nothing too impressive. Beyond the obvious ability to shift from one form to another, we heal faster than humans. I'm quite a bit stronger than an average man and bigger than the average wolf. But I can't do anything special. I'm not fast, as you well know after nights of following behind me. My pace must drive you mad."

"Not at all. You've made excellent time. You mustn't think less of your skills simply because they're different from mine. Your sense of smell is extraordinary. I'd have wasted invaluable time searching Báthory's other castles were it not for your help." He gives my knee a gentle squeeze. "Speaking of your tracking ability, do you think you could sniff out Janos?"

"Of course." His smokey scent will be so easy to follow I can track it without shifting.

"I'd like to find out what he's learned. He's likely to be in the closest village and may have already worked out a method of entry."

"How much longer until dawn?" After many nights of this, I'm getting better at timing sunrise myself, but Bowie can pin it down almost to the minute.

"An hour fifteen," he says. "Hopefully, that's enough to find Janos. He'll know where we should sleep as well."

"What if he's already inside?"

"Then we're on our own getting in, but we can count on his help getting out."

I stand, offer Bowie my hand, then tug him up with me. His eyes reflect the heavy burden of his worry. He's beginning to look gaunt, and I wonder if one feeding was enough. "Bowie, you should drink."

He just shakes his head. "Not now. We should go." He glances wistfully back at the castle. "Unless…"

"Unless what?"

His gaze lands on mine. Intense. Determined. "Maybe I should go in after all. Now. Before this goes on any further."

My gut reaction is absolutely not. It's far too dangerous. But the drive to free Cecily must be impossible for him to bear, especially now that we're so close. "Bowie, you're not invincible. There isn't enough time, and you've no knowledge of a safe place to hide from the sun within those walls."

"But—"

"You mustn't go in alone and without a plan. Please. Let's find Janos and see what he's learned."

Bowie lets out a pained sigh. He glares at Csejthe, the mighty fortress on a hill, prison and death sentence to so many young girls. I feel his pain, but we can't give in to impulses.

His shoulders sink, but he nods.

Relief loosens my chest. "Come, let's go. Janos went this way."

I lead him back to the road and toward the village.

* * *

JANOS WAITS for us outside of a small pub, long since closed for the night. "Took you long enough," he teases. "I'd have thought with four legs, you'd be quicker." He extends his arm toward me.

I still don't like him, but I take his wrist and nod my greeting. His arm is cool, like Bowie's, and thickly muscled. His grip is firm. He meets my eyes and flashes a smile.

"What have you learned?" asks Bowie, straight to the point.

"That this is going to be tricky. Come, let's not talk here."

Trencin is a small village, much like Varad, with few businesses and public buildings. We follow Janos along the hard-packed dirt road lined mostly with private dwellings that double as small specialty shops, a bread bakery that smells of fresh dough even at this hour, a potter with the scents of earthen clay spilling pleasantly to the street, and on the corner, a forge with the tang of fire and metal.

Janos leads us past a row of well-kept cottages farther toward the stables. A church stands opposite, with a sprawling cemetery along the hill rising behind it. A strong scent snags my attention. I catch a whiff of recent death, rot and stench giving way to hordes of insects devouring their feast.

"Wait." I take Bowie's elbow.

"What is it?" His eyes study mine.

Janos has stopped, staring at us both as I've halted in the middle of the road.

I tilt my nose to the breeze, sniffing. Layers of death—fresh, ripe, old, older still. Turned earth and too many people for the size of this village.

Creeping toward the church, I fight the urge to hold my breath. The scent is strong enough Bowie and Janos must detect it as well. Janos takes the lead, forging ahead to circle the building and plow straight through the older section of the graveyard. We come upon a long row of freshly churned dirt piled into mounds. Pine trees watch over the deceased, their spicy scent mingling with the remains.

As branches sway overhead, we scan the morbid sight with its far too many recent occupants. A crow's call rings out on the wind.

"This is where she buries them." Bowie's voice is a haunted whisper.

I take his hand in mine. My chest is tight. The pit of my stomach has turned to lead. There's nothing more to say. My thoughts drift to lives cut short, to the grieving families, and the injustice that allows such horrors to continue.

Bowie turns away, tugging my hand. "I can't stay here."

We leave, heading back to the road and wherever Janos was taking us before I caught the ghastly scent. I want to ask Bowie if he's all right, but I know he's not. I'm not. Our footsteps sound loud in the otherwise silent street.

"To the stables," says Janos. "There's a man you should speak with."

Following him, we cling to each other's hands as we approach the old barn. I'm grateful for the smell of horses overcoming less pleasant odors. We pass through a gate in the fence and walk through the turnout into the structure.

As we enter, dozing horses wake. They're keen at sensing danger, and most will shy from a werewolf. I don't know if it's the same for vampires, but my presence here will upset the animals. I hope we don't stay long.

A man rises from his seat on a bench and nods a greeting. He looks and smells human to me, but I'd have to get closer to know for sure. Brown hair, brown eyes, tan skin as if he spends a lot of time outdoors. A young man, my age, perhaps a few years older, and nervous as a cornered barn cat.

"Petru," says Janos. "These are the men I told you about." He turns to us. "Gentlemen, this is Petru. He's Csejthe's coachman. He knows much of the keep's layout and can direct us to Báthory's court master, Benedikt Deseo, who will support our cause."

Brilliant. This is more than we ever could have hoped for.

Bowie's brows draw tight. "Báthory's own court master is against her?"

Petru gives a shaky nod. "Much of her staff lives in fear. Including Deseo." He pauses. "We've all heard the screams."

Perhaps this won't be as difficult as I thought.

Petru continues, "She's well protected. Her personal guard and servants are loyal. Anyone who objects or causes trouble disappears."

As I'm wondering how Janos found this man and convinced him to risk his life to speak to us, I notice his gaze hasn't wavered from Petru's face. Something intense is shining in his eyes, a deep focus that raises the hackles on the back of my neck. My ears twitch beneath my hat.

Janos is using his vampire persuasion on Petru.

I'm concerned the man is unwilling. That he risks himself unknowingly. But when weighed with the safety of the remaining victims, the scale tips decidedly in favor of Cecily and the girls. Still, my stomach is unsettled at the thought of using coercion.

"Where does she keep the girls?" asks Bowie.

A bewildered expression crosses Petru's face. "I don't know. All over? I've heard there are cages in her personal quarters. There are whispers of girls locked in closets without food for days. There's her school and the chambers of the noble girls who, despite their status, aren't off-limits when Báthory's worst moods strike. Some are just regular staff, young seamstresses and kitchen maids. They have the run of the house, live in servant's quarters, and scramble to avoid her wrath."

My heart sinks. It's one thing to find Cecily and get her to safety; surely we can do that. But to scour the castle beneath Báthory's nose, identify and rescue each victim, that's a monumental task if they're truly scattered everywhere. And how will we get them to safety? Ivaz has promised wagons, but when?

Janos scowls his displeasure. "How many men make up her guard?"

"I can only guess," says Petru. "Perhaps half a dozen men assigned to her alone, and another fifty guarding the grounds. Those men are loyal to the money in her coffers more than the lady herself. She pays them well. Though they may not like her, they'll follow her orders."

"What do you know of the official investigation into her crimes?" asks Bowie.

Petru shrugs. "Only that it exists. A man came through asking questions last week. The countess was furious. And Gyorgy Thurzo—her caretaker appointed to help her run Csejthe—is said to be planning a visit. Báthory has ears everywhere. She knows of the king's orders and believes herself above the law. Deseo says she's convinced Thurzo will be on her side, but he thinks not."

"Why does Thurzo's opinion matter?"

"He is King Matyas's second-in-command. His majesty

values Thurzo's advice, but it will take a vote of the parliament to lay formal charges at the feet of a noblewoman. If anyone is in a position to sway them, it's Thurzo."

I can't help but think none of this matters. The courts, the nobles, the king, his advisers, none of them is more important than the girls who are in jeopardy at this very moment. My goal remains the same: get in, find the girls, get us all out. Let the law sort out what remains once the young women are safe. I'm sure Bowie feels the same.

Horses stamp nervously in their stalls. My presence has been tolerated long enough. "What else do we need to know?" I ask, hoping to leave so we can come up with a plan.

"Deseo will know more. You must speak with him. I've told you everything," says Petru. "If she ever finds out, she'll have me killed."

"We won't let that happen," says Janos. "Stay here in Trencin. Keep your ears to the wind for Ivaz. Take this." He hands over a black velvet coin purse. "Be ready with the wagons when we need you."

Petru stuffs the purse inside his vest and bows his head. "Be careful. She's cagey."

"Don't worry," says Bowie. "Her days are numbered." There's steel in his voice I haven't heard before. I want to speak with him alone, but Janos is unlikely to leave us be. Plus, the two of them have precious little time before sunrise.

Bowie turns to Janos. "You know a place?"

"Of course. This way."

* * *

WE LEAVE the poor horses in peace and head toward the hilly forest. I have little hope for a place above ground, but beyond *dry* and *doesn't smell of onions*, I'm not feeling picky. We're so close to our goal it's hard to wait another day.

Janos picks up the pace as the sky begins to lighten. Birdsong flutters from treetops as we rush uphill. I glance ahead but see nothing that looks like shelter through the dense layers of surrounding branches. If I'm nervous about the oncoming sunrise, how must the vampires be feeling?

"Janos, are we close?" asks Bowie. He doesn't sound nervous, just resigned. I have yet to see him sleep in the ground, but perhaps today is the day.

"Nearly there," says Janos. "We'll make it."

Crunch, crunch, crunch.

Dried leaves and brush snap beneath our tromping feet. Heading uphill seems like heading closer to the sun, but I keep quiet. They know what they're doing. Probably.

"Hellfire, Janos," says Bowie. "It's now or the earth, man. Are we there or not?"

The alarmed pitch to Bowie's voice sends a spike of fear through me. I'll dig a hole and bury Bowie myself if I must in order to keep him safe.

"Yes, yes, here we are." Janos guides us to a hidden cave, the entrance overgrown with ferns and bushes. "Come along," he says calmly as if the two of them weren't minutes away from burnt flesh and crispy skin.

I couldn't handle the stress of being a vampire, not without a safe, cozy home to call my own and the knowledge I'd be protected within its walls.

We duck to shuffle through the cramped entrance, single file, with Janos bringing up the rear. Luckily, the inside is larger than it appeared from the outside. The stone walls open to a roomy cavern, tucked deep within the mountain, far enough I can't see the end from where I stand. The scents of dust, ash, and—is that bear?—meet my nostrils. I sniff more carefully. Definitely bear, though faint, so with any luck, the animal won't be returning anytime soon.

"There. That wasn't so bad," says Janos.

"You cut it close," Bowie gripes, wiping dirt from his shoulder. "However did you find this?"

"Asked the locals. They said there were caves and pointed me in the right direction."

"Will they suspect we're here?" I ask.

Janos shakes his head. "No. I made them forget." He says it with the kind of nonchalance I could never fathom. Wouldn't want to. Making another person forget their memory is…shady at best, unethical at worst. I don't like it.

Nevertheless, I'm glad to be alone. Mostly alone. I ignore Janos in favor of Bowie. "Are you all right?"

"Fine." He wraps his arms around my waist and sighs into my throat. His soft breath ruffles the fur on the back of my neck. "Antsy. I don't feel much like resting."

"Me neither." I hold him close, relishing this moment, even if Janos is watching like a creepy weasel.

The muscles of Bowie's back shift beneath his coat as he rests his weight against me. I know we have important things to discuss, plans to hash out, but as far as I'm concerned, this moment could stretch forever.

"You know who likes hugs?" asks Janos. "I do. I like hugs."

Bowie chuckles. I feel it against my chest and tug him closer.

"You get plenty, I'm sure," says Bowie. "Won't Thomas and the twins be anxiously awaiting your return?"

"Bettina has the twins. And you know Thomas will be there, but not waiting. He'll have acquired his own harem if I'm not back soon."

Bowie absently strokes the place where my hair turns to fur. "All the more hugs to welcome you home." His lips move against my skin.

I want him to bite me. I wish Janos weren't here.

"As sticky sweet as you pair of cinnamon rolls are together, can we break it up and work on the plan?"

With a kiss to the sensitive spot just beneath my ear, Bowie pulls away. I let him go with reluctance.

"Come farther back," says Janos. "I swiped a stack of blankets from the stables and bought some ham, bread, and wine for Andras."

My ears perk up at the mention of ham. Perhaps Janos isn't all that bad.

He spreads the old horse blankets on the ground. We sit. I take the food he offers, suddenly starving, and dig in.

"Have you a way into the castle?" asks Bowie.

Janos shakes his head. "Nothing easy, no. I've considered posing as vendors, but we'll need a wagon and stock. There's—"

"No time for that," Bowie finishes. "Anything else?"

"Hidden tunnels. From the church to the castle, but I can't distinguish if they're real or rumor. Everyone and their friend's uncle in this town have heard of them, but no one's been inside or knows where the entrances lie. I have an idea of where to search, but again…"

"No time." Bowie presses his lips to a frustrated line. "And what if the castle's side of the tunnel is locked or otherwise barred?"

"Ah, I have a set of skeleton keys." Janos slips a ring of various-sized brass keys from a hidden pocket within his shirt-sleeve. "All the main tumblers have been filed down, leaving only the crucial parts behind, which will conquer nearly any lock."

"You know how to use those?" asks Bowie, skeptical.

"It's not hard," says Janos. "They work like any other keys."

"Hmm." Bowie's expression blanks in thought. "Maybe the tunnels aren't a bad idea if we could find them in a hurry. But if we don't, well, that's time wasted, isn't it?"

I swallow a mouthful of bread and ham. "What if we let the guard catch us? Commit some minor offense within sight of the walls, something harmless like drunken arguing or petty theft, and let them drag us in?"

"And when we're thrown into the dungeon," says Bowie while Janos jangles the keys, "Janos can just let us out."

"It could work," I add.

"It's not the worst idea," says Janos.

I gulp down a swallow of strong ruby-red wine; it's dry and more bitter than I'd like but better than the nothing I brought with me. "Anyone got anything better?"

"Not I," says Bowie. "Getting arrested should be swift, which is what we need. It's unfortunate we might be recognized afterward, though. We'll have to lie low until we find this castle court master, Benedikt Deseo, and see if he can't guide us to Cecily and the others."

Janos tucks the keys back into the special pocket in his sleeve. "Getting out without causing a ruckus might prove impossible."

A dark look clouds Bowie's handsome features. "I'm not opposed to a ruckus."

CHAPTER 22

e approach Erzsébet Báthory's castle at dusk to give us as much time as possible to find all the girls. No one wants to spend the day within its gloomy walls, so the plan is to be out before dawn.

The night is overcast, with thick, drooping gray clouds that threaten rain and thunder. My stomach roils with nerves. Not only must I act out a scene with the others to get us thrown in jail, but I also must be careful no guards notice my ears or tail.

I'm not often around humans, and never many at once. Thinking of everything that could go wrong helps no one, but my mind won't stop tossing out every terrible possibility.

"Ready?" Bowie takes my elbow. I smell the wine on his breath. We've all swished it around our mouths, counting on the guards to assume we're drunk.

We aren't the only ones milling the streets of Trencin. People proceed with their tasks in the village at the base of the castle walls, coming and going: a man on horseback, a boy leading goats, women bringing in laundry from the lines. They'll all be startled as our plan unfolds. Either they'll watch, or they'll duck away to avoid the castle guards.

I take a deep breath, let it out through my nose. "Ready." I'm really not, but I've committed to this, so we may as well get it over with.

"Let's go." Bowie heads down the middle of the street most easily observed from Csejthe's gates, and I follow along.

I'm carrying an obvious leather coin purse and toss a large flank of a butchered pig loosely over my shoulder. It's Janos's cue that we're ready for him to rob us.

Quick enough, his stumbling steps pick up speed from behind. Bowie and I pretend not to notice, walking as if we're just headed home from the shops.

Janos plows into me, snatching the purse and pig in a clumsy motion, then lunges to get away.

"Hey!" I yell loud enough the guards must surely hear. I grab the purse's strap and yank.

Janos doesn't let go. The tug sends him staggering off-balance. He really does look drunk.

A quick glance at the guards indicates they've noticed the ruckus. Now for the follow-through.

"Stop! Thief!" Bowie shouts, then joins the fray. He swings and lands a satisfying blow to Janos's jaw.

Flailing backward, Janos falls to his rump and sends the pig flank flying.

"I'm no thief." Janos clambers to his feet and stalks toward Bowie. "That's my coin purse, and you know it. You're the only thieves here!"

At this point, I'd expect the guards to intervene. That's what we were counting on. One of them orders a command to another, but they're far enough away I can't hear what's been said.

"Hey!" At least I know my line. I dart in front of Bowie and shove Janos back to the ground. They know not to tousle me much—it's crucial my hat stays firmly on my head—so after this, I mostly leave the fighting to them.

Bowie kicks Janos while he's down. "What'd you do to earn that much coin?"

"None of your business, cocksucker." Janos latches onto Bowie's ankle and bites.

Bowie gives a pained cry.

I grab him beneath the armpits and drag him from Janos's rabid attack.

One of the guards yells from atop the battlements. "Ho there. Desist at once."

Finally. It's about time they get involved.

Janos flies to his feet and rams into us both, knocking all three of us to the ground. Our drunken brawl becomes a wrestling match.

"Everyone inside," shouts the guard. The onlookers scatter. "You heard me. Inside!"

It's clear the villagers fear the guard's wrath because they abandon the scene and clear the streets.

Bowie and Janos tumble in the dirt, leaving me mostly out of it. I crawl toward the purse, figuring that's what the guards would expect. The pig lies abandoned on the other side of the road, a damn shame because my wolf would have gulped that down in four bites.

Why aren't the guards pouring out of the gates to arrest us? How much longer must Bowie and Janos trade hits before we're dragged to the dungeons? Are thievery, public drunkenness, and fighting in the streets tolerated in Csejthe?

"Stop at once," orders a guard from the safety of the battlements. "Or you will be shot."

I snap my head to the wall.

The threat gets everyone's attention. Shot? That's not part of our plan.

Bowie and Janos spring apart, then freeze.

"Archers at the ready," shouts another guard.

Moons and stars, this can't be happening. I hold up my hands. "Wait! Don't fire!"

A line of archers stands poised, their arrows pointed ominously toward the three of us. Bowie and Janos raise their hands too.

My eyes land on a new figure as she joins the burly guards.

A raven-haired woman, her tresses teased high upon her head. Rubies drip from her neck like blood, matching the red lacing of her gleaming black gown. Dark eyes study us with intense ferocity. Her crimson-stained lips purse into a scowl.

Countess Erzsébet Báthory.

Who else could she be? I stare into the eyes of evil, willing her to call off the archers. We'll come inside without struggle; that's been the intention all along. No need to shoot anyone.

Bowie inches backward toward me.

"Freeze!" orders the guard, halting Bowie's progress.

I itch to be closer to him as well. Those arrows are wooden. What if one pierces his heart? I shudder. I can't bear to think about it.

Janos continues the charade. "These men accused me of stealing, but I'm no thief. They're the thieves! I'll simply take my purse and be on my way."

"You'll do no such thing," says Báthory, her voice carrying without strain. She places elegant hands on the battlement's stones, fingers splayed wide. "You shall remain perfectly still, or I'll have you all killed."

We don't move a single muscle between us.

Janos stammers, "Milady, I beg you. Don't fire. We won't cause you any further trouble."

I have to wonder if Bowie is quick enough to dodge an arrow aimed for his heart. He's fast, but are his reflexes that good? I hope we won't have to find out.

"Ah, but you've troubled me already, haven't you? All three of you." She points us out one by one. "Sneaking about asking nosy questions, your tongues flailing worse than a gaggle of children sharing someone else's deepest secret."

My jaw drops. Fear prickles up my spine.

We've underestimated the enemy.

Báthory chuckles low and sinister. "Ah, you thought I didn't know. I'll say this. Whatever it is you think you've discovered, you're wrong."

This was a mistake. We should have searched out the tunnels. Gone in under cover. Getting arrested was my idea. This mess is all my fault.

She continues, "You'll suffer for disrespecting the noble Báthory name, but first, you'll tell me everything you know. Guards—"

In a panic, I dart in front of Bowie, shielding him in case she orders them to fire.

"Arrest them," she finishes, and my shoulders sag in relief. That's what we wanted anyway. Perhaps our plan could still work if she just— "No, wait. Archer." She singles out one man. He listens for her order, fingers twitching around the bow. "Shoot the one who moved in the leg."

"No!" yells Bowie as the archer fires.

Bowie's yanking me away, even as the pain lances through my thigh.

I yowl. The pain erupts through my leg and radiates from toes to fingers. My wolf breaks free, forcing a shift. Distressed and terrified, we prepare to fight or flee.

Bowie's weight drops over me. "Stop, please! We'll tell you everything!"

I flick my gaze around wildly, seeing Bowie's hair, the dirty street, the stone towers, and the crazed woman. The whites of her eyes are huge as her blackened pupils bear down on my animal form.

"What the devil in hell have we here?" In her stunned question lies a hint of glee that strikes terror into my soul.

Oh no, oh no, oh no.

I've shifted right in front of them! I'm tangled and helpless in my clothes. The scent of blood scares me witless. Pain disorients all my senses.

Too much, too much, too much.

"Hold your fire." I hear the order echoing as if we're in a tunnel. "Seize them and bring them directly to my chambers."

Thump, thump, thump.

The sound of dozens of boots pounds the wooden stairs.

Bowie's hands fist in my ruff. His words in my ears. "Andras. You're all right. It's all right. You must drink."

No! My mind is in chaos, but I know Bowie revealing the power of his blood will only put us in greater danger. I turn my head.

"No," says Janos. "Beauregard, don't. He's a werewolf. He will heal."

Thump, thump, thump.

"I must." Bowie sounds frantic, even through the fog in my mind. "He's bleeding too much."

"Not yet." Janos. "Wait and see."

Their voices fade. Words stop making sense. My leg throbs.

I blink.

Blackness.

IMAGES FLASH and vanish in my mind: boots, rope, dirt, knots.

Black.

Bowie's weight is dragged away.

Black.

Snippets of sound. Too dangerous—Fashion a muzzle—Let me carry him.

Black.

* * *

I COME to with the taste of Bowie's blood in my mouth. I swallow, confused but aware something's gone terribly wrong. The more blood slides down my throat, the more I remember. Our plan failed. Báthory on the battlements. The arrow in my thigh.

Horror dawns as I blink open my eyes. Wolf form in front of strangers. Farkas would banish me for this.

Lapping at Bowie's wrist helps the pain in my thigh to subside, but it means another terrible secret has fallen into Báthory's hands because we're not alone. I lift my gaze from the polished wood floor with its gruesome brownish-red stains to discover we're in a cage—Bowie and I in one, Janos in another not far away.

It's a macabre sitting room, part parlor, part dungeon. The sheer opulence overwhelms my senses. The room smells of blood, fear, and Báthory herself. Sweat and stench are baked into every crevice.

An array of terrifying tools hangs from hooks along the walls: blades, pinchers, wrenches, whips, scissors, pins, and needles. All of them are well used if the scent coming from the wall is any indication.

I must whimper because Bowie attempts to soothe me by stroking my fur.

"By god, the wolf wakes." A woman's voice, coming from somewhere behind me. Assessing. Intrigued.

Glancing around, I see that beyond the cage's bars lies a collection of lounges and chairs plush with gold velvet cushions. Oversized patterned drapes in bronze and brown hang from ceiling to floor, framing small windows. I get the impression of height as the view is of sky and clouds. The walls are painted in intricate, colorful detail: lines, dots, stars, swirls—too much for the eye to take in, too busy.

Janos stands in his cage, scowling, his eyes darting from

Bowie and me to just beyond us and back. The urge to turn my head and behold our captor myself swells, but I ignore it. Best she thinks me weak and injured, though Bowie's blood has already worked its magic.

Whatever poison races through my veins is thwarted. I test my leg. The arrow has been removed. The site of the injury doesn't hurt. Still, I remain limp, half sprawled in Bowie's lap as he takes his wrist from my mouth to his lips and licks the wound closed.

Well, that's that. She's seen all our tricks. Nothing good can come of this.

I hear a snapping of fingers, then Báthory's voice, curt and demanding. "Ficzko, fetch the witch Marjarova. Tell her of the wolfman and bid her come."

"Yes, Countess." Odd shuffling footsteps scamper off. A door slams shut.

Báthory continues, her voice aimed in our direction, "You will teach me everything. Your powers will become my powers."

"We will teach you nothing for free," says Janos. "Our secrets have a price. One you may not want to pay."

Her answering cackle makes my ears twitch. "You're in no position to bargain, demon. I own you both and your wolfman. If you fancy living, you'll do as I say."

Janos huffs. "You won't kill us. Our power holds you captive as surely as your bars hold us."

His stubborn arguing only serves to pull another round of amused chortles from Báthory. "Believe that if it helps you sleep at night, but rest assured. I have ways of making people talk. And you have much to lose."

A shiver begins in my spine and trembles to my extremities.

"Look at me, wolf," she demands.

My fear keeps me frozen.

"He's not well," says Bowie. "There's only so much my blood can do. He needs a doctor."

"He looks fine to me," she says, her tone clipped, annoyed. "Look at me, or I'll take your eyes so you can look at nothing at all."

Cringing, I lift my snout from Bowie's thigh. His hands on me lend me strength. My body is fine, but my mind is racing. This wasn't supposed to happen. How will we save Cecily now?

I slowly turn my head, feigning a struggle, and my eyes land on the devil herself.

Báthory glowers, her irises nearly as black as her pupils, skin powdered ghost white. Her dark hair is styled into an evil halo around her oval face, adding inches of height to her average frame. Stained red lips form a bitter smile, the kind of grin you'd expect from a sly fox while she tricks her prey into a snare. The kind who enjoys watching the victim's agonizing struggle before the inevitable death.

Wicked intelligence gleams in her gaze, a frightening blend of cruelty and ambition. She stalks forward, hands on her hips, the black satin fabric of her gown swishing over the macabre stained floor.

She's a viper hiding in plain sight. Her unthinkable acts are reflected in her predatory gaze, her obvious enjoyment of my fear, of Janos's protests, and of Bowie's protective nature.

We are no match for such malevolence, but I must remind myself that her villainy is contained in a package of flesh, bones, and blood, same as any man or woman. And people can be killed. She can't be allowed to continue her reign of terror. No matter the cost, the world must be rid of such a monster.

"Feeling better?" she asks without a hint of earnest concern.

"He needs a doctor," Bowie repeats. "If you send for one, he might recover."

Her brows narrow as she levels her threatening gaze on Bowie. "Liar. He's recovered. What magic lies in your blood? I will have it for myself."

Bowie tenses. "It doesn't work that way. You must be gravely injured for my blood to be of any help. Unless you want one of your archers to shoot you with an arrow, it will do nothing."

"I don't believe you," she spits. "Lie to me again and see what it costs you. Put your hand through the bars."

Bowie doesn't move. He's frozen in place, as am I, my heart pounding loudly against my ribs.

"He can't," says Janos. "He's already given too much. If he loses more blood, you'll kill him, and then what will you have gained? Another corpse? Surely you've had your fill of those."

Báthory's vicious glare turns to Janos. Bowie and I have a brief moment to remember how to breathe. He hugs me close, and I settle against him as much as I can without drawing attention.

"I think you're all a nest of liars, nosing around, asking questions whose answers don't concern you. Why should I believe a thing you say?"

Janos grips the bars, knuckles white. "Because three hostages are better than two. If you must have blood, take mine."

Bowie shudders. I hope he stays quiet and lets Janos make this sacrifice.

"You'd have me believe you're the same type of creature as that one?" She points to Bowie.

"I am."

"And if his blood is no good without a mortal wound, then why would yours be?"

"I'm older than he is. It's me you want."

She saunters toward the other cage. I let out a breath. Not relief, not in the slightest, but the farther away she moves, the easier it is to remember I have lungs.

"Put your hand through the bars."

Janos hesitates, reluctance evident in his tight, rigid posture.

"Do it, or I'll drain your"—her eyes dart between Janos and Bowie—"lover?" She studies Janos's response, which is to scoff and feign indifference.

"Coworkers, at best," answers Janos. "Our boss isn't the sort of man you want to cross. If we don't return soon, he'll come looking. He knows where we've gone."

"You continue to think words will gain you the upper hand. You're locked in a cage in my personal chambers. I'm not afraid of your *boss*. Send him along. As you can see"—she gestures to an empty cage—"I have plenty of room for guests."

It's one thing to hold grown men in these abysmal conditions, but as I imagine young girls in the same predicament, my mind rebels. Unthinkable.

"Your. Hand," she snaps. "Now."

With a resigned sigh, Janos shoves his hand through the gap in the bars, in a fist, palm down. I'm grateful to him for sparing Bowie. I wonder if he knows as well as I do that Bowie doesn't drink enough. I'm not sure how much blood he can spare before that becomes a new problem for us, and though I wish no harm to Janos, he earns my respect with his selfless sacrifice.

Báthory plucks a gleaming sharp dagger from her torture wall and returns to the cage, an eager flare in her dark gaze.

Janos yanks his arm back in. "I can do it myself."

"And spare me the pleasure?" she asks. "You'll do no such thing. Give me your hand."

He extends it again, strong and steady. I admire him for not trembling. There's no fear in his eyes, only hatred. He doesn't flinch as she drags the blade across the meaty-soft flesh of his palm.

A line of blood wells to the surface. The scent blooms strong in my nostrils. Báthory's eyes widen. She takes his wrist and yanks him forward, his shoulder against the bars, arm extended as far as possible.

"My guards are stationed just outside," she warns. "Remain still, and I won't call for them to pluck off your *coworker's* fingernails one by one. Understood?"

"Understood."

Báthory stares at the blood. One crimson drop falls to the floor, a new stain among many on her polished wooden planks.

Bowie's hands tighten in my fur. We press against each other.

She bends at the waist. Her tongue darts out to wet her unnaturally red lips.

And she drinks.

What have we done?

If I thought her eyes were black before, I'm sure of it now. As the power of Janos's blood courses through her veins, her irises gleam pure ebony.

Báthory drops his hand, and Janos tugs it back inside the cage. He licks the gash she made in his palm, settling back against the bars as far from her as he can get.

Her gaze flits wildly around the room, landing on nothing in particular, just bouncing from one corner to another.

I have an idea of what she's seeing. When I drink from Bowie, it's as if all my senses sharpen and hone to become nearly otherworldly. Colors are brighter, details crisper, and everything vibrates with life. If that's what she's experiencing now, we'll have a hell of a time convincing her to stop after one drink.

"What is this magic?" Báthory inspects her hands, marveling at the buffed nails and bejeweled fingers. "What are you creatures?" Her gaze shifts from Janos to Bowie.

I figure it won't matter at this point if we tell her the truth. It's obvious she must be killed. Her lust for inflicting pain has signed her death sentence in my eyes. If only she would leave us alone, perhaps we could escape.

"If I tell you," says Bowie, "will you send for a doctor? He will also need food if he's to heal."

"Yes, yes, whatever." She waves a hand absently in the air, intent on the information.

"Why should I believe you?" asks Bowie.

She giggles, an airy, mad sound that buzzes around my twitching ears like hornets. "Because the alternative changes nothing. You talk, and perhaps I give you what you want. Or you don't talk, and I work my way down a list of unpleasant activities until you change your mind."

A low growl rumbles in my chest. I do not like this woman threatening my Bowie. I'll rip her spine out through her throat before I let her lay one finger on him.

"Oh," she tuts. "He seems to be doing better after all. Now tell me what you are, or I shall have his claws removed one by one and strung for a necklace."

With an irritated sigh, Bowie answers, "He is a werewolf, and we are vampires. Be warned. Our kind won't tolerate our kidnapping lightly."

Her thick black brows arch to crescents. "A werewolf. And vampires. So the legends are true? How did this become so?"

If Janos cares that we've told her the truth, he doesn't show it. Stoic and silent in his cage, he watches their exchange intensely.

"Creatures don't become so. We are born how we are born," Bowie explains. "Now, the doctor? Please? Or else the poison will overwhelm my blood, and he could still die."

"I think you lie, pretty man." Báthory approaches the bars of our cage. "But I understand. You go ahead and keep your secrets while you're able. I've ways of extracting secrets you can only imagine. Perhaps when I return, you'll be more inclined toward the truth."

She stands so close it's all I can do to resist forcing my snout between these bars and biting at her ankles. I hate her for what she's done and what more she threatens to do. I hope our arrival has at least spared Cecily and the other girls from her attentions tonight.

She spins with a flourish and strides confidently from the room. A door shuts. We're alone.

Taking a deep breath, I force myself to stay calm. The urge to panic, to let go of control, duck my head and shiver in a corner rises strong, but I can't allow myself an attack now. I must shift and help the others.

Bowie strokes my fur. "Are you all right?"

I look up. But our signals won't be enough. Using the strength his blood has given me, I call to my human form and shift.

The change rolls through me with steady ease, thanks to Bowie's healing blood.

He takes me in his arms. I lean in and hug him around the waist.

If anything, the room smells even worse to my human nose. Old blood, body odor, urine. The scents are at odds with the luxurious decor just out of reach of the cages: the fancy furniture, the oil paintings, and plush pillows. I glance at a row of small windows. That could be a problem come dawn.

"Will your keys work these locks?" Bowie asks Janos.

"Yes." He's already pulling the skeleton key set from his sleeve. "One of them should."

Flicking my ears, I hear evidence of men standing outside. "Shh, we must speak quietly. We're under heavy guard." I point to the door. "Four men, just outside."

Bowie blows an irritated breath through his nose. "Thank you. Are you really all right? Your leg. I was so worried."

"You've healed it. I feel fine. But you? I must have drunk a lot of blood. How are you?"

"Fine, fine. Don't worry about me." He hands me my clothes. "I grabbed these as they dragged me away from you. But I lost our satchel."

"Thank you." I stand and get dressed, all the while looking him over. The more time I spend around him, the more I notice the signs when he hasn't fed enough. It's in the faint hollow of his eyes, the gray tint to his creamy skin. He definitely needs to feed. I reach for him, and he lets me pull him to his feet.

Janos tinkers away in his cage. One key clicking and clunking in the lock at a time. They jangle from the chain, the sound loud in my ears. I worry about the guards, but their hearing isn't as good as mine.

Turning my attention back to Bowie, I tilt my neck and push my throat toward his mouth. "Take some back. You need it."

"I don't." He remains rigid when all I want is for him to melt against me and take what I offer.

"Please, Bowie, I feel as strong as a herd of horses thanks to you. I have it to spare, and you must feed."

When still he resists, Janos chimes in to back me up. "Beauregard, don't be stubborn. Cecily needs you at full strength. Bite him."

Bowie's eyes meet mine. He looks painfully torn.

I palm his cheek and place a kiss on his lips. "Let's save her, Bowie. Come. Do it for Cecily." Pushing him like this isn't a good feeling, but we don't have time for a heart-to-heart. We need to get out of here before Báthory returns. "Please?"

"You're sure?" he asks.

I nod and pull him close.

He lets himself be drawn in. His breath ghosts over my throat. I take his waist, and he takes mine.

The bite, when it comes, is a deep, sharp kiss. Fangs slip cleanly through flesh with very little pain and quite a lot of pleasure. I'm in no mood for hard cocks and sweaty skin, but his bite offers another form of pleasure I'll gladly savor. A sense of peace washes over me, rinsing away the bad smells, the frightening futures, the fear that took hold the moment our plan went awry.

A calm determination remains in its place, a growing confidence that we're strong enough and clever enough to escape Báthory's evil clutches.

Bowie doesn't drink much. When he finishes, he stays close, licking and kissing the punctures while I run my hands along his back.

I gain strength in his presence, and I wish we could linger in this moment, but the click of a lock and Janos's triumphant "Yes!" brings us snapping back to reality.

Grinning, Janos swaggers from his cage and approaches ours.

"Well done, brother," says Bowie.

Janos winks at him and begins working on our lock. He looks me over. "Feeding him has made you stronger, not weaker. Hasn't it?"

I'm not sure what the significance behind his words means, but he's not wrong. "It has."

Narrowing his gaze, Janos smirks as he turns the key in the lock. "Interesting" is his only response before the gate clicks open and Bowie and I are freed.

Janos kisses Bowie's cheek.

I growl. I don't mean to, but the noise is out of my mouth before I considered making it.

"Take it easy, wolfy." Janos backs off. "He's your man."

The wolf inside me likes the sound of that. So do I.

* * *

"Now what?" says Bowie. "We're loose but stuck in this cursed room. Four guards, we can manage, but not without a significant amount of noise."

"Well, we can't stay here." Janos glances toward the windows. "Sunrise won't spare us in this chamber, and I'd rather not have to beg her for anything else."

I study the space. We're in a set of adjoining rooms. "Let's see if there's another way out."

We leave the macabre cages behind and explore the suite. To my utter horror and surprise, just past the makeshift prison lies a proper bedroom, quite regal, with an enormous monstrosity of a bed covered in absolute piles of silks and furs. If this isn't the countess's bedroom, I'll eat my tail. To think she lives so close to where she tortures her victims is horrifying.

The look on Bowie's face says he agrees.

I peer out the window to find we're high up in one of several towers. My stomach protests. I step away from the window. Jumping from here is not an option; it's way too far to fall. Beyond the bedroom is a garderobe, and that's all. It looks like there are no obvious exits besides the one under guard.

"Hellfire." Bowie must have come to the same conclusion. "We'll have to fight our way out."

It's not ideal. But two vampires and a werewolf against four humans is a fight we can win.

"We must prioritize speed," Bowie says. "The less noise they make, the better our chances are of sneaking through the rest of the castle unnoticed."

Janos nods. "According to Petru, the castellan, Benedikt Deseo, is our best bet at locating all the girls. Once we're past the guards, he's who we'll need to find."

How we're going to find one man in this huge castle is beyond me. "I think I can sniff out Cecily. We can start with her and whoever she's with."

"We should split up," Janos suggests as he plucks daggers from the wall of doom. "With any luck, Ivaz will have arrived and arranged wagons by the time we've found the girls."

I have my doubts, but I keep quiet. *Out* is the first goal; we can focus on *away* once that's been accomplished.

"What's the plan to find each other again once we've split?" asks Bowie, accepting a weapon from Janos. "This place is huge."

"Petru says the stable master, Daniel Vas, is safe, and the stables shouldn't be difficult to find. Let's meet there."

I feel sorry for the horses already.

Janos hands me a blade. "If we're forced to ground before we've found the girls, the earth will be the safest resting place."

Bowie's expression indicates his reluctance.

"You can take Andras with you."

"You can?" I hadn't realized that was a possibility, having imagined myself sleeping over whatever patch of ground Bowie chose. That would have been fine on our journey, but here on Csejthe's grounds, it's basically an X marks the spot. Vampire hides here.

"Yes, but it's awful."

"Hopefully, it won't be necessary," says Janos. "Let's go. Me first, then Bowie. Andras, stay out of the fight if you can. We should be able to subdue them without you."

I don't argue. I hate to fight, but I'll be ready if they need me.

We line up at the door. My nerves are alight with anticipation. I grasp the handle and mouth, "Ready?"

They nod, and I yank open the door.

Janos races through, Bowie at his heels.

The brawl is lightning fast. A silent strike from Janos to the throat of the first of four men. The bleeding guard's lips form a silent scream as he goes down. Janos finishes him with a squelching stab of his dagger.

Bowie strikes a second man before he can raise an alert. An arc of blood sprays from the sliced artery.

The smell hits the air as Janos dives for the third guard. Before the man can unsheathe his sword, Janos has swiped his blade across his throat.

Our advantage lasts only seconds, and a loud cry of alarm from the fourth shatters the silence. I punch him too late to stop the scream. Bowie steps in to finish him off.

I'm stunned by the violence, though I knew it was coming. Four men conquered without having landed a single blow. They stood no chance against vampires.

Bowie wipes his blade and tucks it into his belt, unfazed. I've never seen this side of him. His eyes meet mine.

"Are you all right?" he asks.

A slurping noise jolts me from my stupor. Janos feeds off a dying man. I cringe.

Bowie takes my elbow and leads me past the carnage. "Talk to me."

"It's fine," I lie. Blood lingers so strong in my nostrils that I itch to blow my nose. "I'm fine."

"Come." Bowie tugs me farther down the gray hall. Wall sconces light the way. Bowie is too kind to call my bluff. "We must flee in case anyone heard the scream. Can you do that?"

I nod, peering ahead. There's a staircase. My instinct says we should head down, but I fear the enemy will be heading up. "Is there another way?"

"There must be many. A servant's passage perhaps? We'll find it."

Janos catches up, and the three of us race ahead, then turn off down another hall.

Bowie checks doors as we go.

I hear footsteps. "Hurry!"

"This way," says Bowie. We flee through a door down a narrow passage to another set of stairs, Janos silently closing the door behind us.

Relief lasts only seconds as a man yells, "Alert the garrison! The prisoners have escaped!"

"Hellfire." Bowie races downward, me on his heels.

"We need to split up now." Janos flings open every door we pass. "Make it harder for them to tail us."

"We'll never find Cecily with the guards tearing through the castle," says Bowie.

I disagree. Maybe we can't find *all* the girls, but we must get Cecily. "I can find her."

"Change of plans," says Janos as we continue toward ground level. "Andras, sniff out Cecily and bring her to the stables. I'll find Deseo and a place to hide. Go!"

Janos vanishes through a door leaving Bowie and me alone.

"Do you smell her?" asks Bowie.

"No, but that's good, isn't it? She hasn't been to Báthory's rooms or dragged through this passage."

"All right, this way. We'll find the great hall and start there. If you smell her before that, let me know."

Bowie sprints off as if he knows where he's going. Maybe he does. He's probably been in dozens of castles. Certainly they'd share commonalities.

As I follow, my mind drifts to the scene outside Báthory's chambers. Bowie calmly silences guards with his dagger. For a man who refuses to feed from others, he managed to kill easy enough.

I know this is different. Lives are at stake. His niece. Innocent girls. Yet I found the act shocking.

My muscles flex with tension as we dart from the endless staircase down a wide corridor. My lungs are tight. My senses heightened. I wish I could tear off this hat so I could hear properly. My ears twitch uselessly from where they're flattened to my skull.

This hall is lit, a public space, and risky. I concentrate on sniffing, hoping for a whiff of mint, willing it to lead us to Cecily.

Bowie slows to a fast walk. Smart, as I suppose two men

sprinting through the halls would attract undue attention. So far, there seems to be no one around. The castle is eerily silent.

I hope Janos has managed to remain undetected. I hear no yelling, no clashing of blades, but I remind myself Csejthe is immense, with thick stone walls, and there's an excellent chance a battle going on at one end would not be heard at the other, even by a werewolf and a vampire.

"Anything?" asks Bowie, his voice barely a whisper.

"Nothing yet."

We push on. A wide staircase opens to an enormous banquet hall, blessedly empty. Keeping close to the wall, under the shadows of a second-story balcony that lines the space, we explore the perimeter.

Crossing to the far side, I finally pick up a hint of the smell I've been searching for.

I cast an excited glance at Bowie. "I've got it."

His face lights up. "Cecily?"

"Yes, this way." I take the lead and track the familiar smell under an arching passageway.

With Bowie at my back, I follow mint as quickly as I can go on silent feet, my ears twitching for sounds of guards on the move.

The castle is a labyrinth of halls and staircases. I've never been in a building so large. Already I'm turned around. If we had to backtrack for some reason, I'd have no idea how to find the tower we started in.

Mint blooms under my nose. Head down, I follow with the tenacity of a hawk diving for field mice. I'm so focused I don't notice trouble until it's too late.

"Andras!" Bowie yanks my elbow, pulling us into an alcove and snagging my attention.

Boots clomp toward us.

Guards.

Lots of them.

e duck as deeply as possible into a windowed alcove, though it's far too shallow to hide two grown men.

My heart races, pounding a battle cry in my ears. My fingers flex on the stolen dagger. I've never used a blade on another person. I don't want to now. But I'll do anything to protect Bowie.

Footsteps draw inevitably closer.

Bowie shoulders in front of me.

I hold my breath.

As they pass by, for the span of a heartbeat, I think perhaps they won't see us. With my free hand, I finger the window in case they do. Surely we're far enough down now to jump if we have to. I risk a backward glance and cringe.

A barrel-chested guard turns his head.

We're caught.

"Ho, there. Stand down!" he orders as Bowie prepares to fight back. The other guards take notice. Perhaps ten in total. We're terribly outnumbered.

Finding the window's latch, I fling it open.

The *shink-shink* of men drawing their weapons slices through the air. Bowie is a good fighter, but against ten men? I don't like his odds.

"Come quietly, and you won't be hurt." The guard looks all too confident with his men at the ready behind him.

That's a lie if I ever heard one. "Bowie," I hiss while shoving the window out as far as it will go. I grab him. "This way!"

With my arm around his waist, I hurl us backward through the opening. Two stories. Should be fine.

We land on hard-packed dirt with a heavy thud, me on my back, Bowie's weight square on my chest. My lungs whoosh out all my air at once. I sputter as he scrambles to his feet and lifts me off mine. As he swoops me into his arms, I struggle to catch my breath.

Bowie races away, and I fling a backward glance at the window. Guards stare out, their faces a picture of shock, and I know why. To them, we've disappeared. I was stunned when I first witnessed the phenomenon as well.

To be on the vanishing end is equally astonishing, but I can't help the triumphant smirk as we leave them behind in a blur. I suck in air gratefully. We're across the bailey and surrounded by the smell of horses in seconds.

Bowie sets me down, his eyes full of concern. "Are you hurt?"

I assess, still recovering my breath. "I don't think so. Perhaps some bruises. It was a short fall, and you're not so heavy."

Relief flares in his gaze. "I've never been so glad to be thin-boned."

Taking in our surroundings, I find we're alone outside an enormous stable, between the turnout pasture and the castle wall. Seeing no guards, I reach for Bowie. "That was a close call."

He returns the embrace, his body still tense from flight. "We'll have to go back."

"I know." Being so close to Cecily and not yet having her safe in hand brings my frustration to a boil. "I had her, Bowie. We were almost there."

Bowie's gaze flicks past me and up toward the wall. "Guards. Into the stables, now."

We creep to the entrance and duck inside. Horses squeal their discontent, snorting a warning to the others.

Danger. Stay alert. Intruder.

I wish I could tell them I mean no harm, but I don't speak horse. Their neighs could attract more unwanted attention. Would guards pay notice to distressed horses? Probably. We'd best be on the move.

A man rounds the corner from behind a set of stalls, checking for the cause of the commotion. A young lad follows at his heels. Both spot us.

My stomach clenches. Bowie could silence them in seconds, but these men are likely innocent. They don't deserve to be caught up in this.

The older man—middle-aged with messy graying hair peeking out from beneath his hat—casts us a wary glance. We must paint a confusing picture. Bowie, who carries himself like a noble but dresses like a merchant, and me, obviously a peasant like himself, neither of us important enough to order horses to be saddled or hitched to a wagon.

But it's his servant's nature that wins out. He gives us a deferential nod. "What will ye be needing?"

The boy behind him isn't so easily fooled. His gaze suggests a level of scrutiny that makes me squirm.

Bowie takes over. "We're here to speak with Daniel Vas. Is he around?"

The man brushes his hands off on his pants and steps forward, arm extended. "He sure is. I'm Daniel."

Bowies takes his wrist. "Bowie, and this is Andras. Is there somewhere we can talk in private?"

Daniel looks around at the stamping, disgruntled horses. "Something you can't say in front of them?"

Bowie stares pointedly at the boy.

"Oh, that's just my apprentice, Tamas. He won't bother ye none."

"All the same if you don't mind. The matter is somewhat delicate. Perhaps Tamas could quiet the horses while we talk?"

Daniel heaves a shrug and nods to the boy. "Go on."

Tamas gives us one last pointed look and makes his way to a snorting red roan, hand outstretched to pet her head.

We walk with Daniel toward the far end of the stalls.

"Apologies for sending Tamas off like that," says Bowie. "I'll come straight to the point. We've spoken to Petru, who says you may be of assistance. We're here to help the girls Báthory has tormented and imprisoned."

I study Daniel's face as Bowie speaks. A blaze of recognition flashes in his widened eyes, followed by a wrinkling of his forehead. Reluctance? Fear? I would blame him for neither.

Bowie continues, "Have you heard from a man called Ivaz? Or anyone asking about horses and wagons being prepared for departure?"

Daniel shakes his head carefully but says nothing.

"I know my questions place you in danger if your answers fall into the wrong hands. Even now, the guards are after us. I don't want to ask you to incriminate yourself. But when the call comes for horses, will they be made ready?"

A long look passes between them. The wickers and squeals have calmed down. Slowly, Daniel nods.

"Good. That's all I can ask." Bowie's hands flourish nervously. "Well, that and to tell no one we were here. Perhaps to shelter us if we must spend the day within Csejthe's walls."

Daniel narrows his gaze. "You can really save those girls?"

"Yes." Bowie's earnest tone conveys the confidence I wish I felt.

"All right," says Daniel. Solemn. Resigned. "You can count on me."

I tune out their conversation as Bowie relays descriptions of Janos and Ivaz. The faintest scent of mint lingers in the stables. We need to get back into the castle. Perhaps Janos has spoken with Deseo. With any luck, we'll find him and the girls already together.

* * *

APPROACHING guards drive us from the stables. With the entire garrison on alert and searching for us, it's impossible to stay in any one place for long. I'm getting used to Bowie snapping me up and carrying me off. He's fast enough we aren't seen, but I can't track a scent at such speed.

Stopping just inside the castle's main entrance is a risk, but we must take it to rediscover the trail. With both of us hyper-aware of our surroundings, we stay close together as we creep farther into the maze of corridors. Passing through foyers and fancy parlors, around the great hall, and toward private chambers we sneak, all the while listening for guards.

I hear chatter and snag Bowie's arm. He's heard it too. Female voices, not guards. Have they been alerted to our presence? Will they shout for help upon seeing us? It's late for them to be up and about.

There's nowhere to hide, and with mint filtering to my nose, I'm hesitant to let Bowie whisk us away again.

"Let's see what happens," I whisper.

Bowie looks unsure, but he nods. "Then we must pretend to belong. Straighten up. Walk to the side and slightly behind me."

I do as he says, making my steps more confident, forcing a neutral expression. When the women appear, I don't make eye contact, but I see their extravagant dresses: lace, satin, and glimmering beads. Noble ladies. They're arm in arm, pressed tight together, and walk as if trying to escape notice.

Since neither the women nor we seem to want to attract attention, we pass by without incident. Bowie and I bow our heads and bend slightly at the waist as they continue. Nothing happens. I release a full breath.

"Did you see that?" asks Bowie.

"See what?"

"The cuts on their hands," he whispers, claiming my arm.

I lean into him. "No. Really?"

He nods.

Horrified, I'm almost glad I didn't notice. "I have Cecily's trail again. This way. We're close."

We must be nearing the finishing school Bowie told me about. This wing of the castle houses primarily young ladies, I can tell by the scents of powder, dried flowers, perfumes, and fragrant oils.

As we round a corner, we spot more guards and back up. I hear no shouted orders or oncoming footsteps, so they didn't see us. But they stand in the way of where we need to go.

"She's through there," I tell Bowie.

He considers. I sense his eagerness. It's in his coiled muscles, the tense line of his shoulders. He's ready to barrel forward, consequences be damned. But he's still my Bowie. Clever and protective.

"I saw two guards. You?" he asks in a whisper.

"Two."

He presses his lips tight together and meets my eyes. "I can kill them before they know I'm there."

Sensing hesitancy, I ask. "But…you don't want to?"

"Báthory's personal guards are one thing," he says, torn. "They're definitely complicit in her crimes. But these men, how much do they know? I can't exactly interrogate them before I strike."

"Could you incapacitate them instead?"

"That's riskier, but yes, probably."

Perhaps he just needs permission. "I support you, whatever you decide." I wish Janos were here. Killing doesn't seem to affect him the way it affects Bowie. "Or I could do it?"

"No," he says immediately. "I don't want your morals compromised, and anyway, my speed is what's needed. Come, let's get it over with."

Bowie vanishes around the corner. By the time I catch up, it's already done. The guards lie slumped on the stone floor, their hearts still beating, but for how long, I can't say. We continue past them to a divide in the corridor.

"Which way?" asks Bowie.

Cecily has been both ways, but the scent is strongest to the right. I take the lead, pausing at each closed door to inhale. We're definitely in ladies' quarters now.

A thick rug, patterned in red and gold swirls, cushions this hall. No expense had been spared on the furniture and decor. Polished wooden display tables line the wall. Vases, knick-knacks, and sculptures decorate their surfaces, gleaming under the light of an excessive number of lit sconces. The aroma of heated oil mixes with rose, lavender, and mint.

I find her door. My heart races, battering my ribcage. The wolf is triumphant, a scent expertly tracked and successful in its conclusion. "She's here."

Bowie clutches his chest with one hand and reaches for the knob with the other. It begins to turn, then stops. Locked. I think of the skeleton keys tucked away in Janos's sleeve and again wish he were here.

"I could force it," says Bowie. "But the noise."

"Which is louder? Breaking down the door or knocking?"

"Generally, I'd say breaking down the door, but Cecily sleeps like the dead. I'd have to knock so loud I'd wake the entire hall."

"Force it, then. I'll stand guard. If there's trouble, we'll snatch her and run."

"What of the others?"

"We come back for them once she's safe."

Bowie nods. "Stand back."

Stepping away from the door, I watch as Bowie delivers a powerful kick directly by the knob. Splintering wood shatters the silence. The bolt breaks clear through the catch plate, and the door slams open.

Loudly.

Bowie races into the room while I hover at the threshold checking for guards. No way that wasn't heard but triangulating where the sound came from may just give us enough time to clear out undetected.

Inside, Cecily has startled awake. The sight of her blonde curls in my periphery sends a jolt of mind-numbing relief to my brain. I'm so overwhelmed my knees threaten to buckle.

Before she knows what's happening, she's in Bowie's arms. Her reflexive struggle is short-lived when she realizes it's her uncle come to save her.

"Bowie!" her shrill voice echoes too loud.

Bowie claps a hand over her mouth. She takes him in with wide eyes, and he drops it.

"How?" she whispers.

"We'll talk later." Bowie kisses her cheek.

I scan the hall. Still nothing, but I need my hearing unimpeded. I tear off my hat and stuff it into my pants. My ears twitch free. Secrecy be damned.

Bowie joins me, carrying Cecily, her legs latched firmly around his waist, arms squeezing his neck. Both of them are crying. Bowie's eyes are pinked over with blood tears.

"I need to get her out. We'll have to come back for the others."

I nod, and we're off. Bowie runs at a pace he knows I can match, back the way we came.

As we leap over the fallen guards—still unconscious but with beating hearts—I hear the telltale stomp of boots. Moons, we're so close.

Bowie whips around to face me. "Incoming! Straight ahead."

"I know." I listen, calculating. Maybe six men. I stand a fair chance. "You go. I'll meet you at the stables."

He balks. "No, Andras, I can't leave you."

"Take Cecily to safety and come back then. You're fast enough."

His hesitation pains me, but this way is safest for Cecily.

"Go!" I take his shoulders and urge him on. "I'll be fine."

With a wail of dismay, he vanishes.

I gulp.

Guards round the corner. "There's one of them."

"Take him down!"

With muscles coiled like springs and my throat tight, I fist the stolen dagger and prepare to fight for my life.

a burly man unsheathes his sword to attack first.

I'm not trained in this kind of fighting or in any kind really, but I'm stronger than they are and faster, with a wolf's instinct for survival and skill at taking down prey.

I'll just think of them as beavers.

Big, scary beavers.

With swords.

On second thought, maybe I should run.

My feet hit the stones before I can second-guess the decision. The guards will have to chase me, and that will give Bowie time to care for Cecily with less chance of me being skewered like roasted meat.

Racing through the castle corridors, I lead them away from the girls' residences and toward the great hall. At least I think I do. It's easy to get turned around in this labyrinth.

Footsteps pound at my heels, but I'm all right so far. And I can go faster than this if I have to. For now, these men must remain on my tail and out of Bowie's way.

A guard yells for reinforcements, his powerful voice echoing off the walls. Their armor weighs the men down and creates a racket of noise in their wake. The whole castle must hear us. At least Bowie won't have any trouble finding me when he returns.

I tug a heavy brass statue to crash down as I pass. It clangs to the ground, forcing the guards to dodge and weave around it. Next, a table, then a tall wooden display case. Glass shatters with a pleasing cacophony of smashing wreckage. Shards blanket the stones.

Ahead lies the enormous banquet room. I've gone the right way after all. Once there, a burst of speed should put me far enough in front to take one of the many passages from the hall before the guards round the corner to see which way I've gone. Then I'll catch my breath and listen for Bowie.

It's a good plan.

Too bad it's not going to work.

A second contingent of guards appears and blocks my path. Eight men, all of them armed, weapons drawn. Their swords make my dagger look trifling in comparison.

"Corner him!" The command comes from too close behind me.

"We've got him!" A yell of triumph comes from in front.

My stomach drops. The wolf pleads for a shift, but I know we'll get tangled in this shirt. With the dagger clenched in white knuckles, I spin to find myself surrounded.

I'm going to die here.

"I want him alive." Báthory's voice, far too calm for the circumstances.

Her words bring no relief.

The guards inch forward, closing in, their scowls tinged with glee. They are as bloodthirsty as their mistress.

Panic rises to a peak, tightening my throat and causing my heart to hammer in my chest. My pulse pounds loudly in my ears. I've got to focus.

"Where are the other two?" asks Báthory.

I flick my gaze in her direction. Four men stand between me

and the countess, with the others along my flanks equally ready to intervene.

"They remain inside the walls," says a guard. "We'll find them."

Planning my attack, I aim for the men in my way first. If I can squeeze past them to plunge this dagger through her breast, my death won't be in vain.

"Restrain him and get to it. It's the others I want, but they'll protect this troublesome mutt." She eyes me, her expression caught between amusement and irritation.

I dive for her.

Ducking beneath a slashing sword, I grab the first guard by the ankle and yank. He thuds to the ground, blocking the attack of the guard next to him.

Báthory stumbles backward, scrambling away from my reach. Her other guards come to her defense. Hands clutch at me from behind. Too many, but I'll go down fighting.

I jerk my elbow back to ram a man's chin, then stab out with the dagger to catch another across the forearm, but my efforts aren't enough. My wrists are wrenched behind my back. Panic rises as I struggle.

A blurred shadow streaks through my vision, laying waste to the men in its path.

Bowie? Janos? I don't know which, but I'm filled with gratitude they're here. Men are yanked off me. My arms are free. I spring to a fighting stance, my goal unchanged.

Grunts and groans pollute the air as the flash of dark lightning cuts a path of guts and gore through the men.

I can't help but cringe. Blood and waste waft to my nose, suddenly so strong they blot out all other scents. My eyes aren't swift enough to follow the trail of carnage spilling out all around me, so I focus on Báthory, who's somehow still standing.

Gripping my dagger, I lunge.

Her evil heart is my target. But before the blade can meet its mark, I'm whipped from the air by the terrible shadow and flung aside like I weigh nothing. I slam into the stone wall with a yipe. My back, already pummeled from the earlier fall, takes the hit hard.

Fighting for air, I keep my eyes on the action.

The shadow comes to a halt. Not Bowie. Not Janos.

Another woman stands before a cowering Erzsébet. "What in the ever-shining stars do we have here?" she purrs.

A petite beauty in men's clothes—black pants and an amber top—with two pearlescent fangs framing her wicked smile, each dripping blood down her chin. She glowers at the countess. Her chestnut hair is wild from the massacre, tousled over her shoulders and hanging messily down her back. Green eyes pass over me before returning to Erzsébet.

Around us, guards lie dead or dying. A low moan of agony rises from a twisted, mangled body unlucky enough to have survived the assault.

The vampiress says to Erzsébet, "You, my dear, have caused me quite a lot of trouble. Where's Beauregard?"

In an effort of visible iron will, Báthory straightens. "Who are you?"

"You'll soon find out," says the vampiress. "We're about to become closely acquainted, assuming, that is, you haven't harmed my Bowie."

I growl low and deep, baring my teeth. Bowie is mine.

Both women spin to face me. Erzsébet sneers.

The vampiress only grins. "Ivaz told me of you," she says. "The mongrel."

I flinch. I haven't missed that name. Testing my back and finding it mostly stable, I rise to a sit. "It's Andras, and I've heard of you too. Bettina."

Bettina's brows, plucked to perfection, arch with amusement. She bows as a man might. "The pleasure is mine, indeed."

There's no pleasure here.

Erzsébet fingers a dagger of her own, partially hidden at her side. Funny she thinks she stands a chance against these creatures. Her minutes are numbered.

I wonder what's keeping Bowie just as another shadowy trail comes barreling down the hall toward us.

Janos materializes and bellows, "The bitch dies!"

He flings himself at the countess, only to be stopped by a dainty manicured hand wrapped neatly around his neck. Bettina lifts him so his feet dangle in the air. He grabs her wrists with both hands.

"No one touches the lady but me," says Bettina. "Understood?"

Janos scowls, even as he nods. Bettina sets him down.

When he can speak again, he argues, "That woman's no lady. She's a killer. Of young innocent girls. A blade across her neck is the least of what she deserves."

"Silence," Bettina orders. "I'll make that decision for myself. More guards are coming. Take care of them." She points toward the hall.

Begrudgingly, Janos leaves to obey the command.

I rise to my feet. "The killer you just spared wouldn't do the same for you."

Bettina blinks. "How would you know, *Andras?*"

The ways she enunciates my name, with such deliberate venom, makes me wish I hadn't corrected her. "She hides a knife in her right hand for which I'd assume you are the target."

"Let her try." Bettina's laughter could peel paint off walls.

I'm not sure which of them I hate more, Bettina or Erzsébet, but the world would be better off without either of them.

Erzsébet tucks the knife into her bodice. She must know there's no point in running, for she doesn't attempt to flee. Her gaze darts between us. Wisely, she keeps her mouth shut.

"No one has answered my question." Bettina stamps her booted foot. "Where is Beauregard?"

I don't owe this woman anything. And I don't know where Bowie is for certain, though my guess is the stables. She'll get no information from me.

Erzsébet clears her throat. "I didn't get their names, but if you mean the dark-haired, prissy one, he's yet to be apprehended. Though what's left of my guard"—she glances over the bodies at our feet without any real emotion—"*if* there are any left of my guard, still search for him."

"You'd better pray to whichever god you believe in that he's not been injured. Beauregard is my youngest child and as such, holds a special place in my heart."

"Your...child?" Erzsébet's expression turns justifiably confused. Bettina barely looks old enough to be a mother, much less the mother of a grown man. In fact, she and Bowie appear to be much the same age.

"Mortals." Bettina rolls her eyes, then glowers at Erzsébet. "You've much to learn, and I assure you, it will be no picnic."

Erzsébet takes a hesitant step forward, over the dead body of a man she'd seen slaughtered, her velvet-slippered foot gingerly avoiding a puddle of blood. She has a sort of hypnotic charm I find repulsive. "You will find me an eager student."

What in the full moon am I witnessing here?

Bettina meets her halfway, takes Erzsébet's chin in her fingers, and tilts her head so they stare one another in the eyes. "Will I?"

"You have my word," says Erzsébet.

I'm disgusted. Men lie dead and dying. Girls have been tortured and killed within these walls. Is Bettina really suggesting Erzsébet remain free?

Bowie appears at my side from thin air. I may never get used to that, though I manage not to startle.

"Are you all right?" he asks, eyes full of concern.

I nod. "You?"

"Yes, fine. What's happened?" Bowie takes in the carnage. "Why isn't she dead?"

Bettina whirls around, putting Erzsébet at her back to face Bowie. I wonder if the countess will grab for her knife, but she remains still. Watching.

"You had me worried sick," says Bettina as she approaches, arms spread, to embrace Bowie.

Growling, I angle between them.

Bettina snarls back. "Out of my way, wolf."

I stand firm. I don't want her wicked hands to touch him. The thought of her scent on Bowie makes me cringe.

"I see you've already met," says Bowie as if we aren't posturing to go for each other's throats. "Bettina, please back up. Andras and I have had a very long night."

Bettina doesn't step back, but she does halt her progress.

"If you wouldn't mind," Bowie continues, hand raised to single out Erzsébet, "I have someone to kill."

Tutting, Bettina shakes her head. "I'm afraid not, dear. The king has plans for the countess, and I have plans for the king. Her murder would impede us both."

Janos returns during this bizarre conversation happening over the bodies of a dozen men. He's brought with him a human man dressed in servant's clothes but with the fine fabric and cut of a noble's. The man pulls a handkerchief from a pocket and presses it over his nose. From the expression on his pinched face, he's as revolted as I am.

"This is the court master, Benedikt Deseo," says Janos. "He knows where Báthory's many victims are housed throughout the castle."

Deseo appears as if he'll pass out at any moment. Meanwhile, the countess has the gall to look put out by this revelation. The fact that she remains alive boils the blood in my veins.

"Ivaz will be along to shuttle the women to safety," says Bettina.

"Girls," I correct. "Your pet project murders children."

Bettina narrows her gaze in my direction. "Your disapproval is noted, and that will be enough out of you. I will only put up with so much on Bowie's behalf. And it's not as if Erzsébet will enjoy her time in my care. She'll be punished in due course."

My mind is rattled. I turn to Bowie. "Let's get the girls and go. Cecily must be terrified."

The mention of her name brings a saddened, weary expression to Bowie's face. He nods, resigned. He must know there's no use arguing with Bettina when she's put her foot down.

Janos pushes Deseo past the dead guards. "Lead us to them."

As we leave, I glance over my shoulder to find the two women eyeing one another, each taking the measure of the other. Though it pains me to leave the countess alive, I think to myself perhaps this is what they deserve.

They can be each other's punishment.

$\mathcal{J}$anos and Deseo collect and watch over the girls as we wait for the arrival of a healer, Ivaz, and extra wagons. Daniel prepares Csejthe's horses and carts in the meantime.

The longer this endless night drags on, the more likely it is we'll end up spending the day within these walls. The thought makes me shiver. As far as I'm concerned, these grounds are cursed, and I want nothing more than to put some distance between us and this terrible castle.

Cecily hasn't been physically hurt. Thank the moon we were fast enough to spare her that. But the emotional trauma of being stolen from her home, from her loving family, and being hauled halfway across the country will be with her for countless nights to come.

Bowie and I sit next to each other on hay bales, both of us watching Cecily as she sleeps beneath a heavy horse blanket. Though my racing heart has finally calmed down, my nerves are worn thin, and I'm unable to settle. I fidget on the prickly bale, leaning closer to Bowie.

"I'm so sorry about everything," he says, his voice a low whisper.

I match his dulcet tone. "What do you have to be sorry about?"

He takes my hand in his and pulls it into his lap. "I'm sorry you got shot. I should've thought of that, but I was in such a hurry to get into the castle. I put you at risk."

"That was my own fault," I argue. "It was my plan."

"A plan I agreed to. I shouldn't have."

I give his hand a gentle squeeze. "You couldn't have known what would happen, and you saved me from the worst of it."

"There's more. I'm sorry I got Bettina involved at all. It seemed like a good idea when I first wrote to her, but I should've known she could never resist adding someone like Báthory to her collection."

Horrified, I fail to hold in my gasp. "You think she's going to make Báthory into a vampire?"

"I hope not, but the thought crossed my mind. I wouldn't be surprised if she does."

"We should kill them both before such a thing can come to pass."

Bowie shakes his head sadly. "I cannot kill my sire. Not only is it forbidden, but…" He hesitates. "A part of me can't help but love her. And I'm sorry for that too."

I can't pretend to understand Bettina's grip on my beloved, but one thing I know for sure is that it's not his fault. None of this is. Yet he's taking all the blame on his slim shoulders. I release his hand and wrap my arms around him. "You have nothing to be sorry for. Your heart is too big for killing, and that's all right."

He grips my waist. "I killed those guards. I wanted to kill Báthory."

"Me too." I've wanted it more than even the first juicy bite when I take down my dinner.

"And Janos. Janos could have killed her."

"He tried. Bettina stopped him before he could land the blow."

"Of course she did." Bowie sags.

"Bettina won't let Báthory continue torturing and murdering girls, will she?" I hate to even think it, let alone ask.

"No, Bettina won't tolerate that for a second. She may redirect Báthory's cruelty or starve her of it just to see what happens. Perhaps she's only acting under King Matyas's orders to be sure Báthory can't escape trial." Bowies heaves a sigh. "What an awful mess of this I've made."

"Hey now, stop that." I meet his gaze. "Cecily is safe, and little Esther's big sister, Bethie, and so are the others. Báthory is caught. The king will have all the evidence he needs, and whatever ulterior motive Bettina has is no one's fault but her own. You have saved these girls, Bowie. *You.* When everyone else turned a blind eye, you refused to do nothing."

"*We* saved them, Andras, together. I could never have done it without you. But I'm glad your opinion of me hasn't been damaged. Tell me what happened when I left you to fight them alone. I was so worried."

"I ran." A grin sneaks across my face. "Seemed like better odds."

"Wise man. Then what?"

I tell him of our chase through the castle halls, the second set of guards, and Bettina's chaotic arrival. "I almost had Erzsébet. Would have if Bettina hadn't tossed me aside like a sack of rotten potatoes."

"I suppose I'm glad she arrived after all," says Bowie. "It was you against a dozen guards and a wretched murderess otherwise. If that had ended poorly…" He doesn't elaborate.

It hadn't occurred to me until this moment that Bettina probably saved my life with her timely arrival. I can't bring myself to care. I still hate her.

Bowie reaches up to touch my ear. "You've lost your hat."

I flick my ear toward his fingers. "I needed to be able to hear as best I could. Guards appeared from every corner. I tucked it into my pants, but it must have fallen out."

"I like the way you look without it. Your ears are beautiful. You're beautiful. My Andras."

My cheeks warm under the praise.

We share a kiss.

"Gross." Cecily sits up from her makeshift bed.

If my cheeks were warm before, they're burning now.

Bowie plucks a piece of hay from her curls. After all this time, her clothes still smells faintly of mint. I'll never eat a mint candy again without thinking of her.

"Kissing isn't gross, young lady," says Bowie. "Take it back."

"I will not. It even sounds gross." Her gaze shifts from Bowie to me. "Why, Andras, your ears really are beautiful. I thought Bowie was just being weird when he said that."

Whoops. I should probably find another hat.

"Are they wolf ears?" She furrows her brows. "Why do you have wolf ears?"

Bowie handles this. "There's a possibility I haven't been entirely honest with you yet, my darling niece. I'll have quite a lot of explaining to do on our journey home."

"Home. I want to go home." Cecily's inquisitive expression turns to anguish. My heart aches for her. "When do we leave?"

"Soon." He strokes her hair. "I promise."

Her eyes fill with tears. "I want my mama."

Bowie opens his arms, and she flies into them. "I know. Me too. We'll see her soon." He settles her onto his lap and rocks her. She's too big for this, but it doesn't matter; they make it work. "You're safe now, Cecily. I've got you."

She cries into his shoulder, quiet sniffles and achingly sad sighs.

We're still huddled together sometime later, when Janos arrives to check on us.

"Is she all right?" Janos asks Bowie.

Cecily lifts her head from Bowie's shoulder and nods, wiping tears off her cheeks with the back of her hand. "Who are you?"

"I'm Janos, milady, Bowie's brother." Janos bows, then takes a seat on the opposite hay bale.

Cecily cocks her head and scrutinizes him. "That would make you my uncle. Why have we never met?"

Janos looks delighted at this, but Bowie shuts it down quickly. "Janos isn't your uncle. Remember how I told you I had much to explain? Remind me to cover that too."

"I will." Her little voice comes out clear and unshaken.

I can't believe her strength. I'm in awe of Bowie's entire family.

Janos looks to Bowie. "The other girls are safe, asleep together in the wagons and ready for departure. Petru, Daniel, and Tamas will drive the wagons out come dawn. The girls with no family will go to Matyas in Vienna, the nobles' and merchants' daughters back to their homes scattered throughout the Kingdom of Hungary. Ivaz and I will watch over them at night."

We're sitting so close I feel Bowie's relief as tension releases from his muscles. "Thank you, Janos. I owe you."

He waves this away. "You owe me nothing, brother. You and Andras will take Cecily yourselves?"

"Yes, of course," says Bowie without a second's hesitation. I doubt he'll ever let her out of his sight again, though I've no idea how a girl of only twelve will make the journey all the way back to Varad. I suppose we'll need a wagon ourselves.

Janos nods. I notice he's wearing our lost satchel. He takes it from around his neck and digs inside. "I went back for it," he explains. "Couldn't have you missing your dolly."

He pulls Marta from the bag and makes a kissy sound as he presses the rag doll to my cheek. I'm sure I flush bright pink, but I grab for the doll anyway and hold her to my chest.

Janos flashes a grin and shakes his head, staring at me. "You were made for Bowie."

Bowie watches me and Marta with a fond expression. I know it's silly for a grown man to keep his childhood dolly, but as I've recently come to know, there are far worse things in this world than youthful sentiment.

"And I was made for Andras," says Bowie. "And his dolly."

Cecily's answering giggles are music to my ears.

* * *

We don't need a wagon after all.

"I can ride," Cecily insists. "I want to. I saw nothing of the cities nor the countryside the entire way here. They kept me stuffed in that smelly old wagon. Get me a horse, and I'll ride."

I've learned very quickly not to say no to Cecily, but I do feel sorry for whatever horse is forced to tolerate my company for the long journey home.

"If you're sure," says Bowie. "But you can change your mind at any time if you grow weary. Promise me you won't be stubborn and suffer just to prove me wrong."

I fail to hold in my laughter. Who does Bowie think he's dealing with? He shoots me an amused glance.

"I promise," says Cecily. "Now let's pick a horse."

We're at the stable in Trencin, having spent the day together holed up in the cave in the hills. Bowie confessed to her his true nature and explained vampires in meticulous detail. Though I'd expected Cecily to be horrified, she wasn't. The only vampire she knows is Bowie, and he's perfectly lovely, so her sense of the creatures may be skewed.

I've stumbled through my explanation of werewolves, with

Bowie's help when I sent him pleading gazes. He's so much better at words than me. She's seen me transform into a wolf and taken it in with the steadfast curiosity I'm coming to associate with her. Wide intelligent eyes, fearless when protected by her loving uncle, she exceeds every expectation I could have of her.

Bowie and I follow her down the aisle of agitated horses. We both have handfuls of apple, carrot, and sugar cubes to hopefully bribe some poor pony into liking us.

Petru is gone already, but another groom tags along, telling us about the strengths and weaknesses of each available horse. We come to a stall with a lovely bay gelding that doesn't seem as fearful as the others.

I offer the horse a carrot, and though his eyes stay cautiously glued to mine, he takes it. The first to do so. "I like him."

"Oh, that old man?" asks the groom. "You don't want him. Bit pudgy, that one, and slow."

Yes, but he might actually learn to like me, I think. "What's his name?"

Cecily and Bowie join me, each also offering the bay a snack, which he takes with a friendly wuffle. As soon as he's done chewing, he's asking for more.

"We call him Sausage," says the groom.

"Sausage?" Try as I might, I can't contain my laughter. Butter, Toast, Beans, and Sausage! We must have him. I hand over my apple gladly. Sausage takes it, and I swear the horse is smiling at me.

Bowie and Cecily are snort-laughing. The groom must think we're daft as bats, but this isn't the kind of story you can explain in a hurry.

"Heavens," says Bowie through his chortles. "Why is the noble steed called Sausage?"

The groom shrugs. "He was saved from a slaughterhouse. Too friendly to be put down, even with all that meat on his bones. Thought it was funny to call him that, so he'd become Sausage after all. Get it?"

"That's ridiculous," says Cecily, grinning as she strokes Sausage's soft nose.

It feels so good to laugh again, like a tiny bit of normal life has crept in to shove aside Báthory's horrors.

Things aren't perfect. We have a long journey ahead. Cecily will need time and love to heal. Bowie and I have much to discuss about our future. We must be certain Báthory is brought to justice by the king so she can never harm again. But despite the loose ends, I feel like everything will be all right as long as we're together.

Bowie leans into me and answers my questioning gaze with a nod. What could be better than a little buttered toast, beans, and sausage?

Sausage knickers as if he's starving and nudges my shoulder to give up the last of the sugar cubes.

Chuckling, I hand them over and gather myself just long enough to say, "We'll take him!"

CHAPTER 27

It takes twice as long to journey back to Varad as it did to get from Varad to Csejthe. Traveling with a lazy old horse and an excitable young lady isn't an opportunity for speed so much as it is for making memories.

Cecily is in good spirits most nights, and when she isn't, we make sure she feels safe and loved until she's all right again.

I fare slightly better on the terrifying floating bridge on our way home, keeping my mind distracted by telling Bowie and Cecily the story of the bridge troll called Arlo that Ava used to tell me.

Sausage has become completely used to me in either form, which makes me worry for his future. If he thinks wolves are safe, he could be an easy target for a pack. Bowie picks up on my worry, like he always does, and assures me Sausage will have a place of honor in Jakob's stables for the rest of his days. That makes me feel better. I've already fallen in love with the sweet old horse.

What's not to love about a big lazy animal who just wants extra snacks?

We don't stay at The Twig and Berries this time around.

Instead, Bowie runs ahead and speaks with Dominus, who has the succubi prepare a room for us at The Peach and Pearl. We shuffle Cecily through as quickly as we can, but she's too smart not to question the establishments. Bowie manages to explain them away without lying exactly, but not telling the entire truth either.

In Debrecen, we stay at Ivaz's hostel, though Ivaz himself isn't present. He's still busy escorting the rest of the girls to safety. Everyone wears a lot more clothes than I remember from last time, and no one dry humps or bites each other in every nook and cranny of the parlor either. It turns out vampires will stay on their best behavior when you have their boss's brother's twelve-year-old niece in tow.

A messenger is sent ahead from Debrecen to let Catherine and Jakob know we'll arrive tonight. I can't believe we're nearly home. I imagine I can smell Ava's cinnamon apple cakes from here. My heart feels too big for my chest, but worry creeps along the edges.

What's next when this is done? I don't want my old life back. Hovering in shadows and cowering from Farkas and his cronies is no way to live.

I'll have to think of something, but not just yet.

Bowie and I have enjoyed our share of quiet, sweet moments together on the journey, but we haven't been intimate, not with Cecily in our care. He's been a pillar of strength for her this entire journey. It's not until we're on the final approach to Varad that his emotions begin to seep through the cracks. With as much time as he spends comforting Cecily, he hasn't had any time to seek comfort for himself.

Bowie. Always a giver. Never a taker.

His eyes fill with pinkish tears as we draw close to his home. Cecily rides atop Sausage. I loop my arm through Bowie's and match his stride. It's an act of pure restraint not to ask Sausage to gallop the rest of the way just so we can arrive a moment sooner. If Bowie could get away with it, I think he would carry Cecily, me, and the old horse to the family's estate himself.

Just when I'm about to suggest he take Cecily and run ahead, a set of horses and riders comes galloping our way.

Cecily recognizes them first. "Mama!" Her excited scream wells with joy and longing.

Sausage must sense the urgency because he picks up his pace. Not exactly a gallop, but as close to it as Sausage gets and faster than I've ever seen him go.

Bowie halts and squeezes my arm against his side as we watch the reunion.

Jakob practically leaps from his horse to gather Cecily from Sausage's back and into his arms. Catherine abandons her mount as well, and the three of them cling together in a tight embrace. Sobs of relief mix with cries of joy as they hold each other.

My heart thumps fast, my chest warms, and my eyes water. But I can't cry now because Bowie needs me. His blood-tinted tears already stain his cheeks, and I know he'd rather not be seen this way. He goes to swipe at them with his shirt sleeve, but I stop him.

"Let me." The wolf wants to lick him clean, and I'm powerless to resist. Quickly, I clean his face so he can greet his family without looking like a creature from a nightmare. I wipe his cheeks dry with my thumbs.

"Thank you." He leans in so I can nuzzle him, pressing our faces together to combine our scents. I love that he encourages this. So does the wolf.

"Go to them," I whisper into his ear.

Bowie draws back to gaze into my eyes, his own stormy blue irises full of emotion. He nods, lets me go, and runs to be welcomed into the group hug.

Catherine clings to him hard, repeating "thank you" over and over.

Jakob tugs him close and plants a firm kiss right on the crown of his head.

Cecily is smushed between all of them so that all I see of her are pretty blonde curls. My smile stretches wide. Seeing the family together after everything we've been through brings a swell of emotion that threatens to overwhelm me. I don't even know what to call it. Happiness isn't enough. Neither is relief, satisfaction, or joy.

When I'm so full of this odd euphoria that I don't know what to do with myself, I notice Sausage wandering off and silently thank him for giving me a purpose.

I gather the horse's reins in one hand and pat him with the other. He presses his velvet nose against my cheek, and I half wish we were alone so I could cry to him. Somehow, I think he'd understand.

Cecily's bright voice shakes me from my stupor. "Someone get Andras. He needs a hug too."

The four of them collect me—and Sausage by default—and we find ourselves swept into the embrace. Jakob's hand lands on my shoulder and squeezes. As much as I love this family, and as happy as I am to see them whole again, my thoughts drift steadily to Ava. I want to ask how she's been and to hug her as Catherine, Jakob, Cecily, and Bowie hug me.

Sausage bears the bubble of affection with the relaxed sort of posture that indicates he isn't bothered but would rather be snacking. I adore him and his predictable nature.

When the chorus of thank-yous extends to me, my cheeks flush, and I inspect the dirt road beneath our feet. I appreciate it, of course, but I'm unfamiliar with this amount of praise. I don't know why it makes me uncomfortable, but I want Ava more than ever.

Bowie, with his uncanny ability to understand what I need often before I realize it myself, makes excuses for us and draws me away from the group. Sausage clomps along.

"Shall we continue up the hill to Ava?" he asks.

I can't believe he's offering to come with me when he must be so eager to return with his family to their estate. It's a generous offer, but I won't be selfish. "No, Bowie. I'll go alone. You stay with Cecily and see that Sausage is taken care of for me, will you?"

He looks torn, glancing to his family, then back to me. "But I don't want to leave you."

"I'll be fine. I'll have Ava." I nod toward the others. "And they need you more than I do."

He hesitates. "Are you sure? I can always come back to Varad after you're settled."

"I'm sure. The time by myself will do me good, help me calm down before I reach pack territory."

Bowie's brows furrow. "But Farkas—"

"Will be asleep at this hour," I assure him. "I just want to see Ava. I don't care about the other wolves."

"But—"

"You should be with your family," I insist.

His face falls into a sad expression that breaks my heart and prompts a surge of guilt. Guilt that Bowie feels obligated to look after me instead of enjoying his hard-won reunion gnaws.

"I'll be fine without you, promise." I take his shoulders and tug him in to wrap my arms around him.

When words fail, touch comes naturally. Pressing my cheek against his soft hair, I drop featherlight kisses to his nape. The wolf wants to take him up on his offer, drag him with us, insist we aren't parted, but I overrule the selfish animal.

As I break away, the need to reassure him remains. "Don't worry about me. Take care of them. And Sausage."

Bowie nods. His lips form a strained smile. "Of course. Give my love to Ava."

I wave my goodbyes to the others and hurry toward the forested hills before I can change my mind.

Ava awaits, and my heart needs her.

* * *

LEAVING Bowie behind is one of the hardest decisions I've ever made, but I know it's the right thing to do. As much as the wolf insists he belongs to us, he doesn't. He has a family that loves him. I won't take him away from them when they need him the most, though after all this time together, it feels strange not to know when I'll see him again.

Tomorrow night? The night after? Next week?

I honestly don't know what's appropriate. My life's been turned upside down—and I'm glad of it—but I don't know how to proceed when a mission isn't guiding our actions. When it's just Bowie and me, how do we fit?

It's the early hours of the morning when I approach Ava's cottage. Too soon for birdsong, hours before the first golden rays of sunlight will reach her tidy porch.

The familiar scents wash over me like a fresh spring rain: garden soil, chickens, freshly laundered bedsheets, the smell of baking and cinnamon, and best of all, Ava herself. My only real family. The woman who raised me when no one else would, who taught me to read and to hunt, who made sure I never had to be sad alone. I take a deep, fulfilling lungful and sigh it out.

Part of me hates to wake her, but the other part knows there's no way I can stand to wait a second longer.

I'm quiet as I enter the house, sneaking on tiptoe to make sure I don't accidentally frighten her. The door to her bedroom stands open, and I peer in to see her peacefully sleeping, nestled in a pile of quilts.

With a sigh, I realize I don't have the heart to wake her after all. I'll have to wait until morning. Turning to leave, I'm considering curling up on her rug when a sleepy voice says, "Andras?"

I whip back around to face her.

Ava blinks up at me. A smile sweeps across her face, and her eyes brighten as she sits up. "It is you! Oh, how I've missed you. Come here." Her arms open wide.

I'm grinning ear to ear as I go to her to receive what is possibly the best hug of my life. "I missed you too. How are you? Is everything all right?"

She doesn't let me go, patting my back and kissing my cheeks. "Of course everything is all right, my dear. Why wouldn't it be? But let's not talk about me when you've obviously been on the adventure of a lifetime. Look at you!" She holds me at arm's length, squeezing my shoulders. Her gaze travels my face, peers into my soul. "You're all grown up."

"I was grown when I left," I huff happily. "Nothing's changed."

"Everything has changed." Ava is right. She's always right. She scoots over to make room for me. "Tell me all of it."

"But it's the middle of the night. I've woken you. Aren't you tired?"

She tuts. "Don't be silly. I have the rest of my life to sleep. I want to hear about your travels. Were you able to help Bowie? What did the two of you do? He was quite vague in his explanations, but Farkas told me of the missing girls. Are they found?"

"Yes," I say with an enormous amount of relief. "They're safe now."

Ava pats the spot next to her. "Come, come. Start from the beginning."

I crawl into bed just like I used to as a child and tell her everything.

Well, almost everything. I leave out all the naked parts. And the bloody parts. And the naked and bloody parts. For decency's sake.

By the time I finish my tale, dawn's warm light streams in through the windows. It's been so long since I've seen sunlight, I marvel at its beauty. At the same time, I miss Bowie something dreadful. He'll be going to sleep now, and for the first day in many, I won't be by his side. The thought makes me sad.

Ava brings me back to myself as she says, "Why, Andras dear, you've left out the most important part."

I cringe. "I did?" Surely she hasn't read my mind about the naked, bloody bits?

"Mm-hmm. The part where you fell in love with the handsome vampire."

My heart begins to race. Heat rushes to my cheeks.

"It's obvious, you know," she continues. "Have you told him?"

My mouth drops open.

I haven't. Why haven't I told him? He's told me. Surely he knows.

"You haven't told him?" Ava scolds.

I shake my head when words refuse to come.

"You silly wolf. Some things must be said out loud."

Bowie's sad expression as I left takes on a new meaning in my mind. He didn't want to be parted either. I decided for both of us and left him out of it, thinking I knew what was best. But when have I ever known that? *Wrong, wrong, wrong.*

"What are you waiting for?" asks Ava. "Go on! Get! Shoo!"

She's absolutely right, and I am absolutely an idiot.

I leap from the bed, shrug off my shirt, and shift. I'm much faster as a wolf.

"And don't come back without him!" orders Ava as I burst from the cabin to race back to Varad.

To Bowie.

hining, I pace outside the massive double doors of Bowie's family estate. I really should have considered the consequences of sprinting here as a wolf. If I shift, I'll be naked, which is awkward. So I haven't shifted, and now the servants are faced with a lovesick predator pining at their door. Also awkward.

Short of howling outside Bowie's window, I'm not sure what else to do.

I'm seriously considering it when Cecily throws open the doors and saves me, much to the servant's disapproval.

"You can't let a wolf into the house!" he protests.

"This one's friendly," says Cecily, bossy as ever. "And he's not here for us anyway. He's here for Bowie."

"For Bowie?" The servant flutters around nervously, torn between protecting his charge and protecting himself, and obviously wondering why neither course of action seems necessary.

"Come along. I'll open the doors for you." Cecily starts down the hall for the stairs.

I trot behind her gratefully, leaving the frazzled servant behind.

We hurry up to Bowie's room. Cecily gives me a quick pat along my shoulders. "I knew you'd be back, but *he* didn't. You naughty wolf. You'll have some explaining to do. Good luck."

I whimper-sneeze as she pushes open the door so I can slip inside. I owe her one.

Bowie's glorious scent overtakes me. I breathe it in greedy gulps. He's washed with that lovely rosewater and lavender soap and smells just like he did the night we met. His scent is like home. Even though we've only known each other for a season, I feel as if it's been a lifetime.

He lies on his back, covers pulled up to his chest, dark hair haloed on the blue satin pillow, hands peacefully resting on his stomach. Prettier than a picture because he's real, and he's mine.

Overcome with love for him, with regret that I left him confused, and with emotions I can't quite categorize, I hurry to leap onto the bed.

Bowie startles awake, but when I press my snout into his daintily curled hand, he settles. His hand slides over my fur.

"Andras." The way he breathes my name seizes at my heart and warms my soul.

I snuffle my apologies against his chest. He buries his hands in my ruff and rubs my neck.

"Shift for me. Please?" That's my Bowie, always so polite.

I should have known he wouldn't let me get away with handling this as a wolf. I won't deny him, but the wolf must have his way too. Before the shift, I settle on his chest to lick him silly. His neck, his jaw, his cheeks. I get a bit of his silky hair in my mouth, but I don't even care. I just love the taste of his skin.

Bowie laughs into the caresses. That's a relief. Not that I thought he'd be mad, but I wasn't sure how he'd react to my turning up in the middle of the day. The sound of his laughter has me relaxing. I push my snout against his ear and snuffle. He pats my flanks, long, slow strokes that make me want to show my belly.

But I owe him a conversation. When the wolf is content to have slobbered all over him, I shift. The change rolls through me, reshaping bones, stretching my legs and arms, rippling up my spine, and replacing fur with skin. Though I'm still a little nervous, I'm happy to be with Bowie, and I have something very important to say.

When the shift is complete, I lie naked on his chest, unintentionally pinning him down with elbows and knees. The cover is still between us. His cool palms rest on my lower back. My face hovers over his as I gaze on him with adoration.

"I love you," I blurt out with all the elegance of a pair of dancing rhinoceroses. Then I smash our lips together because kissing Bowie can fix anything, even ridiculously long-overdue love confessions. "I love you so much," I say into his mouth.

Bowie returns the kiss awkwardly, his lips fighting a smile the whole time. So I draw back to admire his happy expression, his sparkling blue eyes.

There's more to say, and the words tumble from my mouth in a rush. "I'm sorry I left without you earlier. I wasn't thinking. Or I was thinking too much because I only wanted to do the right thing and thought your family needed you, but I'm your family too now, aren't I? And I didn't realize that you might need me, not until I'd already gone, but I know now. I do. I won't forget again."

He grabs my face. Laughs. Holds me still while he laughs some more.

"Bowie?" I start to feel self-conscious.

"It's all right, darling. Everything's all right. That's just the most I've heard you say at once, unprompted, and in one breath, perhaps ever?"

I'm just glad he's still smiling.

"I love you too." He tugs me down for more kissing. I melt

against him, surprised he can still breathe with me sprawled all over him like this. His satin cover is soft and cool against my skin, but it's Bowie I want to feel. His hands on me aren't enough; I want everything.

He breaks from our kiss. "I'm so glad you came back. I didn't want to sleep without you."

"Me either."

"Did Ava send you, or did you figure things out on your own?"

"We may have arrived at the conclusion together."

"Ah, that's the best way." His grin brings me joy. "Do you think she might like to stay here with us?"

My lips part stupidly. "We could live here? Ava and I?"

"Of course." He's quick to add, "Or I can come to you, but we mustn't be parted again."

I couldn't agree more.

Bowie caresses my nape, where hair turns to fur, and follows the trail of it down my spine. Tingles erupt. I cuddle into him.

His fingers creep down my lower back, and when I settle in to enjoy his touch on my cheeks, they lift away. I'm about to protest their absence when he slaps my ass with both hands.

I startle. "Hey!"

"Get under the covers with me this very minute, or I'll do it again."

The initial sting fades to a pleasant warmth. "That's hardly a punishment."

His hand curls around the base of my tail and gives a little tug. "Don't tempt me."

I crawl off him. He shoves the covers down to reveal he is naked also. Moons, he's lovely. I could stare at him all day and have often stared at him all night.

Climbing under the satin with him, I duck my head to lay kisses on his throat before he catches me drooling. The wolf wants to mark him, claim him as ours, mix our scents until one can't be distinguished from the other. I can't say I disagree.

Bowie comes alive against me, rolling in to be closer, tucking his leg between mine. "Your skin on mine reminds me of what it feels like to have the sun shining down on a warm spring day."

Wrapping my arms around him, I feel a little shy about responding with words, but for Bowie, I'll try. "Yours is the opposite, though just as nice, like a crisp evening breeze on an early fall night."

This sentiment earns me a sweet nuzzle of Bowie's cheek against mine and a tantalizing thrust of his hips.

I want him. I always want him. And the pent-up desire from weeks of holding back urges me to shut up and let this happen. But that part of me is stupidly overcome by the part that can't forget we're in his sister's house in the middle of the day.

"Should we? I mean, are you sure because—"

Bowie quiets my protest with a kiss, then whispers against my lips, "We most definitely should." Another kiss before he draws back. "Darling, this house is enormous, and we practically have our own wing."

The *we* and the *our* stand out to me, causing a rush of warmth in my chest.

Bowie continues, "As long as you can refrain from absolutely screaming when I take you, they'll never know."

My mouth opens around a gasp as a picture of Bowie over me and thrusting dances through my mind. I'll bite my tongue if I have to, but I must have him, screaming or not.

"Yes, please, that," I stammer, my imagination taking over and running away with the scenario of Bowie fucking me. I've never done it that way, never had a safe opportunity, what with hiding my tail and all.

"Anything you want, dearest. I'm for you."

"I want you to fuck me." *I want to smell like you, and I want you to smell like me*, I think while the wolf inside me chants *mate, mate, mate.*

My cock has gone from plump to hard just picturing it. I feel Bowie's against my stomach. He presses his hips forward. I match his motion. We both release a sigh of pleasure.

"I have you," says Bowie. "Turn over."

My body obeys gladly, shifting on the feather-soft bed to lie prone. Anticipation tingles along my skin, a needy sensation that makes me want to beg for his touch. But I don't have to because it follows immediately: the weight of him along my back, his mouth on my shoulder, his teeth scraping against my flesh.

"Bite me," I plead.

In these past weeks as we've traveled home, Bowie has moved past his reluctance to feed from me, with each session coming more naturally than the last. I love it. The sharp twin pinpricks, the sucking sensation, the smell of my blood in the air, knowing it's nourishing my beloved.

"Not yet," he teases, dragging his fangs along my throat. "Later. When you're coming with me inside you."

"Moon and stars, I'll come now if you keep talking like that."

His answering chuckle puffs against the fur on the back of my neck. I want him to clamp his jaw over my nape and hold me down.

I'm not sure how he always knows what I'm thinking. Bowie swears he can't actually read my mind, but he rises and grips the back of my neck with his hand and squeezes.

"Yes," I moan. My hips lift my ass off the bed to press into him. "More."

"Patience," he murmurs, letting me go to reach the bedside table. He'd better be going for oil. That's the only acceptable excuse for the current lack of touching.

I whine into the bedsheets. This feels new for me. To be waiting. Not to take charge like I've always had to, to protect my secrets. Bowie is safe, and I like this feeling, this suspenseful expectation of euphoria.

As he returns, the bed dips, his weight shifting over me. His hands land on my arched back, so cool against my hot flesh I'm surprised there's no steam.

Bowie parts my thighs with one of his, the smooth slide of soft skin on skin sending a shiver straight through me.

I thrust against the sheets.

He takes pity on me and slides his hand under my hips to grip my cock. "On your knees for me. Let me see you."

I rise to obey. A flutter of anxiety comes, but I let it go as Bowie's stroking keeps me from worrying about what I might look like. One hand forms a perfect channel for me to push into, and the other lifts and massages my sac. I imagine what his elegant fingers must look like touching me there, and I shudder.

A bead of moisture leaks from my tip. Bowie swipes it up to swirl over my crown. His hands on me feel marvelous, wringing out whimpers and moans I can't hold in, though I try to at least keep them quiet.

"Do you want to lift your tail, or should I?" he asks.

I'm so delirious with pleasure I've nearly forgotten I have a tail, much less that it's curled over my ass, blocking his way. I fling it up, exposing myself further, then bite into the pillow while waiting for him to touch me there too.

The seconds that pass form an eternity of anticipation. Of curiosity. Of bashful self-conscious jitters. But when the soft, oil-slick pad of his finger nudges between my cheeks, I melt into his touch like a plummeting drip of hot wax down a candlestick.

Moaning my delight, I press back for more, and he gives it— massaging, circling, teasing.

"You sure you've never done this?" asks Bowie.

I register the jest in his tone but answer in all honesty. "Never. Couldn't before you."

His fingers work magic on my body. In my body. "I won't lie and say I'm not glad. To be your first. To have this for myself." His words add another layer of pleasure.

"Only you," I murmur. The more he probes and stretches, the more my curiosity blooms with each new sensation. "Will it hurt?"

Bowie's thoughtful silence is loud in my ears. "Perhaps a little. How are you now?"

"Good," I moan the word out on a breath. "Did it hurt your first time?"

"Yes, but only because we didn't know any better, and I was impatient."

Impatient. I can relate. I'm feeling that now. I want him, all of him. I want us to be joined. "Please." My whimpers are growing desperate. "I don't care if it hurts."

"I do."

Bowie's gentle nature threatens to undo me along with the steady slick and sweet motion of his fingers. I've gathered fistfuls of satin in each clenched hand.

"Now," I whine. "Don't make me wait anymore, please."

He drops cool kisses on my heated skin, distracting me while his fingers vanish to be replaced by what I really want. An achingly slow stretch pulls another moan from my throat. Bowie clutches my hips in tight fingers, holding me firm, grounding me in the moment. And oh, this moment. I'd linger here forever, marveling at the miracle of him inching inside me. Nothing hurts. The sensation is new and different but welcome. All I want is more, more, more.

"Move, Bowie." The words huff out as a demand. Bossy. Needy. I shift to angle back against him, but his grip prevents the leverage I seek.

"Trust me, Andras," he purrs. "You don't want me to move now, or this will be over before we've started."

Oh. *Oh.* He's close? Already? I've been so consumed in the

world of ecstasy he's created, it hadn't occurred to me he could be on edge same as me. My cock throbs in sympathy. I stop trying to rush him and settle in to enjoy the unhurried pace.

Bowie releases my hips to slide his hands up my back, raising a trail of gooseflesh in his wake. The fronts of his thighs meet the back of mine as he bottoms out. I press back, eager for everything he has to give. Together like this, I know in my heart and soul that Bowie is my forever. All I need is him.

We find a rhythm, rocking together, breathing and panting in tandem. Bowie wraps his arms around my chest and lifts me from the bed, both of us on our knees, his chest against my back.

I drop my head to his shoulder and offer my throat, which sparks a tremor in him I feel inside my body—a marvel I note for future encounters because the sensation wrings a groan straight from my core to my lips.

We're a sea of motion as his fangs find my neck and bite down. The welcome zing of pain transforms quickly to pleasure as Bowie grips my cock and begins to stroke.

He's everywhere. In me, on me, around me, sucking me. I never want it to end, but the inevitability seizes us in its clutches.

Quaking together, we tremble against each other as the peak takes us as willing hostages. I spill into his hand. He spills into my body. The euphoria of paired sensations overtakes me. I press my body back against his, my throat arching to take his fangs deeper. The scent of blood wafts between us, tangy and metallic and glorious.

The wolf is content in Bowie's arms. I'm riding high on the aftermath. My muscles begin to relax one by one.

Gently, Bowie licks the wound closed and slips from my body. He lays us down against the satin, still holding me close.

I turn in his embrace. I need to see his face, to kiss his

perfect lips, to know he's as affected as I am by our union. One look says he is.

Bowie's eyes glisten with warmth. His cheeks are flushed a pretty pink with my blood. He gazes at me as if I'm his whole world, and I understand because he is mine.

Our kiss holds all the words and sentiment I struggle to say. I wrap my arms and legs around him and squeeze until I don't know where I end and he begins.

He pushes hair from my face and studies me. "What did you think?"

I grin. As if he doesn't know. But just in case there's a hint of true vulnerability in his question, I answer seriously. "I loved everything. I love you. I want to do that often and with enthusiasm until I'm too exhausted to walk."

Bowie's chuckle warms my heart. "Good." His nails ruffle the fur along my spine. "That sounds like an excellent plan with which to begin our future."

Our future. I'm going to embarrass myself and cry.

Slowly, Bowie leans in. I close my eyes so he can drop fluttering kisses on the lids. "Don't cry," he whispers, his breath on my cheek. How does he always know? "I have you."

"We have each other," I say, returning his kisses.

Mongrel is gone. I'm Andras now, and I belong to Bowie as he belongs to me.

* * *

For more in this world, check out the next volume, **Changeling**, coming soon! Be the first to know about bonus scenes and giveaways by joining Lee's Newsletter. Please take a moment to leave a rating and review to help other readers find Bowie and Andras. Thank you for reading.

Parts of this novel were based on the true and terrible murderer, Erzsébet Báthory—the most prolific serial killer of all time. To stay as close to historically accurate as possible, the countess had to go on living in my novel in order to face the real-life trial to come. If you're curious what happened, I'll summarize, but let me also recommend *Infamous Lady: The True Story of Countess Erzsébet Báthory* by Kimberly L. Craft, Esq. This book was extraordinarily helpful in writing Mongrel, as was *A Concise History of Hungary* by Miklos Molnar.

Erzsébet was found guilty of the slayings based on copious testimony, but because of the noble status of her family and her immense riches, she was protected from a death sentence. Thurzo condemned her to house arrest against King Matyas's wishes. The king wanted her dead so her wealth would revert to the crown. House arrest only achieved the cancelation of Hungary's debt to Báthory, no small sum, but her assets and properties were passed down to her three surviving children.

Legend says the countess was walled off in a small room in her tower to live out her remaining years in solitude. But conflicting tales indicate she was actually in the dungeon below ground, and yet others say she had the run of the castle. In any event, she spent her last four years confined to Csejthe's walls writing letters to her powerful family in an effort to clear her name and escape her fate. She never confessed to her crimes.

On August 25, 1614, the countess died alone. Or did she? Though people have searched all the likely burial sites, her body was never found.

I blame Bettina.

Beneath the Opal Arc

~A rare male witch who saves the world

~The vampire who saves him

In a race to safety will love flourish or will war tear them apart?

Across the Sapphire Sea

~A possessive lover bent on discovering a hidden cure

~A feisty fledgling eager for a hint of independence

Can their love last or will ancient secrets shatter their bond forever?

Beyond the Ruby River

~An Ancient Egyptian leading a simple Life

~A demon half-breed, his incubus lover

Will their love last forever or is each soul destined to pine for the other for eternity?

Slay My Love

~A sweet talking vampire

~A duty-bound slayer

Will love triumph or will one have to kill the other to survive?

Changeling

~ A bored incubus

~ A faerie who's just learned his heritage

Are they exactly what the other needs, or will ancient curses tear apart?

Feral Dawn

~A lone werewolf

~An injured vampire left for dead

Can a disgraced vampire & an outcast wolf find love,

or will the ghosts of their pasts divide them?

Forbidden Bond (They Bite Series: Book One)

~A vampire heir at a werewolf university

~An alpha wolf who hates vampires

Can love conquer all—or is war inevitable?

Forbidden Love (They Bite Series: Book Two)

~An esteemed vampire surgeon

~A young, injured werewolf

Can love flourish between enemy species despite a society in turmoil?

Forbidden Need (They Bite Series: Book Three)

~A jaded vampire too damaged for love

~A lovesick shifter who refuses to give up

Will destiny unite them—or will old enemies reign?

A Bridge to Love

~A sweet messenger werewolf

~A lonely troll stuck guarding his bridge

Can love blossom across a massive cultural divide,

or will Arlo and Toby always be alone for the holidays?

ABOUT THE AUTHOR

Lee Colgin has loved vampires since she read *Dracula* on a hot sunny beach at 13 years old. She lives in North Carolina with lots of dogs and her husband. No, he's not a vampire, but she loves him anyway. Lee likes cookies and pizza.

Connect with Lee

Email: LeeColgin@gmail.com
Facebook: www.facebook.com/groups/leecolgin
Twitter: www.twitter.com/leecolgin
Website: www.leecolgin.com
Newsletter: http://eepurl.com/gJEu35

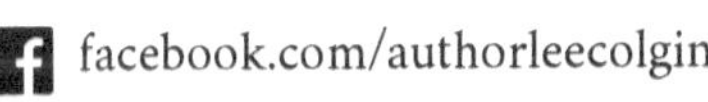 facebook.com/authorleecolgin

 twitter.com/leecolgin

instagram.com/circus_stella

www.ingramcontent.com/pod-product-compliance
Lightning Source LLC
Chambersburg PA
CBHW030811210726
48290CB00002B/526